The Girl Behind The Mask

D0924389

Also by Stella Knightley

The Girl Behind The Fan (June 2013)
The Girl Behind The Curtain (August 2013)

About the author

Stella Knightley is the author of twenty-six novels published under other names. *The Girl Behind The Mask* is the first of three books in the *Hidden Women* series, which blends the daring stories of historical women of note with an erotically-charged contemporary love affair which will delight the fans of *Fifty Shades*. Stella grew up in the west of England and now lives in London.

STELLA KNIGHTLEY

The Girl Behind
The Mask

HODDER

First published in Great Britain in 2013 by Hodder & Stoughton
An Hachette UK company

First published in paperback in 2013

1

A CIP catalogue record for this title is available from the British Library

Paperback ISBN 978 1 444 77705 5
Ebook ISBN 978 1 444 77704 8

Printed and bound by Clays Ltd, St Ives plc

Hodder & Stoughton policy is to use papers that are natural,
renewable and recyclable products and made from wood grown in
sustainable forests. The logging and manufacturing processes are
expected to conform to the environmental regulations of the
country of origin.

Hodder & Stoughton Ltd
338 Euston Road
London NW1 3BH

www.hodder.co.uk

To Mark, for his encouragement,
his patience and his love.

Prologue

It should not have been so easy, escaping the watchful eye of the chaperone, but fortunately the woman Gaetano Giordano chose to care for his only daughter Luciana was as eager to have some fun in the city as her angel-faced seventeen-year-old charge. The chaperone shared a glass of wine with the priest in the salon on the *piano nobile*, while Luciana, in her cell-like bedroom on the floor below, prepared for her daring escape.

Moored beneath her bedroom window was the small boat the priest had arrived in, rowing himself to avoid awkward questions as to who needed to confess when all decent people should be tucked up in bed. Dressed in the boy's clothes she had stolen from her brother, Luciana found it no trouble at all to let herself over the sill with a twisted bedspread for a rope. She landed with a gentle 'pouf' on a pile of blankets the priest had collected for the poor. Gathering herself quickly, Luciana unwound the rope by which the boat was tethered. She found the oars, carelessly hidden beneath the blankets, and slotted them into their locks. Pulling her simple white half-mask down over her nose and with a three-cornered hat to cover her hair, Luciana pushed out into the canal.

Luciana rowed like the boys she had played alongside during long summers on the lagoon, when her father was away on business and the maids were too busy flirting to watch her. No one would have suspected that beneath the tricorn were the soft, dark curls that could have inspired love poems. And under the cloak and the billowing white shirt . . . Well . . .

Luciana abandoned the priest's boat at the entrance to the Grand Canal. Quick as a pickpocket, she weaved her way through the revellers on the Rialto Bridge. It was Carnevale. Again. Just that morning in the chapel, the priest had complained that these days Venice was all 'Martedì Grasso and no Lent'. Silly old hypocrite. Everyone wore masks, from the very highest to the lowest of the low, all making the most of their anonymity as they crowded the waterside. Pillars of society pinched bottoms. Well-born ladies, ordinarily so refined you might think they never passed wind, were lifting their skirts in the hope of feeling more than a breeze between their thighs.

Luciana smiled. She recognised so many of them: associates of her father, friends of her late mother, pious fellow members of her church's congregation. All of them kidding themselves that a papier-mâché snout could hide their identities, while giving themselves away with familiar hand gestures and rip-snorting laughs. Luciana was cleverer than that. She had to be. If she got caught now, it was straight to a convent. So she kept her small hands stuffed deep inside her pockets and walked with her feet turned out, just as her brother did. She set her rosebud lips into an unsmiling line that even her childhood nurse would not have recognised. When acknowledged by someone keen to know more, Luciana merely nodded and kept on her path. She did her best not to meet anyone's gaze. She would not stop. She would not speak. She had an appointment to keep.

Passing through the deserted Rialto Market – as extravagantly vaulted as any cathedral – Luciana pulled her cloak a little tighter to her neck. A gaggle of prostitutes, taking advantage of the revelries to stray from the *Carampane*, took her for the boy she pretended to be and offered to teach her something useful in return for a couple of coins. The most daring flashed her ample breasts as added enticement. Luciana held her cloak right up to her mouth to cover her grin.

'Oh, he's not interested in us, girls,' the prostitute called after Luciana's back. 'He must be looking for an education of the Greek kind.'

If only you knew, dear ladies.

Luciana pressed on. The prostitutes could have no idea how close they had come to discovering Luciana's real mission. They doubtless would not have understood it. Looking up to consult the painted name, Luciana turned a corner into a *calle* she would not, without her disguise, have walked down in the daylight. Not alone at any rate. She crossed the *Ponte delle Tette*, the 'Bridge of Tits', and braved more lurid catcalls from the girls who were plying their trade there. Luciana pushed on into a quieter part of town. Quiet enough to be dangerous. But her disguise gave her a sense of invulnerability and her purpose gave her the courage to tackle any number of robbers who might lurk in the dark.

Just as promised, she found the house with the monkey's-head door-knocker, right where the street took another turn. This was the place. This was the house that

3

held the key to all Luciana wanted to know. Acting quickly, before her bravado deserted her, she grasped the monkey's head and hammered to announce her arrival. The sound echoed down the alleyway before being swallowed up and spat out in a different accent by the water that threaded through the city like blood through veins. Luciana thought she saw a shadow at a window opposite. She pulled her hat down further. No one must know she was there.

It was a while before anyone responded. Had the servants taken so long to answer a call at Luciana's father's palazzo, they would have been turned out. But maybe there were no servants in this house.

Luciana stood in front of the polished bronze monkey's head, feeling both a longing to be inside and a longing to run away. She did not know the owner of this poor-looking house, who had agreed that it might be used as a secret rendezvous. Exactly whom was she meeting anyway? Why had she given her trust to a man she barely knew? What if, in asking for his assistance in acquiring the education her father had forbidden her, she had unwittingly invited instructions that would lead her to her death?

At last the door opened wide and it was too late to change her mind. Luciana's lips moved but she could not find any words. She was transfixed, hypnotised, by the dark laughing eyes that met her own. Seeing her new teacher standing on the threshold of the house, filling the whole doorframe with his broad shoulders in a plain white shirt, Luciana was suddenly taken by the urge to throw her arms around his neck and beg him to bite her with those straight white teeth. His mouth, so sensual and generous, spread into a warm but wicked smile.

When he took her hand to lead her into the house, Luciana felt the prickle of arousal over every inch of her skin. Confused and excited by the emotions the sight of her new friend aroused in her, Luciana had the distinctly unnerving feeling that he would be teaching her a great deal more than philosophy.

I

Venice, last January

You never forget the first time you see Venice.

Leaving England on the 7.40 a.m. flight from Gatwick, all I could think about was how much I wished I were still in my bed. I left the house in pitch darkness. The cold London air bore intimations of snow. Now, just two and a half hours later, I was standing by the waterside in bright sunshine. The quay at Venice's Marco Polo airport certainly made a change from the Victoria platform for the Gatwick Express. Though it was still only January, the warmth of those unexpected rays coaxed me to unfasten my coat and loosen the thick woolly scarf I'd expected to be wearing until April. I lifted my face to the sky and let the light pour over me like a creature coming out of hibernation. I stood there in a dream state, letting the heat find my winter-weary bones, until I realised that the crowd behind me was at last boarding a boat.

The yellow-hulled municipal ferry spluttered across the shallow water, trailing a thick cloud of grey warning smoke in its wake, but nothing could detract from the beauty of that morning for me. The sunshine reflected by the shallow sandy-bottomed lagoon made it seem as though the whole world was bathed in lemon and pink and baby blue. I found myself a spot by a grubby salt-splashed window and, while my fellow passengers attended to their endlessly chirping phones, I watched life on the water. A handsome water-taxi skimmed by like a flying fish. There was just enough time to see its passengers embrace. A moment of affection for them. A small stab of poignancy for me.

On the portside, an island loomed. I craned to see a boat-yard, a tiny church and a simple cottage with washing all aflutter on the line outside. And then the ferry passed Murano, where the glassmakers ply their trade, hugging close to the coast so we could almost see into the islanders' houses. Next came San Michele, the island of the dead with its high cemetery walls and sad cypress trees. A brief moment of introspection seemed to fall over all the passengers in the ferry as we lowered our eyes in respect.

Then finally, Venice itself, almost close enough to swim to. It was exactly as it looked in the pictures. A jumble of proud campanili. Red bricks. White marble. Warm terracotta and mustard-plastered walls. A thousand wooden poles studded the water, marking out the safest routes to shore. Venice owed her success in no small part to the treachery of the lagoon, where her ancient enemies had found themselves grounded by unmarked shallows.

And there! At last! My very first gondola. I was so surprised to see it – a genuine gondola, with sleek black hull and six-pronged ferro on the prow – that I automatically turned to share my delight. But this was a quotidian view for the Venetian grandmother standing beside me.

'*Sì, gondola,*' the woman said, as though she thought me a bit slow.

'*È la mia prima,*' I explained.

The woman smiled and nodded. '*Sì, sì.*'

She knew it wouldn't be my last.

As the boat's captain threw the engine into reverse to bring the footbridge closer to the dock, the other passengers started to gather themselves, sensing the end of the journey. As I stepped onto the land and looked about me with appropriate wonder, I had the feeling I was just beginning mine.

2

'Sarah Thomson! Welcome to Venice, my dear.'

I recognised Doctor Nick Marsden from the one time we had met before, in the dusty senior common room of his historic Oxford college. How different he looked here in Italy. The tweedy professor had shrugged off his shabby cardigan with the patches on the elbows and was wearing instead a jacket that revealed an athleticism I certainly hadn't noticed at that first meeting. His one concession to the season was a boldly striped collegiate scarf wrapped around his neck. His chestnut hair, which had been greased back when we first met, flopped forward engagingly, curtaining his clever blue eyes. The general impression was of a man in constant motion. He bounded towards me, smiling as though I was a long-lost friend rather than the pesky distraction he probably thought me – arriving on a Sunday as I was.

'How was your journey?' he asked,

'Good. Great,' I told him. 'Early start but . . .'

'Seeing Venice for the first time soon makes you forget how tired travelling's left you, eh? What do you think of *La Serenissima* so far?'

'It's exactly as I imagined,' I said. 'I mean, more precisely, it's exactly like the pictures. The seventeenth-century Canaletto pictures.'

'Isn't it just?' Nick smiled as though I had complimented his own work.

'I thought. I don't know . . . I thought there would be more modern buildings.'

'Ah, Venice is very good at resisting change,' said Nick. 'Though you'll see that the nineteen-seventies made it as far as your apartment.'

'I'm sure it will be lovely,' I said.

'If you like brown,' said Nick. 'Follow me.'

Nick insisted on taking my bags as we navigated the next part of the journey. It was a good job he was so chivalrous; the university-owned apartment where I would be spending the next month was in the Dorsoduro. I kept up with the directions as far as to which vaporetto stop I should get off at, but after that, Nick led me at high speed over a series of hump-backed bridges and through a warren of *calli* I knew I would never remember.

'I'll draw the fastest route to the university on a map,' Nick promised, as he raced on ahead of me shouting street names I could never quite catch.

'It's like a labyrinth,' I called to his back.

'You'll get used to it in time.'

But I wondered how anyone could ever get used to Venice. The city's streets really were like a film set. If they hadn't been thronged with tourists in 21st-century clothes, I might have thought I had stepped back in time. Every turning brought something ancient and different to marvel at. As Nick strode ahead, I skipped to keep up with him, desperate for just a moment's pause as I caught tantalising glimpses of a thousand and one things I wanted to study more closely.

'Best ice cream in Venice on your left,' Nick tossed over his shoulder. 'Good restaurant, miserable owner on your right.'

He covered another bridge in three steps. His legs must have been twice as long as mine. He darted out of the path of an oncoming postman with his trolley. He almost ended up in a canal to avoid a dawdling *nonna* with her shopping bags. Then he skidded to a halt in front of a building painted in dusky red, three storeys high with peeling shutters of faded Loden green at its windows.

'And here's Ca' Scimmietta,' said Nick. 'I'll let you in. The door is sticky. Hell, every door in Venice is sticky. It's the damp.'

He grinned at his own joke and took out a key. There was a brass lock on the door, but that had long since been retired in favour of a more prosaic Yale. The old knocker, however, was still in place. While Nick struggled to get the key to turn, I rested my hand on the laughing face of a monkey that was ever so slightly more human than animal in its expression. Its muzzle was smooth and almost golden from the polish of a hundred thousand caresses over the years.

'Ca' Scimmietta means house of the little monkey,' Nick explained. 'Though no one knows why this fancy creature's on the door here. It was clearly nicked from a much bigger house.'

'Perhaps I should investigate,' I suggested. 'There's nothing I love more than a historical mystery.'

'Reminds me a bit of my grandmother,' Nick mused as he gave the monkey an affectionate pat before he finally got the door to open by using the magic combination of swearing in three languages while shoving it hard with his hip.

'*Voila!* You'll get the hang of it in a couple of months.'

I foresaw a couple of months' worth of bruises.

I followed Nick inside. The large stone-floored hallway was dark and lined with bookcases stuffed and groaning with textbooks: medical, mathematical, you name it.

'Feel free to leave your own contribution,' he said. 'Though it'd be nice if someone left a thriller for once.'

Like the medics and mathematicians before me, I was in

Venice to study. I was a doctoral student in London, special-
ising in women's self-representation in the eighteenth
century. That is to say, the diaries and letters of those women
lucky enough to have had the education to write them. My
research into a particular Venetian noblewoman had reached
a dead end and I hoped to find much more here in the city
where she'd actually lived. Nick Marsden, a fellow specialist
in my field who split his time between Venice and Oxford,
had been only too happy to help. Especially when I told him
about the grant I'd managed to wangle. Academia is all
about the money.

Now he showed me round the university's apartment for
visitors at the same breakneck speed with which he had navigated our route from the vaporetto stop. He was correct in
his observation that the nineteen-seventies had got as far as
Ca' Scimmietta. The kitchen was early Conran brown –
complete with a ceramic chicken – and the bathroom was a
classic avocado.

'Bidet,' Nick pointed out. 'If you ever feel the need to wash
your feet.'

He continued to whirl around the flat, pointing out all the
mod-ish cons.

'Boiler is in this cupboard here. Very temperamental. Best
to plan a day ahead if you fancy a bath. Or just jump in the
canal. Water's a similar colour. Vacuum cleaner. Never really
worked. There's a dustpan and brush under the sink. Washing
machine. Turns most things out dirtier than they started . . .'

'Great, great,' I muttered. 'No hot water. No vacuum
cleaner. No washing machine.'

'No point trying to use the microwave either. It's just for
show.'

Still, Nick's enthusiasm made it seem as if living in such a
shambolic place could actually be an adventure.

There was only one room left.

'Bedroom.'

He pushed the door open but then stood aside, as though respecting the privacy of the room I had yet to occupy. Likewise, I found myself poking my head round the door as though someone had already claimed the room and we were just sneaking a look.

'Wow,' I breathed.

'Yes,' said Nick. 'It is rather amazing, isn't it?'

I was lost for words as I gazed at the bed I would be sleeping in for the next couple of months. In contrast to the Seventies nightmare that was the rest of the flat, this room had been left untouched for much, much longer. In the centre was an enormous four-poster complete with burgundy velvet drapes. The bed had been carved from solid oak and was darkened with years of old varnish.

'Too heavy to move,' said Nick. 'That'll be the only thing that saved it from ending up at auction.'

'It's incredible,' I said, running my fingers over one of the intricately carved posts decorated with animals that might have been fashioned by the same hand as the monkey knocker.

Nick remained by the door.

'Well, I hope you can get a good night's sleep in it,' he said. 'Knowing all those creatures were looking down on me would give me nightmares.'

'Thanks,' I said.

Nick was already heading back to the kitchen.

'I got a few provisions in. I hope you're not vegetarian.'

Fortunately not. Most of Nick's provisions were cured meat.

'Obviously, you can get fish just about anywhere. There's a fish stall in the Campo Santa Margherita. A fruit and veg boat pulls up right beside the bridge to San Barnaba. You'll like the owner. Terrible flirt.'

There was a bottle of prosecco too. Nick waggled the bottle in my direction.

'To toast your arrival in Venice?' he suggested hopefully.

'I suppose it is almost lunchtime,' I replied.

'Good girl.'

He poured out two small glasses and we toasted my arrival and then settled down to discuss the weeks ahead in a vaguely professional matter. Three hours later, after Nick had eaten most of the provisions and the bottle of prosecco was finished, I finally had my new apartment to myself.

I went into the bedroom and opened the stiff metal shutters. In the mid-afternoon light, the bed didn't look quite so Gothic, though it was covered in an impressively thick layer of dust. I leaned out of my new bedroom window and took in the view. Across the canal, a Venetian housewife was sweeping clean the pavement outside her front door, piling the rubbish against her neighbour's step instead. An elegant older gentleman walked a small white dog around the detritus. A young couple, obviously tourists from their bright waterproofs and bulging backpacks, took photographs of themselves with the humpbacked bridge behind. When they kissed, I felt my heart tighten.

I'd heard that Venice was legendarily tranquil, on account of there being no cars, but from where I stood now, I realised that the city was far from silent. Neighbours talking. Water-taxis idling. The occasional crescendo of students singing in the bars on the Campo Santa Margherita behind. And every quarter-hour, the chiming of church bells that seemed to come from every direction. The water distorted everything. Echoes abounded. The air was abuzz.

Exhausted from my early start and fuzzy-headed from my unexpected lunchtime drink with Nick, I lay down on the dusty bed and listened to the busy, noisy world outside.

London, with all its sadness, suddenly seemed so very far away. I was glad of that for the moment. After all, I had not come to Venice just for research, I had also come to mend my broken heart.

3

That afternoon, in the 'four-poster of doom', as Nick had dubbed the bed with its curious animal carvings, I had a dream about Steven – the man I'd left behind. It was inevitable, I suppose. As hard as I tried not to think about him, I could not keep him out of my subconscious. There are no restraining orders for the heart.

In my dream, we were in our bedroom back in London: a room far plainer than the one I was in now. Steven's style was rather minimal. He said he liked to keep things simple in every area of his life.

If only that had turned out to be the truth.

But for now, in my dream, Steven smiled at me the way he used to, full of softness and warm affection, and opened out his arms for me to step into them. I walked eagerly into his familiar embrace. He stroked my face, murmuring sweet nothings, telling me how beautiful he found me. How beautiful he'd always found me. I rested my head on his shoulder and pressed my hand against his heart.

'You're mine,' he said. 'You'll always be mine.'

I lifted my face towards his and waited for his kiss.

Together we sank onto the bed we'd bought together when I thought we had a future and Steven began to undress me, kissing me all the while. I kissed him back, greedy to have more of him. His tongue flickered against mine. I sucked on it as he pulled away. Released from my mouth, he dipped his head to kiss his way down my neck. He unbuttoned my blouse, revealing my nakedness beneath. I twisted my fingers in his thick dark hair and sighed with pleasure as he moved his attention further down my body, kissing a trail from my throat down to my eager, aching breasts.

Cupping my breasts, Steven kissed each one in turn. He always joked that they must be treated equally and he always kept his word. I let out a groan of delight as he moved to tongue my waiting nipples into hardness. He traced the curves where the soft mounds met my ribcage and I arched my back to be closer to him. Steven instinctively knew how to get the best response from me. After seven years, he knew my body almost as well as I knew it myself.

Moving down the bed to start again from my feet, Steven slid his hands along my calves, following close behind them with his mouth. He kissed a damp path along the inside of my legs until his hot lips reached the tops of my thighs, leaving me breathless with anticipation. Coyly, I rested my hands on my pubic bone. Steven moved my hands away with his lightly stubbled chin. He planted kisses on the newly denuded skin above my bikini line and nuzzled my small neat triangle of hair. He looked up at me, catching my eye to smile his approval. Steven liked me almost bare.

I knew what would happen next. It wasn't long before his darting tongue found my clitoris, already swollen and quietly aching for his attention. He flicked the little nub from side to side with his strong pink tongue. He sucked it between his lips. He nipped at it gently with his perfect teeth. The mix of pleasure with just a salt sprinkle of pain drew a sharp breath from me but I begged him to go on. That little sliver of pain was what made it so good.

I twisted luxuriously in the ecstasy of Steven's warm mouth upon me. I could feel myself growing wet, wet enough to take him in easily in one deliciously welcome stroke. Moving his attention from my clitoris, Steven stretched out his tongue and probed deep inside me, pulling my legs apart and holding them steady so I couldn't roll away and escape. Not that I ever wanted to escape when he was making love to me. I wanted to feel myself pinioned beneath him, unable to do anything but give in to his desires.

'Please,' I begged him. 'I need you inside.'

'Not yet,' he told me.

'Please.'

He ignored my pleading and continued to work hard with his mouth. Every stroke of his tongue brought me closer to an orgasm. I felt my thighs growing tense as I braced myself against him. I kept pushing up, up towards him. My legs were beginning to shake. My breath grew shallow. I felt his fingernails digging harder into my flesh as he tried to keep me still. To stay in control.

'Please be inside me!' I cried.

This time, he would let me have my way. Steven was more than ready. He moved up the bed until he was lying directly on top of me, then slid his hand down between our hot bodies and guided his stone-hard penis between my legs. I drew breath sharply at the first thrust, quickly relaxing again when I felt his pelvis touch mine. Holding himself high above my body, Steven gazed at my face steadily as he began to move. My eyes wandered over the taut planes of his chest. His veins bound his rock-hard muscles like tightly wrapped cord. His pectorals flexed powerfully as he swayed forward and took all his weight on his beautiful arms, and I thrilled to the utter delight of being so expertly and completely filled by the man I loved.

My eyes drifted lower. The sight of Steven's long smooth shaft plunging into me was every bit as good as the feeling it gave me inside. To see his prick glistening with my juices as he pulled nearly all the way out was almost too much. I felt the walls of my vagina begin to pulse in appreciation. It was a steady, rhythmic pulse that began to spread slowly throughout my limbs like a single drop of red ink colouring a whole glass of water like blood.

I lifted my legs from the bed and wound them tightly around Steven's waist, at the same time grasping his buttocks with my hands and using them to bring him further inside me still. My fingers dug hard into his firm warm flesh as I grew more and more excited, forcing him to increase the pace of his movement to keep time with my racing heart.

'Harder,' I told him and he responded instantly. His teeth were gritted in ecstatic determination as he thrust into me powerfully with strokes that hammered against my swollen clitoris and drove me to the edge. Deep down inside, I had the sensation of standing on a ledge with arms stretched wide. I could hear the rush of my own blood in my ears. Now for the jump. I felt perfectly weightless as my orgasm set in and quickly took hold of every nerve in my body. There was no going back.

I was coming long before him. My vagina contracted and throbbed around his penis as though trying to pull him inside me for always. Steven continued to thrust, his face smiling down on me. I shut my eyes as though to lessen the intensity, but my mouth was spread in a wide, wide smile.

As my climax subsided, Steven pushed against me once more and this time he stayed there, holding himself tight against my body as his own orgasm took off. I opened my eyes again just in time to see him coming. Just in time to see his composure lost completely as his thrusts became uncontrolled and a cry he could no longer hold inside exploded from his lips.

Lying in his arms as we recovered ourselves, I felt happier than I had done in a long while.

Until I woke up, that is.

* * *

My short sleep had been profound, in the way a slightly drunken nap often can be, and it was a struggle to open my eyes. When I did, the first thing I saw were the heavy deep-red drapes of the bedcurtains, casting strange shadows that seemed to be falling towards me. The window I had left open was letting in a bitter chill. It was dark already and, now the sun had gone down, the winter reasserted itself in earnest. For just a moment, I didn't have a clue where I was. The haunting sound of bells nearby added to my disorientation.

Sitting upright against the unforgiving oak headboard, I remembered the day's events. I was in Venice for the very first time. I was alone. I looked at my watch. Though it was pitch-black outside, it was still only six in the evening. Five o'clock back home in the UK. I needed to get up, get unpacked and start to sort out this new life of mine. But something kept me on the bed. I pulled my knees up to my chin and wrapped my arms around them, self-comforting like a lonely child, making myself small.

The sense of adventure I'd felt when I stood on the quay that morning seemed to have deserted me in the dark. I fumbled around to find a switch for the bedside lamp. In the feeble glow of an energy-saving bulb, the animal carvings on the bed seemed to undulate until I could have sworn they were actually breathing. I squeezed myself tighter. It was just wood. Nothing alive. But there is something about Venice, something about its timelessness, that automatically makes one think of ghosts. And wasn't a ghost exactly what I had come in search of? Luciana Giordano, born 1736. Died ... Well, no one knew exactly when Luciana died, but it had certainly been a long while ago.

I knew I should probably unpack my suitcase and hang my clothes in the mothball-scented wardrobe, but I chose instead to pull out my laptop. I needed the bright modern glow of the screen to link me firmly to the present and remind me that London was just an email away. Plus I had such a short time in this new city to find out about Luciana's life, I might as well start right now.

As Nick had warned me, the Internet connection in my new apartment was patchy to say the least, but it was enough to enable me to pick up my emails. And there it was: an email I'd been awaiting for a very long time. At last I had a response to my request to visit a private library in a palazzo on the Grand Canal that held what remained of Luciana's correspondence.

Yes,

it said.

By all means. Please email to arrange a time.

In a more enthusiastic moment, I might have punched the air. It had taken months to track down Luciana's letters. It had taken even longer to persuade the owner I should be allowed to see them *in situ*. Now I had received my answer. It was brief, but it was definitely positive.

Squashing my feelings of loneliness and trepidation for the moment, I concentrated instead on my reply to Marco Donato, owner of the most extraordinary private library in Venice. This was what I had come for.

I wrote:

Thank you for your kind agreement to let me see Luciana Giordano's letters. I would be delighted to visit them at your earliest convenience. I can come to the library any day you prefer.

I was astonished to receive another email in response just three minutes later.

Really, Miss Thomson, you should play much harder to get. But ten o'clock on Tuesday morning will be fine.

Sincerely, M. Donato

4

Luciana Giordano was her father's favourite. In many ways, this was an ideal situation for a girl to find herself in. In other ways, it was a disaster. Never had a girl been so closely guarded as Gaetano Giordano's beloved only daughter.

Gaetano had not wanted to move to Venice, but his growing export/import business demanded he move his family from respectable Turin to the sinful city on the sea. Venice was still at the centre of the eighteenth-century universe, with links to the whole of the Mediterranean, Constantinople and the world beyond. However, Gaetano feared for the moral purity of his good Catholic children in such a hotbed of turpitude and debauchery. His prejudices about the city were only intensified when his wife succumbed to a fever and died just a year after they arrived there. It was exactly as he had suspected. The very air of Venice was foul with pestilence.

After the loss of his angelic wife, Gaetano was determined that his only daughter would not suffer the same fate. But how do you protect a young girl from a whole city? Well, for the most part she was kept in the house: a grand Gothic palazzo in Cannaregio. On those rare occasions when she was allowed out, Luciana was forced to wear an ugly mask with a hooked nose filled with purifying herbs. Wearing such a mask hadn't saved the plague doctors of the seventeenth century and it wouldn't prove any more effective in keeping Luciana safe from the common cold, but Gaetano insisted Luciana wear it until she was thirteen years old and – according to the physician – her lungs could be considered fully formed. Her childhood nurse called her 'the pigeon' for her black cloak and her pointlessly pointed beak.

But that was far from the worst of it. Desperate in what seemed like unending grief for his late wife, Gaetano went to great lengths not only to keep Luciana's lungs healthy but to keep her mind pure as well. To that effect, he took an even more old-fashioned step than having the poor child wear a plague mask when venturing outside the house. It was Gaetano Giordano's opinion that beyond rudimentary reading, writing and arithmetic, education for women led only to trouble. To keep Luciana from discovering something that might set her on the path to certain ruin, Gaetano banned his daughter from reading anything but the Bible.

'Maria, what exactly does it mean when it says that Onan spilled his seed upon the ground?'

Maria the chaperone snapped the Bible shut on Luciana's fingers.

'You wicked girl. You know you're not to read that.'

'But it's in the Bible,' Luciana protested. 'What can possibly be wrong in my reading God's word?'

'You evil child! You know exactly what's wrong with it.'

Luciana shook her head, eyes wide and innocent.

25

'Oh!' Maria snatched the Bible away altogether. 'Do some sewing instead.'

Luciana delighted in tormenting her chaperone. The woman was an idiot, chosen specifically for her inability to stretch the boundaries of Luciana's little world beyond showing her new stitches. She didn't know enough to be dangerous, though she was very good at making sure that Luciana went no further than the tiny courtyard at the heart of the palazzo – unless they were going to church.

Maria could not, however, stop Luciana looking out of her bedroom window at the front of the house when the rest of the household was asleep. Once everyone was quiet, Luciana would sit on the sill, imagining herself as a princess in the tales her mother used to tell her at bedtime, before she died and all the happiness drained out of the house like the colour leaching out of badly dyed cloth in a downpour. Luciana's father had covered the house with mourning drapes and they hadn't been taken down since. He was trying to keep Luciana's mind covered with mourning drapes too.

Like her father, Luciana thought she would never stop missing her mother, but eight years after their bereavement she felt equally sure that her mother would not have wanted the house in the Cannaregio to stay mired in the darkness of mourning for ever. As much as her father was serious, Luciana's mother had been rather frivolous. She had enjoyed music, adored dancing and liked to wear beautiful clothes. She liked to laugh and to gossip. She had loved her brief sojourn in Venice. She would never have blamed the city for her illness.

Luciana had tried to explain her mother's point of view to her father only once. It earned her the threat of a year in a convent. Being shut up at home was bad enough, but at least she had the view of the canal from her window. The convent her father spoke of was on a desolate scrap of an island way out near Torcello. There were thick bars on the windows there and no one passed by but the seabirds.

So, Luciana became a creature of the night. By day, she was the perfect daughter. She read her Bible and sewed dresses for the poor. But she lived for the moment when the house grew quiet and she would creep from her bed to sit on her windowsill and watch and learn about the big bad world outside.

She soon came to know the routines of the people in her immediate vicinity. For example, every evening at nine, the gentleman of the house directly across the canal would kiss his wife on the forehead and send her off to bed. Half an hour later, he would leave the house for what could only be an illicit rendezvous. He certainly had a shifty look about him as he pulled his hat down over his face and set out in a rowing boat. Half an hour later still, the wife would appear on her bedroom balcony and watch for the arrival of her lover, who stayed until one o'clock in the morning, leaving moments before the husband returned. Their shenanigans filled Luciana with delight as they timed their comings and goings like characters in a play.

Luciana also timed her night by a boatful of revellers who could be heard long before they were seen. The boat carried three musicians who played the same tunes every evening, while the passengers sang along in voices that got louder the more they drank. They were always much noisier when they made their return journey. Luciana came to know the songs by heart and once earned herself a switch across the hand by humming the tune to a particularly lewd one as she went about the house.

'Where did you learn such filth?' Maria asked her.

'I must have heard it in my sleep. I didn't even know what the words meant,' Luciana lied.

The people across the canal and the singing boat were some of Luciana's favourites. She also loved to watch the gondolas carrying grand ladies and their menfolk to the opera. Though Luciana herself was always dressed plainly, modest as any novitiate, she soon had a very broad knowledge of the fashions of the day and longed to swathe herself in an extravagant red domino cloak.

But the boat Luciana most looked forward to seeing was a stealthy affair. A simple black gondola propelled by a single, black-clad gondolier, it moved through the water with nary a sound. The gondolier was so skilled he made not the slightest splash as he rowed. Luciana was fascinated by the simple craft, which was such a contrast to the flagged and flounced pleasure boats that thronged the canals every night. Whom did it belong to? Where was it going? Who hid beneath the plain black canopy of the gondola's *felce*?

Luciana imagined a widower, like her father, who in the grip of his grief had turned his back on frivolity and lightness. But then her imagination roamed further from what she knew. Was the occupant of the gondola a wealthy courtesan, keen to deflect attention on her way to visit a notable lover? Was it a straying husband on his way to see a courtesan? Was it a nobleman? Perhaps even the Doge? Luciana leaned as far out of her window as she could to watch the gondola pass by.

She was so absorbed in the tableaux that unfolded beyond her window each night, she gave no thought to the notion that she too might be observed. From beneath the canopy of the simple black gondola, Luciana's admirer looked forward to seeing her just as much as she longed to see him.

5

The next morning – my first full day in Venice – I headed in to the university to meet the people who would be my colleagues for the next few months. I followed the directions Nick had scribbled down after half a bottle of prosecco and got lost three times. I had to make a pit stop at a coffee shop.

Fortified by the coffee – and boy, it was strong – I continued on my way. It was another bright and beautiful day, despite being so early in the year. The sunshine soon bleached out the slight sense of dread with which I had woken. Venice was doing its utmost to make me welcome. A stallholder, setting up for the day, proffered a freshly caught mackerel in my direction, as though the shining fish were an ornament cast in silver just for me. Using my best Italian, I promised I would be back later and the fishmonger gave me such a wicked grin, I started to worry I had inadvertently promised I would drop by for more than the ingredients for that night's supper.

The university was situated on the Fondamenta Soccorso, in a beautiful building that made even the colleges of Oxford and Cambridge seem ugly. The students were beautiful too. Even the security guards, like almost everyone I had seen in Venice so far, looked as though they were actors, cast in the part, rather than ordinary men doing an ordinary job. No wonder Nick Marsden felt the need to up his game when he came to do his sabbatical in the city.

Nick was already in the office. Unlike me, he didn't seem in the least worse for wear for the previous day's bottle of prosecco. As enthusiastically as he'd shown me the flat, he showed me the tiny cubbyhole that had been allocated to me and explained everything I might need to know, from the procedure for taking books out of the university library to how to persuade the temperamental coffee machine to serve up something faintly drinkable.

'Actually,' he said, having gone through the complicated sequence of punches and kicks the machine required before it would spit out an approximation of an espresso, 'don't bother. Far easier to go to the café on the corner.'

I was happy with that.

Later, he introduced me to other new colleagues, including Beatrice from Rome. I was especially keen to meet her as our areas of interest overlapped. Beatrice, known to her friends (which definition now seemed to include me) as Bea, was writing a thesis on the legendary Giacomo Casanova, concentrating on his intellectual achievements rather than his romantic conquests. We'd already corresponded by email about the possibility of my getting access to the Donato library. Bea was sure that some of Casanova's letters must be languishing there too.

'I'm going to the library tomorrow morning,' I told her.

'You're kidding,' said Bea. 'How on earth did you swing it? Did you find the magic word? I've been trying to get into that library for years. Never heard a thing.'

'I just wrote a letter.'

'A letter? Not an email?'

'Not an email. Not in the first instance, anyway. I thought perhaps I might be writing to someone who appreciates tradition.'

'But what did you say?'

'Nothing unusual. I just went on and on about how Luciana's correspondence might hold the clue to one of the biggest literary mysteries of all time.'

'*The Lover's Lessons*,' said Bea, referring to the novel that had obsessed me since I'd first heard about it five years earlier. 'Well, I suppose if you decide Luciana isn't the author, it will at least lend some more weight to my theory that Casanova is.'

'I will report back on everything,' I assured her. 'And I'll do my best to make sure you get access to the library too.'

'Well, I don't know how you did it, but I am very envious indeed.'

'It's like you've scored an invitation to Willy Wonka's Chocolate Factory,' Nick added.

'What do you mean?' I asked.

'I mean,' said Nick, 'that nobody ever goes in and nobody ever comes out. The Donato library is as much a mystery as your anonymous novel.'

'As is the owner,' Bea told me. 'No one has seen him in nearly fifteen years.'

'They say he only comes out at night to drink the blood of young virgins,' Nick continued, really warming to his theme.

'Oh well,' I said. 'In that case, I'll be *perfectly* safe.'

Nick's blush was a delight to behold.

Despite his curious reputation, now that we had made contact Marco Donato could not have seemed, to me anyway, more helpful. That afternoon, I received further instructions regarding my first visit to his library. The building in which it was housed was on the Grand Canal, in one of the few significant houses that remained under private ownership and had not been turned into apartments, a gallery or a luxury hotel. I was instructed to arrive at ten o'clock precisely. The letters and some pages from Luciana's only surviving diary would be ready for me. I would be allowed to remain in the library for exactly two hours.

I understand that very few people would think a morning spent looking at old letters could possibly be exciting, but I anticipated the following day as eagerly as a child looking forward to Christmas. I felt certain that Luciana's correspondence would provide the missing piece of the jigsaw I had been putting together for years.

The Lover's Lessons, an anonymous erotic novel about a young girl's sexual awakening, caused an absolute scandal when it was first published in 1755. It claimed to be written by the young woman herself, a virgin at the time she began the life journey that led to the creation of the extraordinary work. The good people of Venice, licentious though the rest of the world believed them to be, were still shocked to read such a candid account of female sexuality. Members of the church called for the work to be burned, which naturally ensured its notoriety, popularity and numerous reprints.

It wasn't long, however, before people began to wonder if the book was in fact a hoax. Intellectuals of the time debated whether it was really possible for a young woman to have such a hearty sexual appetite; the narrator claimed she was befriended by a courtesan and indulged in a lesbian affair just a few weeks after losing her virginity. They concluded that it would have been highly unusual. Far more likely was that a man had written the book in the guise of a woman to extract maximum outrage from his musings. For months on end, the gossip in the coffee shops and gambling houses concentrated on the true identity of the author. Venice already had a long history of erotic writing, beginning with fifteenth-century writer Pietro Aretino. Giorgio Baffo, a well-known erotic poet of the time, was flattered by the gossip but denied any involvement. Eventually, Casanova himself emerged as the most likely candidate. When asked if he was the person behind the novel, he neither confirmed nor denied it.

As the centuries passed, Casanova's name was so often associated with *The Lover's Lessons* that the theory of his authorship of the work passed into fact. However, I was not convinced. For my master's degree, I had made long study of Casanova's work and I felt instinctively that *The Lover's Lessons* came from a different pen. The phraseology and the vocabulary were subtly different. Though he had risen to dizzy heights in Venetian society, even partying with the Doge before he wound up in prison, Casanova's beginnings were quite humble. I felt there were qualities in *The Lover's Lessons* that betokened a more refined upbringing and a genuine feminine sensibility.

Luciana Giordano came to my attention shortly after I first suggested that Casanova was not the author of *Lessons*. I had been trawling through Casanova's diaries again, matching the acronyms he used to describe certain of his lovers with women known to have lived in Venice at the time. At first Luciana seemed an unlikely associate of the well-known bad boy, but further investigation into her life suggested that the highly born girl had gone right off the rails. She was admitted to a convent in 1754. Back then, a girl of her class didn't end up in a convent unless she was orphaned, or she was in *serious* trouble. Since records suggested that Luciana's own father had sent her to the island convent near Torcello, disgrace was the only possible motive. But how had she disgraced herself? I felt there had to be a man involved. With my very own history of falling for bad boys, I was determined to find out.

At the end of my first day in my new office, Nick wandered over to my desk and suggested I join him for dinner. I happily accepted his invitation. Despite my enthusiastic promise to the fishmonger, I really didn't feel like cooking for myself. To be honest, I also wouldn't have known where to start with a fish that didn't come in fingers. Neither did I feel like being alone. No matter how many times I checked my email, I had to accept that Steven was in no hurry to make contact. Left to my own devices, I knew, I would dwell on his continued silence. Dwelling is never a good idea when you're on your own in a strange city.

So I went with Nick to a bar on the Campo Santa Margherita, where we drank cold white wine, despite the chilly weather, and ate yet more prosciutto. Fearing I might well start oinking if I had to eat any more ham, I tried to slip a piece to the bar's resident dog. The dog turned its nose up at my offering.

'Ah,' Nick observed. 'He only eats beef. Unlike me. Prosciutto, chicken, fish; I can't resist any of it. Italy has made me into a dustbin.'

'You look very well on it,' I said, as Nick patted his stomach. It was true. He did. And the enthusiasm with which he tucked into whatever was put before him was actually rather attractive. A healthy appetite in one area usually translates into others, after all. While Nick tried to catch the eye of the waitress, I remembered a conversation I'd once overheard on the Tube. Two girls were discussing one's latest boyfriend.

'Does he, you know . . . does he go down on you?' the first girl asked.

'He's a chef,' said her friend. 'He'll eat anything.'

Having asked for the bill, Nick returned his attention to me. He cocked his head to one side and I had the feeling I was being appraised. I also had the feeling that I'd passed. That was perhaps confirmed when Nick gently probed for information about my living situation back in London. I told him I was staying with a friend, which was the truth. I had been staying with a friend in the six weeks since Steven and I fell apart. I hated to admit even to myself that the situation showed no sign of changing.

After dinner, Nick insisted on walking me back to my apartment. He offered his arm as we weaved along the narrow *fondamente*.

'It's quite icy underfoot,' was his excuse.

I was grateful for the support.

When we reached the apartment, Nick hovered as I tried to open the door myself, but in the end had to lend his physical assistance. I provided the magic swearwords. When the door swung open, I sensed he was waiting for me to invite him in. I didn't. Though Nick didn't seem like the kind of man who would ever pull rank, technically he was my superior. Inviting him in would be a bad idea and not just because we had to work together. I'd known him for such a short time I couldn't really call him a friend. I was vulnerable. I'd had half a bottle of wine. At best I would end up boring him with my love-life woes. At worst . . .

'Got to be on form for my meeting with Marco Donato,' I told him.

'Of course,' said Nick, kissing me lightly on both cheeks, Italian-style. 'The man of mystery. I'll see you tomorrow.'

I watched him go. When I got upstairs, however, I began to think perhaps it would have been nice to have company for a little longer. Was it arrogant of me to have thought Nick wanted anything more than a coffee? Perhaps he just wanted some company too. I took off my coat and stood in the middle of the apartment's dingy hallway, feeling my mood come back down. This was, after all, the worst part of the day. Alone at last. Absolutely alone. And in Venice, too. Steven had always said he would take me to Venice . . .

6

I undressed quickly and slipped under the covers of the creaky old four-poster. It was cold that night so I pulled the curtains around the bed, creating for myself a red velvet cave. Thanks to the wine, I fell asleep as soon as my head hit the pillow – and found myself dreaming of Steven again.

It was so vivid. This time he was in the room in Venice with me. He was standing by the window. The moonlight threw shadows across his face, enhancing the high cheekbones and strong jaw that made every woman look twice. His eyes were dark and almost unreadable. Frighteningly so. I hesitated by the door until he beckoned me over. He reached out to touch my face. I stepped towards him, looking into his black eyes for an answer. He closed them as though to shut me out, but at the same time he started to kiss me.

The kiss quickly became passionate. We were so hungry for each other – starved for love after our time apart – that now our appetites had been aroused again, there could be no holding back. As he probed my mouth with his tongue, Steven's hands roamed the curves of my body. I did not protest as his hands moved beneath my clothes. Within moments I was helping him to unfasten the buttons on the back of my dress. As I lifted my arms to pull the dress off over my head, he was already kissing my gently rounded stomach. His tongue traced the edge of my black silk knickers. His fingers sought out the clasp of the lace-trimmed bra that flattered my bosom so well. He'd picked it out for exactly that reason. I remembered how proud and excited I'd been when he told me how he'd gone into Agent Provocateur and got hard while he chose those scraps of lingerie and imagined how I would look in them. Now he changed his mind about letting my breasts free and instead pushed the lace cups down so that my nipples spilled over the top. He'd told me before that sometimes he liked to see me half-dressed. He found it erotic to imagine me caught out and fucked quickly with no ceremony.

While Steven devoured my breasts with kisses, I worked at getting him out of his own clothes. I was desperate to feel his bare skin upon mine. When he was naked and I was in nothing but my bra, he pushed me down onto the bed. I pressed my body against his, luxuriating in the feel of his brown skin against my belly and my thighs. I breathed in his warm scent. He murmured words of love in my ear. Steven filled all of my senses.

He kissed me again, while his fingers tiptoed down to the place where my legs came together. He found my clitoris and stroked it carefully. I moved my pelvis to meet his hand, willing his fingers to stray inside. I knew I was already wet. Steven smiled broadly when he felt it too. He kept his eyes fixed on mine as he dropped his head to my breast and bit down hard upon my nipple. The shot of pain made it all the more delicious when he soothed it away with his tongue. All the while, he finger-fucked me, lubricating my swollen clit with my own love juice.

When the teasing of Steven's fingers became too much to bear, I begged him to enter me. I knew he was ready. I could already feel his penis pressing hard against my thigh. All I wanted now was to have him inside me properly. Filling me. I wriggled my hand down between our warm bodies and sought out his familiar erection.

I guided Steven towards my longing vagina. Our eyes

remained locked as he gently pushed into me and began to move carefully and slowly. With each stroke I felt myself opening up to him, pulling him deeper. He never took his eyes off mine, as though our minds were making love as well as our bodies. I abandoned myself to the sensations he aroused in me, feeling an orgasm build inside me like the unfurling of a flower towards the sun. As Steven came, he begged me to hold him more tightly. He called out my name. I called out his in reply. In ecstasy. And in love.

But calling out Steven's name woke me from my dream. I sat up in bed and pulled the covers closer around me.

'Way too much wine,' was what I told myself. I lay back on my pillow again and put a cold hand to my forehead.

The monkeys on the bedposts seemed to be laughing. They looked at me in definite amusement. I wondered who had slept under their watchful gaze before.

7

Tuesday morning. The day of my first appointment at the Donato family library. I was awake early; I had yet to get used to the bells and how surprisingly noisy this city of waterways could be. At six o'clock, a water-taxi idled right beneath my window for what seemed like an hour, thoughtless as any London cabbie running his diesel engine while he waited for his fare to arrive. Giving up on silence, I got out of bed and shrugged on the huge woolly sweater that was a permanent feature of my wardrobe from October to April back home in England.

Of course, I would dress more carefully for my visit to the library later on. More specifically, I would be dressing carefully for my first meeting with the library's owner.

Marco Donato was, as my new colleagues had suggested, something of an enigma. An Internet search of his name threw up two different men. The first was Marco Donato Senior, who had made his money in shipping. The Donato family had run a popular cruise line in the 1950s, sailing out of Venice to points all over the Mediterranean. There were several pictures of Marco Senior on his ships, dining with the huge Italian celebrities of the time. I discovered that a relatively famous movie had been filmed on one of the boats, and Marco Senior had subsequently left his wife for the female star. Only to go straight back to her when he realised the star couldn't cook anywhere near as well as his long-suffering missus . . .

I liked the look of this first Marco. He had an easy charm about him that was doubtless born of necessity. His Wikipedia entry explained that his beginnings had been humble. Having struggled through a childhood of appalling deprivation, young Marco had given everything to succeed in the world, making his first investments with the money he saved from tips earned while working as a waiter. First of all, he bought a single water-taxi. Then another. Then a fleet. Twenty years later, he owned one of the biggest oceangoing liners in the world. He kept the first water-taxi, however, and would ride out in it on a Sunday morning. The modest boat was always as smartly turned out as a billionaire's Riva, all gleaming brass and polished wood.

The second Marco Donato – the one who'd been writing to me – was this dashing entrepreneur's grandson.

There's an old saying: shirtsleeves to shirtsleeves in three generations, which refers to the idea that it takes three generations to make, consolidate and then squander a fortune. Marco Donato Junior certainly seemed to be doing his best to prove the adage true. His grandfather had made the family fortune. His father had diversified the family's interests and begun to invest in the trappings of class: the houses, the library, and the right education for his son. But Marco Donato Junior was a playboy through and through. Most of the photographs I found in my online search for him were from the mid to late 1990s and the majority of them seemed to have been taken in nightclubs.

Marco Donato Junior was the ultimate gilded youth. Where the grandfather's character and ambition had been born of hardship, the grandson was definitely a product of pure privilege. You could see it in his face. He was handsome as any Michelangelo statue, with sculpted cheekbones and seductive dark eyes beneath a mop of softly curling black hair. His lips were full and sensuous. His habitual expression was a cat-that-got-the-cream grin.

He was tall and broad-shouldered. Obviously a keen sportsman. When he wasn't being photographed in clubs, he was often pictured on a horse or with a racket in his hand. I couldn't help noticing he had excellent biceps, which were showcased to perfection by his designer polo shirts, especially when he was resting an elbow on the windowsill of a soft-top sports car: another favourite pose.

Like his grandfather before him, this younger Marco seemed to enjoy the company of celebrities. He was frequently photographed alongside film stars and musicians. He was certainly never pictured alone. Those companions who weren't bona fide celebrities still had a touch of stardust about them: invariably female, young and slim with enormous, sometimes awe-inspiring, breasts. He didn't seem to discriminate with regard to nationality or colour. As long as they had the legs and the tits.

Marco Donato Junior clearly loved life and it seemed to love him right back.

Though the photographs of this Marco's philandering grandfather had intrigued and amused me, I was surprised to find myself feeling slightly ruffled when I looked at these newer pictures. Every image seemed to tighten an invisible band around my heart.

Was I envious? Jealous? Perhaps. There was no rational reason for it. Good-looking but obviously far too pleased with himself, Marco Donato Junior was hardly my type. My overall impression was that he was an over-privileged boy with too much time on his hands. Likewise, I knew I wouldn't have matched up to his feminine ideal. I'm slim but I have the figure of a boy. Much as I like my breasts, I know they're never going to stop traffic. I certainly couldn't compete with the groomed beauties of Donato's world. I didn't want to in any case. It shouldn't have mattered in the least how Marco Donato conducted his private life. I didn't need him to fancy me. I just wanted him to allow me access to his library. I didn't really need to know anything about his personal life at all. But I couldn't help delving further. I told myself it wasn't prurient; it was the historian in me that made me want to know more. And Marco Donato Junior did have a certain mystery to him.

It was odd, given how gregarious the man had obviously been in his younger days, that he was so very secretive now. The photographs of the young Italian, louche and delicious as any dark-eyed stud in a Caravaggio painting, stopped around 1999. There was simply nothing after that. Nothing at all. No pictures. No gossip items. I wondered what had happened to make the playboy stop playing, but my searches on the Internet proved fruitless. There was no mention of a wife, who might have put her foot down about his partying. It was as though he had just vanished. From the party scene, at least. He was obviously still alive, since he was sending emails to my inbox. Well, someone using his name was.

That morning, I sent one more polite email to confirm I would be at the library at the appointed time.

I am very much looking forward to meeting you,

I concluded.

And I found I *was* very much looking forward to meeting him, to the extent that I put on make-up before leaving the house, as though I was heading out on a date rather than a library visit. I was not just casually interested, I was intrigued. Though I was barely conscious of the feeling at the time, seeing all those photographs of Marco Donato draped in beautiful women had made me want to experience what those girls must have felt in his orbit. A psychologist would have recognised my reaction at once. There is a little part of every woman that wants the man who has already been approved by the sisterhood. You would think that knowing a man had had so many partners would be off-putting, but in fact it can have quite the opposite result.

They call it the Casanova effect.

8

The Palazzo Donato was a beautiful place – even by standards in Venice, where everything is astonishingly beautiful. Rising four proud storeys above the waterline, the house was built in the Byzantine style popular in the fifteenth century, when connections with the Near East were strong and influence flowed back and forth between Venice and Constantinople like the tide. The details round the extravagantly arched windows on the terracotta-coloured facade were picked out in fresh white paint. In front of the house was a well-scrubbed wooden deck, surrounded by the candy-striped mooring poles that littered the city. Tied to one of the poles, which were painted in the burgundy and yellow Donato colours, I recognised the old water-taxi that had been the first step in building the family fortune. It still looked well cared for. The wooden hull was recently varnished. The brass oarlocks shone as bright as gold.

I had splashed out on a water-taxi of my own to get to the library that morning. Though I had been in Venice for three days now, I was no closer to knowing my way round than I had been on that first morning. I still got lost within fifty feet of my apartment and I could not risk being late. Not when it had been so difficult to persuade Donato to let me visit in the first place.

'This is the house,' said the taxi driver.

'Thank you.' I counted out the fare I had negotiated at the start of the trip.

'I'd love to have a look inside,' the driver continued. 'My father told me in the nineteen-sixties, this was *the* place to come for a party. Everyone came here. Film stars, millionaires, politicians, rock stars. Even the president of the United States.'

'Kennedy?' I suggested.

'Maybe.' The driver shrugged. 'It was the same in the nineteen-nineties, with the grandson. Parties, parties, parties. Every night. All the famous faces were here. One night, he had Prince fly in to play a song for his girlfriend's birthday. We thought he would have Prince here to play for the millennium too. You know, 1999.'

'Of course.' I remembered my own Millennium Eve, spent in a suburban semi, getting drunk on a bottle of schnapps my cousin had stolen from her parents' drinks cupboard. Sixteen years old and stuck in Guildford, with no hope of even being allowed out of the house to see midnight, a party in a palazzo with real live celebrities was beyond my wildest imaginings.

'That party never happened,' the driver sighed. 'No one knows why. It would have been an incredible night.'

'Well, yes. I suppose it would.'

'And now this place is just a library.'

I had explained my mission to the water-taxi driver as he brought me to the house.

'Such a waste.' He shook his head. 'Great house for a party.'

'Great house for a library,' I countered.

'If you like that sort of thing.'

Fortunately, I did like that sort of thing and as the taxi driver helped me on to the pontoon in the wonderfully gallant style I had quickly come to expect from Italian men, I could feel my excitement growing. I was now only minutes away from seeing the letters and diary I felt sure would prove my theory about *The Lover's Lessons*. I was also only moments away from meeting the mystery man himself.

I was almost trembling with anticipation as I tugged on the brass bell-pull and heard the chimes announce my arrival deep inside the house.

After a moment, I realised the water-taxi driver was still hovering. He too wanted to see behind the door that had so long been closed to anyone but the few people who worked inside.

'Call me when you want to go back,' he said hopefully.

'Of course,' I said, though I knew I wouldn't. My budget didn't stretch to two water-taxi rides in one day. Now I just wanted him to go away so I could savour this moment alone. I turned back to the house. At last he got the hint and the landing platform bobbed furiously as the water-taxi roared off at top speed. I had to spread my feet for balance to keep from tumbling into the canal.

It seemed like an age before the door was opened. As I heard the creak of a lock being pulled back, I straightened myself up in expectation of meeting the master of the house – after all, he was the one who had been corresponding with me – but a crooked-looking man, who must have been in his seventies, came to the door instead.

'*Signorina* Thomson?' the man asked.

'*Sì, sì*,' I confirmed. Perhaps Donato was waiting for me inside. A multimillionaire hardly needed to open his own doors, did he?

'*Avanti*,' the man said, ushering me through and closing the door quickly behind me, as though to shield the house from prying eyes. Donato was obviously serious about his privacy. 'This way. Please.'

I stepped into the lobby. I had been expecting incredible luxury but the stone floor was plain and cold. The walls were covered in thick tapestries. It was dark and I couldn't see what the tapestries depicted. The whole effect wasn't especially welcoming. In fact it was austere.

I followed the old man through a series of corridors that were as narrow and convoluted as the Venetian streets outside, until eventually we came to another heavy door. The man pushed it open, putting his shoulder against it for leverage. I made Nick's joke about the damp. He didn't laugh.

'Come on.'

The door led onto a courtyard with an elegant formal garden.

'Oh, how beautiful.' I couldn't help but exclaim at the view of neatly trimmed hedges and elegant lemon trees, especially after the severity of the entrance hall.

'*Sì*,' said the man. 'Come on.'

We crossed the garden at a clip. I wished I had time to linger, to look more closely at the silent fountain in the centre, and also up at the arched galleries that surrounded the courtyard. As I glanced in that direction, a gilded sundial directed a shaft of weak January sunshine right into my eyes, forcing me to look back down, catching sight of a beautiful statue of a woman as I did so. On the other side of the garden stood the marble woman's stony partner, with his hand extended towards her. There was so much to look at. I wanted to pause and imagine what it must have been like to live here when the house was first built. Who had designed this haven from the bustle outside? Who had commissioned the beautiful marble lovers? Why did they look so sad?

But the old man was not having any of it. He was already pushing hard against the door that would take us back into the house on the other side of the courtyard. I just had time to glance up again and – I was sure of this – see a figure quickly conceal itself behind a curtain in one of the upper rooms.

'This is the library,' said the man as he opened another door and stood to one side to let me pass. 'The papers are there.' He indicated a desk with a curt nod of his head and there, as promised, was the box that must contain Luciana's letters. '*Due ore,*' was the man's last comment before he closed me inside.

Well, I thought as I listened to the old man's footsteps retreating slowly down the corridor. I guess I'm not meeting Donato today after all. While the air still reverberated to the sound of the door closing behind Donato's servant, I took my first proper look at the library.

It was an incredible room. The kind of room I dreamed of having for myself. Not that it would have fitted into that tiny flat back in London, where Steven and I had stuffed books onto an overflowing set of shelves from Ikea, or stacked them in precarious piles in every spare corner: by the bed, by the bath, in the kitchen. What luxury to have so much space for books. The ceiling in this secret library was two storeys high. It was crammed with volumes, but at the same time, the stacks had been carefully arranged so they did not encroach on any of the windows. The room was brilliantly lit, even on a January day. There were two desks, which faced each other like companions, and a number of comfortable chairs arranged in various corners and round a huge fireplace set with a fire to cut through the winter chill. Above the fireplace hung a portrait of a woman in eighteenth-century dress. She was beautiful, with intelligent brown eyes that reminded me a little of Bea. She looked down upon me kindly, I thought. I wondered who she was. There was no name on the frame.

It would be a pleasure to work in a library so well appointed. I was already wondering how I could extend my visit beyond the two hours I had been promised.

Two hours would certainly not be long enough to study Luciana's correspondence with the attention it deserved. But, remembering that two hours might be all I ever had here, I stopped admiring the scenery and sat down to the task ahead.

The letters of Luciana Giordano were collected together in a beautiful box, covered in the kind of multicoloured marbled paper for which the master stationers of Italy are justly famous. I opened the box gingerly, unsure how robust it would be. Though it was undoubtedly much younger than the letters it contained, it was still ancient and fragile. I had to take care.

I automatically held my breath and closed my eyes as I let the hinged lid fall open. I knew that when I opened them again, everything would be different. Because this wasn't just a box full of old paper to me. I was about to touch something that my heroine had touched, three centuries before. The letters inside this box contained her own true thoughts. The implications were momentous. Luciana Giordano and I were about to make contact across the years.

9

The diary of Luciana Giordano, 11th November, 1752

I have to write quickly, as in just half an hour Maria will be awake and at her daily business of bothering me to within an inch of my life in the name of preserving my dignity and reputation. What a night! When the household was asleep, I took up, as usual, my place by the window to watch the nightly circus unfold. Truly, I cannot imagine anything the good people of Venezia might see at the *Teatro San Benedetto* could compare with what happened here on our little canal last night.

It all began as usual. The husband from the opposite house left at his customary time. I checked his exit against the bells. He kissed his dear sweet wife on the forehead and sent her to bed. He didn't look up to see her watch from the window to make sure that he had really gone. He never does. Poor fool.

Fifteen minutes later, the lover arrived. He tied his boat out of sight of the main canal and made his way to her building like a cat sneaking after its prey. Hearing his signal – which is not unlike a cat's meow; I have been practising it myself – the wife threw her window wide and let down a rope, as long and thick as Rudaba's hair in the Persian fairytale. Her lover was up it like a monkey and did not even wait until she had closed the shutters to start

51

kissing her and loosening her breasts from her bodice. I have to admit, I was quite aroused by the sight, though I fear it will be a long time before anyone but Maria loosens my stays.

They only half-closed the shutters this evening – though it's grown so cold these past few days I would have thought they would catch their deaths – so I was able, if not to see what was going on, to hear what was going on very easily. Such grunts and groans! It's hard to imagine they were doing something pleasurable. I thought the act of love was supposed to be accompanied by tender sighs and sweet declarations, not howling and curses to raise merry hell.

Anyway, the grunting and groaning took the usual amount of time and came to its crescendo with a particularly anguished wail on the part of the lover. After that, I heard the wife giggling so I assumed the lover was not hurt. Indeed, he came to the window moments later, throwing the shutters a little wider to let in the air. Frustratingly, he had his mask on. Perhaps he had not taken it off. Maria tells me there are people in Venezia who wear their masks so often that even their friends and relations are unable to recognise them bare-faced.

My father thinks the practice of wearing masks in this town has gone much too far. My brother says my father disapproves of the widespread use of the mask precisely because it is so levelling and liberating. When everyone is masked, a pauper may talk to a duchess. The Doge can move among his people unknown and thus learn exactly what they think of him. My father thinks masks encourage dishonest behaviour. My brother argues the exact opposite. How can the Doge govern properly if he does not know the true will of the people and how can he know the true will of the people but by being anonymous? Indeed, how can the ordinary people make their true feelings known except from inside a disguise?

All I know is I wish I had a mask. But I do not want the one kind of mask my father has offered to buy me. Despite making me spend my childhood in a plague doctor's mask to keep me from my mother's terrible fate, these days he says if I want to hide my face from the sight of God in broad daylight, then I must wear a *servetta muta*, a mask only held in place by a button between my teeth so I may speak no evil while I am wearing it. Apparently, the *servetta muta* is very popular with the husbands of Venezia.

Anyway, the lovers finished their exertions, but that was not to be the end of the evening's entertainment. I heard the bells of the *Chiesa degli Scalzi* sound the quarter to. And then I saw the husband. He was early! Oh! If only I could have given the poor wife a warning. Instead, the husband and the lover met in the most unfortunate circumstances. When the lover let himself down from the wife's balcony, he almost landed on her husband's head.

You have never seen such a pantomime. It drew a crowd until the canal was quite solid with boats. No one could get by but nobody cared. Here was a fabulous free show.

I was so absorbed by the spectacle I didn't notice at first that the black gondola had stopped right beneath my window. I slipped back behind the curtain, hoping to hide myself, but I was too late. The gondolier looked upwards and caught my eye. He gave me a smile. I stayed behind the curtain but he beckoned me back out. He looked towards the canopy and its mysterious occupant and, while I watched, a hand, in a white cuff that was stark against the darkness, snaked out and handed the gondolier a letter. The gondolier duly spiked the letter on the end of his oar and – horrors – passed it up to me.

I did not know what to do. My first thought – the thought my father would have liked me to stick with – was that I should tell the gondolier to take the letter back. How insulting to be passed a note in such a manner! But my second thought was that I was desperate to know who had written it. Until that moment, I had not even known whether the mysterious occupant of the *felce* was a man or a woman. I guessed now, from the size of the hand in the frilly white cuff, it was a man. Though having said that, Maria does have rather large knuckles.

So, what did I do? Well, I nodded to the gondolier. Curtly, as befits my status compared to his. I wanted him to know it was inappropriate of him to smirk at me as if we were equals. Then I snatched the letter from the end of his pole and retired to my room, slamming the shutters behind me.

And here I am. Though I am happy that the gondolier can report back to his master that I accepted the letter quite coolly, I cannot tell you how excited it has made me. This is the first letter I have received in years. The last was from my grandmother, writing to console me after the death of my mother, her only daughter. I treasure that letter and read it often, but how I have longed for some lighter correspondence. There's not much joy to be had in reading when the only reading matter available to a girl is a letter of condolence or the Bible. The Bible lately is a lot more boring, since Maria has taken a sharp knife and cut out all those pages that make reference to breasts or emissions. The book is a good third less thick.

Well, I have something much more interesting to read now. The letter is addressed to 'The Nocturnal Madonna of the Open Window'. The seal bears a monkey's head. It is not a crest I recognise, as I surely would had I seen it before. A shiver goes through me as I slide my thumb under it. It seems to be the emblem of a great man.

The handwriting is impressive too, with grand sweeping strokes and luxurious curlicues. And the words . . .

To the Nocturnal Madonna of the Open Window. For the past four weeks, I have had the pleasure of seeing your face as I make my leisurely way to the Rialto. At first, I felt sure I would have the greater delight of making your acquaintance on dry land, but my inquiries led me no closer to knowing who you are and why you sit at your window night after night when a beauty of your tender years should be dancing. Please, forgive my impertinence, but I find I can stay away from you no longer. The sight of your shining hair tumbling through the window is the only sight Venezia has worth seeing. Tell me, fair maiden, how I may know you better, or otherwise tell me to forget you and I will have my gondolier choose another route to my house. You may return correspondence by the same manner tomorrow night. GC.

Oh. I have read the letter a dozen times or more. He has noticed me. And I thought I had been so discreet. But, how wonderful! His language is both eloquent and daring. I feel my heartbeat grow faster as I press his words against my breast. He has inquired after me. I have to know more about him too. *GC*? What does that *GC* represent?

I must write my reply, of course, and then the only thing to do is make sure Maria doesn't find it before I have a chance to pass it to his gondolier tomorrow night. That hateful woman is like a dog in search of a rat when it comes to secrets. I am amazed she has not already found this diary, as she found the small bottle of perfume I secreted under the mattress last year. I will tuck the letter inside these pages. May there be many more to come.

10

I glanced up at the clock and did a double take. It seemed as though I had entered the library only minutes earlier, but now the clock was telling me I had just two minutes left until the old retainer would return to escort me from the premises again. What a disaster. Even with my enormous Italian–English dictionary alongside me, I had only managed to read four pages of Luciana's scrappy diary. Her handwriting had been difficult to decipher at first. So much so that I began to wonder if she was writing in code. Then there was the complication that Luciana's Italian was quite unlike the modern Italian I had studied at school. Or even the Latin. And she used plenty of Venetian slang. I had no hope whatsoever of translating *that* in a hurry. The Venetian dialect was as foreign to me as the Arabic from which much of it derived.

I stared at the clock as though willing the hands to travel backwards. I felt as though I had only just started to hear Luciana's voice, but at midday on the dot, the door to the library swung open and the old retainer waited impatiently while I gathered my notes and my dictionary. Please God, I muttered to myself, don't let this be the last time I am here.

I expected the old man to accompany me all the way back to the waterside, or to the street, but instead when we got to the courtyard, he merely asked me whether I would be going back by boat or on foot.

'On foot,' I replied.

'Then you need that door there,' he said. 'Go straight

down the passage and you will emerge on to the Calle Squero. I trust you'll find your own way. I have work to do.'

Then he turned, leaving me quite alone in the hall.

Obviously, I could not have failed to notice that my presence at the house was not entirely welcome, but with the old man gone, I couldn't resist taking a longer look at the courtyard garden and the surrounding galleries as I passed through. The fountain still wasn't playing, but a leaking washer somewhere in its plumbing meant that every so often a drop splashed from the fountainhead into the surrounding stone bowl, where years of such innocuous drops had eroded a little dent. Two sparrows were taking it in turns to wait for a glittering drop to fall, taking a sparrow-sized shower before they dried themselves off in the sunlight. It was magical.

Though it was still only January, there was life in this sheltered garden. London's greenery was still deep in hibernation, but the first signs of spring were already in evidence on the edge of the Adriatic. I ran my fingers along the sharp edge of a box leaf. There was even a flower: a single winter rose, proud and beautiful and brave. I don't know what possessed me in that moment, but suddenly, without thinking about the consequences – like Beauty's father in 'Beauty and the Beast', always my favourite fairytale – I reached out and plucked the trembling white flower from its stem. I was immediately ashamed. Hiding it inside my cupped hand, I quickly headed for the door the old man had pointed out to me, my heart quickening from the excitement of my petty theft. Nobody stopped me of course but, just as when I first crossed the courtyard, I had the distinct impression that I was being watched.

Back at the university I drafted an email to Donato, thanking him for allowing me to use his library. However, I suddenly decided that it was important to make a better impression.

An email would have been easy but I had actually started our correspondence with a proper, handwritten letter and perhaps that was what had made the difference. So I got out the fountain pen that my grandfather had given me on my eighteenth birthday. My lucky pen. I hardly ever used it, not least because after years of working on keyboards, I found it difficult to write more than a few paragraphs without getting cramp. But when I wanted to make a real impression, to convey to the person receiving my words that they were truly heartfelt, I brought out the pen.

> *Dear Mr Donato,*
>
> *I want to thank you for your kindness in allowing me to visit your library this morning. I cannot tell you how much it meant to me to be able to see Luciana Giordano's correspondence. Reading her letters, holding them in my hands, made me feel as though Luciana and I were actually talking to one another across the centuries. How wonderful it was to read a page from her diary, so vibrant and funny. It was as though she had written it yesterday. I can't thank you enough for that experience.*
>
> *I know it was no small matter for you to let a stranger into your house and for that reason I hesitate to beg your further indulgence, but I must tell you that Luciana's writings are extremely important to my research and possibly to the wider academic community. If you were to see your way to allowing me access to those letters even one more time, it would make an enormous difference.*

Though I wrote the letter in English, I signed off with a florid Italian turn of phrase, courtesy of Bea. At five o'clock, the post-boy popped his head round the office door to see if anyone had any mail to send. I picked up my letter and almost handed it over, but then decided against it. Donato's house was just a twenty-minute walk away, assuming I didn't get lost. It seemed ridiculous to let the post-boy take it only for it to travel to the outskirts of town to the sorting office and perhaps spend three or four days languishing there before it reached its target.

So I delivered the letter on my walk home that evening. Though I was starting to be able to orient myself I still managed to take a couple of wrong turns. Not that wrong turns in Venice are ever such a disaster, since they almost always turn up something beautiful or interesting. I felt I could wander the *calli* of Venice for a thousand years and never get bored. Eventually, however, I came to the street entrance of the palazzo – the one through which I had left at midday. There was no letterbox that I could see, so I rang the bell. It was at least five minutes before the old retainer appeared. He didn't exactly exude warmth as I greeted him and showed him the letter.

'It's important he gets it quickly,' I tried to explain in my faulty Italian. 'Is he here in Venice at the moment? Because if he isn't, then I'll email him too. I don't want him to think I'm not grateful for being allowed in the library this morning.'

'He's here,' the old man said, nodding. 'He is always here.'

'Oh.' I was surprised and, if I'm honest, a little offended then that he had not made the effort to meet me. 'OK . . . I'll just leave this with you.'

The old man took the letter, closing the door simultaneously, leaving me on the street wondering whether he would really pass on the letter or use it as kindling.

I waited for a moment or two, toying with the idea of knocking on the door again and asking, since Mr Donato was in, whether his servant wouldn't mind if I delivered my thank-you note in person. But my bravado soon deserted me. If Donato hadn't wanted to see me that morning, why would he want to see me now? Or perhaps he had seen me. Perhaps his was the shadow that had lurked in the gallery bordering the garden. Yes, that was it. He had seen me all dolled up in my very best pencil skirt and decided I wasn't worth getting to know, unlike the long-legged, large-breasted supermodels of St Moritz and Saint Tropez. I felt myself growing hunched at the comparison.

My mobile phone vibrated in my pocket.

It was Nick.

'*Aperitivo?*' he suggested, in an exaggerated Italian accent. 'Look for the Ponte dei Pugni. There's a bar right at the foot of it. You can't miss it. Everyone spills out onto the bridge.'

'OK,' I said. 'Why not?'

I needed company again. I felt oddly downcast by Donato's decision not to make my acquaintance that morning and that small rejection somehow amplified the much larger hurt I was already feeling with regard to Steven. Plus, there was something about the Donato house. It seemed to have thrown a shadow that remained with me as I walked away. There was sadness there, most definitely. But why? I glanced up at its shuttered windows one last time as I got to the end of the street. Perhaps I was going bonkers, but I was sure someone was watching me again.

I I

12th November, 1752

Night could not come quickly enough. Even though it is November and the days are supposed to be short, I felt as though darkness would never fall. The hours I spent sewing in front of the fire seemed like a year. And then, even when it was dark, I had to wait longer. Maria normally sends me up to bed at the earliest possible opportunity, but tonight of all nights she was not in any hurry. I asked if the priest was coming to take her confession. She bristled and told me the priest has gone to visit an elderly relative in Padua. Besides, she added when she realised her answer might have told me too much, she had no reason to confess. Unlike some. She nodded her head towards the windows and the darkness beyond. I knew she wanted to gossip about the people in the house across the canal but of course, she couldn't gossip with me. More's the pity for her. I could have added some real colour to her hearsay.

Instead we had to sit in silence, both of us frustrated. Her without the prospect of divine intervention. Me just waiting for the end of this interminable day. If only I felt Maria could be trusted. If I could have told her exactly what happened on the canal beneath my window last night, how quickly our evening together might have passed.

Anyway, I digress. At last, at last, the time came when Maria suggested I go to my bed. I had been hinting for several hours already. Yawning and sighing, complaining of dropped stitches. But I know Maria dislikes being alone in the darkened rooms of the palazzo. My father is away on business. My brother has accompanied him this time. There remains only me to keep her company. Both Maria and I knew that Fabio, my father's boatman and general factotum, would have taken advantage of the absence of the master of the house and gone to visit his sweetheart. Lucky Fabio, having a sweetheart whose parents don't care about her reputation at all.

So, I went to bed. I made a show of reluctance, of course, but Maria said it was her duty to ensure I didn't fall asleep in church the following day. I agreed that would be a terrible shame, though church is where I have my best naps. Maria rarely notices because she is so busy mooning over the priest.

Maria unlaced my dress and helped me into my nightgown. She unfastened my hair and combed it out. I have told her several times she doesn't need to comb my hair. I am perfectly capable of doing it myself. But tonight she insisted. I don't know why. She certainly doesn't seem to enjoy the job. Though I suppose I should be grateful she doesn't seem to be doing the task for the pleasure of hurting me either. When she finds a knot, she very rarely bothers to untangle it. At that point she hands the comb over to me.

I washed my face and hands and Maria joined me by the prie-dieu as I said my night-time prayers. I prayed for my father and my brother, my mother in Heaven, for Maria – I was rewarded with a sort-of-smile for that – and for all those on the water that evening. Maria's brow wrinkled.

'All those on the water?'

'I heard there might be a storm,' I said.

While Maria fussed about the room, letting down the curtains round the bed and blowing out most of the candles, I completed my prayers in silence. I wasn't sure what God would make of my request for the safe passage of my gondolier and his master, but I made it all the same.

'Goodnight,' said Maria.

'Goodnight,' I answered from my place on the pillows. Knowing she would turn round when she got to the door, I made a show of finding it hard to keep my eyes open. I let my body go limp and my eyes fall shut. I was the very image of an innocent girl in her dreams.

But as soon as the door shut behind my chaperone, my eyes were open. I listened to the sound of her footsteps in the dark. I listened for the creak of the board halfway down the corridor. She was going straight to her own room. Good. I waited for a minute or two more before I swung my legs out of bed and found my still warm slippers on the floor. I wrapped my dressing gown around me and padded to the window. Softly, I opened the shutters. There is always a danger that one of them will squeak but tonight they were good to me, complicit in my plan.

The night air rushed in. It was so cold my first breath almost stopped my heart. Such a night! Who would be out now by choice? Mist swirled along the water, curling its way up to my balcony. I listened to the *campanile* strike twelve and hoped I would not have to wait too long.

There was, of course, no scene being played out at the

house across the canal that evening. I'd overheard Maria and the cook saying it would be a couple of weeks before the husband ventured out alone again. I leaned as far out of my window as I could to see the distant entrance to the Grand Canal. Thanks to the fog rolling in from the lagoon, I could see next to nothing, but the voices of the revellers let me know they were still there. Snatches of song, shouts and whistles met my ears, though they were softened and distant, like the voices of the dead.

You can imagine then how ghostlike was the black gondola this evening. Just this once, I heard it before I saw it. I heard the gentle slap of the oar in the water as the gondolier steered skilfully towards my house. Then I saw the polished *ferro*, and the gondolier's hat. He lifted his lantern towards me. The light shining on his face, illuminating that alone, made him look like some sort of floating demon. I ducked back into my window. He whistled up.

'Hey! Hey! It's the Madonna of the Window.'

I leaned back out, putting my finger to my lips. He was going to get me into trouble.

'Have you written your reply?' he asked.

I showed him the paper, folded and sealed with a piece of string and a plain blob of wax from my bedtime candle. I don't have a seal so I used the end of my pen to scratch my initials into it. I hoped my correspondent would understand this embarrassing lapse.

The gondolier reached up his oar and I fastened my letter to the end of it. He plucked the letter off and passed it into the *felce*. He tipped his hat at me and began to row away at once.

* * *

Now I feel horribly foolish. What have I done? I have sent a letter containing all my innermost secrets and frustrations to a man I do not know. He might be anybody. How could I have been so insane as to believe I could trust someone who doesn't show his face, even in this town where no one shows his face? I imagine my letter being passed from hand to hand in some tavern. Oh, what an evening's sport I will make for a bunch of men on the Rialto. What if the letter falls into the hands of someone who knows my brother? Or, far worse, my poor papà? I can almost hear the gates of the convent closing behind me.

I cannot sleep. I can do nothing but lie on my back and stare up at the canopy, imagining the stream of events I have just set in motion.

12

I was quickly learning that an *aperitivo* with Nick always turned into an event. When I met him at the bar, Bea was already there. There were other faces I recognised from the corridors of the university and a whole host of other people I didn't know yet, but who greeted Nick like an old friend. The proprietor of the bar seemed especially happy to see him. When Nick wrapped his arm round my shoulder – treating me to a cloud of his delicious aftershave – and took me into the bar itself, to see the sort of food that was on offer, the old proprietress gave him a beaming smile. She gave me an altogether more appraising look. It put me in mind of Donato's old retainer.

'And what can I get for *her*?' the old woman asked, jerking her head in my direction.

I tried not to take offence. Instead, I smiled and said '*Grazie, grazie,*' a million times as Nick picked out a selection of small bites – *cichetti* – he thought I might like. Then Nick ordered me a spritz – Venice's signature tipple, a mixture of white wine, soda water and Aperol – and we went back outside. Despite the freezing weather, international students in their North Face puffa jackets and locals looking altogether more glamorous in their Prada and real fur thronged the bridge.

'This bar has been here for centuries,' Nick explained. 'Bea thinks Casanova might have mentioned it.'

'I worked it out from the location,' Bea explained.

'I don't suppose it's changed much,' said Nick.

Bea picked up a crostino and examined it. Her nose wrinkled. 'This has certainly been on the counter for several centuries already.'

It was true that the quality of the *cichetti* Nick had picked out was variable, but no one came to this particular bar to eat. They came to be seen. They came to meet old friends. They came to flirt with strangers. After two glasses of spritz, which I'd quickly got a taste for, I forgot about the cold. After three, I was delighted to join Nick and some other guys for dinner. When I finally pushed open the door to my apartment at midnight, I had the feeling I was going to have a slow sort of morning the following day.

I fell into the spooky old four-poster quite gratefully. I pulled the red velvet curtains closed to keep in the warmth and snuggled deep beneath the scratchy blankets. Laying my head down on the pillows, I thought about my morning at the Palazzo Donato.

I drifted into sleep thinking especially about the secret courtyard. I heard the drip, drip, drip of the broken fountain. I saw the statues – parted lovers frozen in time – eternally beckoning to each other across the crooked path. I saw the playful sparrows jumping in and out of the water as sunlight turned the droplets on their wings into dazzling sequins. I saw the fruit trees waiting for the first breath of spring. I saw my hand closing on the stem of the single white winter rose, breaking the sap-filled green stalk to set the blossom free. And then another hand, large and masculine, was suddenly closing around mine. I felt hot breath on the side of my face.

'What will you give me in return for my most precious possession?'

I turned in horror. Towering over me was a man in a

half-mask similar to those sold in every tourist shop in the city. He was smiling but with no intention of putting me at my ease.

I apologised for my clumsy theft, my face reddening with shame as I struggled to find the right words. I tried to step backwards but the stranger held on to my hand and unbalanced me. The rose stem was squeezed inside my palm. I waited to feel a thorn pierce my skin, but no pain came. The masked man stared at me. Behind the mask, his eyes were dark and almost animal. Like a bear's. I was hypnotised. As I looked closer, they started to change. Far from being hard, now they seemed sad but kind. They were at odds with his cruel, twisted smile and I felt my fear begin to ebb away.

'It's yours,' he said eventually. 'It was waiting just for you.'

And then suddenly that cruel mouth was upon mine, kissing me passionately. Our two hands were still joined together round the flower. His free hand was round my waist, posed as though we were dancing. He kissed me until I ran out of breath and started wilting in his embrace. The rose was forgotten as we unlaced our hands so I could wrap both my arms around his neck. He picked me up. He was strong and certain. He lifted me as though I weighed less than the broken flower. I knew he would not drop me.

He carried me into the house, past the door to the library and on down the corridor. Still carrying me, he pushed open a door with his shoulder and took me into his chamber. In the centre of the room was a high four-poster bed made up with bright white sheets. He laid me down upon it.

Helpless with desire, I sank into the pillows. I reached my hands up to him. He stripped off his shirt. His back was wide and strong. His arms, as I had gathered when he carried me, were hewn from thick hard muscle. I stared at his body. On his chest was a scar that looked like an exploding comet. It sat over his heart. When he leaned over me, I touched it with a tender finger. Without speaking to me, he pushed my hand away.

He started to undress me. I was wearing clothes I did not recognise as my own. They were not even from my own time. I was dressed in a long velvet gown like the ones I had seen in paintings of Luciana's contemporaries. While my terrifying lover struggled to unfasten the laces that held the bodice closed, I could feel the bones of a corset straining as my breath grew more ragged. Unable to untie the ribbons, my lover was angry enough to rip them instead. I gasped as I felt the bodice loosen. It was as much from relief as from the indignity.

He devoured me with kisses. I lay helpless on the pillows as he touched every part of me greedily and without restraint. He treated me as though I were his possession. But at the same time, I knew I was precious to him. He would not hurt me. He wanted me to feel pleasure in everything he did to me. He pulled my legs apart with rough enthusiasm. I gasped at his erection. When it pressed against me, I felt like a virgin again.

I gave myself to him without question. I abandoned myself to the bliss of our two bodies melting into one.

'Take off your mask,' I begged him. 'Please take off your mask.'

But he would not. He simply would not show me his face. No matter how urgently I asked him.

Waking up alone in the darkness, I blinked away the last of the dream, wishing at the same time that I could close my eyes and go back to it. Three erotic dreams in as many nights. I sat up and caught my breath. Was there something about the air in Venice that was making my imagination so wild, or was it just that I'd had too many spritzes? I fetched myself a glass of water in the hope of making the next morning's hangover less hideous. While I was out of bed, I checked my phone and my emails.

A text from my mother. An email from an old friend. There was still nothing from Steven in response to my own last angry message. Getting back into bed, I closed my eyes and pressed my eyelids with my fingers to stop the tears from coming. I was as lonely as I had ever been and somehow the dream of my strange lover in the palazzo garden had only made things worse.

13

I spent the next morning looking at the notes I had made in the library. The white rose I'd plucked from the garden was pressed into my notebook, already a paper-thin ghost of itself. I felt a rush of shame as I admired my stolen bounty and remembered the previous night's strange dream. Though I had not been given express permission to do so, I'd also taken a few sneaky photographs of the letters with the camera function on my phone. I'd taken some sneaky photographs of the library too. I thought about sharing them with Bea and Nick but decided against it. Not yet. I suddenly felt a strange obligation to keep Palazzo Donato's secrets.

At midday, the post-boy came into the office, pushing his little trolley. He had books for Nick and Bea. He had flyers regarding a Martedì Grasso party being organised by the students' union. And for me he had a single letter.

I knew at once whom this letter was from. The envelope, made of thick creamy vellum, did not bear a stamp. It had been delivered by hand. My name and the university address were written in extravagant cursive. It was, I thought, exactly the kind of handwriting I would have expected. I could imagine its owner using his expansive script to sign off large cheques and hotel invoices. Maybe even signing the odd autograph. I tucked my thumb underneath the envelope flap and levered it open. Inside was a single sheet of expensively heavy paper.

*By all means, you must come back to the palazzo and
continue your research. How could I stand in history's way?
My housekeeper will be happy to let you into the library at
ten o'clock each weekday. I ask only one thing of you: that
you tell me more about your research. I would like to know
about the contents of Luciana's diary and letters and their
significance. I have always meant to read them myself, but
never seem able to find the time. Also, how does a woman
from the United Kingdom come to be so interested in an
obscure Venetian merchant's daughter in any case? I would
like to know. You may email your response. Your handwriting
gives me a headache.*

Oh. I was delighted to receive such a letter but I was shocked
by the bluntness of Donato's last comment. I had to agree,
however, that he had a fair point. Handwriting had never been
my strong suit. Even with my grandfather's pen. But he had
also said he wanted to know more. That was the real surprise.
I had to indulge him, so I emailed my response right away. I
confirmed I would be delighted to take Donato up on his offer
and would present myself at the library the following day.
Then I offered him his due. I told him a little about the diary
entries I had read so far and – somewhat shyly – about myself.

I became interested in history thanks to an enthusiastic
teacher at school. A woman who truly made the past come
alive for the time I was in her lessons. She encouraged me
to study history at university and that is where I met the
tutor who brought my attention to eighteenth-century
Europe. She was a specialist in 'self-representation': history
directly recounted by the people who were living through
it. Letters and diaries. Novels, too. Back when it wasn't the
done thing for women to have their say about anything but
what they would be making for dinner, an anonymous
novel was one way for a woman to tell her truth.

A little later I came across *The Lover's Lessons* and was fascinated at once. Not just by the scandalous aspect of the content, but also by how very real the narrator seemed. I knew that for years people had assumed the author was a man, but I found it hard to imagine any man of that period capturing the thoughts and feelings of a young girl quite so delicately and well. The more I read, the more I became convinced I was reading the writing of a real woman. Of course, the book was always touted as having been written by a real woman, but I don't think anyone really believed it even at the time. After all, what kind of Venetian girl would have had the education and the freedom to even imagine such a thing as writing an erotic memoir? Despite the widespread debauch of the Carnevale, most young noblewomen in Venice prior to marriage were every bit as closeted as their counterparts in any other part of Europe.

So, I turned detective and determined to find out the truth behind the scandal. I made a shortlist of possible candidates for the author. There were a couple of courtesans who might have fitted the bill. Certainly, they would have known all about the demi-monde the author describes. But would they have known about life in a less exotic household, such as that of a respectable merchant? And after years in the sex trade, would they have been able to summon up the innocence and naivety that gives the book its unique voice? Would they have had the time to get the words down?

I came across Luciana Giordano when I discovered her letter to a cousin in a book on the voices of Venice. I had read just a couple of sentences when the thought came to me that I was hearing the same voice that narrated *The Lover's Lessons*. The same phrases. No one is truly anonymous when they write. A sentence written down contains as many hallmarks of the author as a voice or a fingerprint. Luciana's turn of phrase was so familiar to me. I determined to find out more.

And that is what brings me to Venice and to your beautiful library. How fortunate for me that you have decided to let me inside. I thank you again for your generosity and hope that we will meet in person very soon.

Yours sincerely . . .

I pressed send and immediately worried that I had sent an email that would bore Donato so rigid, he would not only fail to reply, he would withdraw his kind invitation to let me use the library as often as I wished. Bea read the email. She told me I was worrying about nothing. Though she added, to tease me, 'If that's the kind of dull note you wrote him in the first place, he must have seen your photo online and fallen in love with you. It's the only explanation for why he let you into the library and not me.'

I told her I doubted it. To my knowledge, the only photo of me in existence online (apart from a rather blurred one taken at my sister's wedding) was my official portrait on the university website, in which I looked like I'd been arrested for shoplifting. I was rather embarrassed about it. Because of that, I told myself Bea was being facetious. Subconsciously, however, the idea worked upon me. Why was I the first person to gain access to the library in so long? Was it just that Donato was interested in getting a free translation of the diaries?

Later that day, I found myself typing his name into the Google search bar again. The search turned up the same pictures I had already seen, and goodness knows I had already studied them closely. But this time, I felt I could start to put a voice to the man in the photographs. We had shared just a handful of exchanges but he had already teased me a couple of times: first about responding to his email granting me permission to visit the library so quickly. Secondly about my appalling handwriting. Were those teases delivered with a sneer or a smile? His interest in my research certainly didn't fit with my image of the playboy prince. Perhaps he was just being polite.

I studied Donato's face in a particular couple of photographs again. He was ridiculously handsome. He didn't seem to have a bad angle. If he hadn't been the scion of a wealthy family, he might easily have made a fortune by his looks alone. He was so much at ease in his body and his confidence was incredibly sexy. It radiated even from the still images on my screen. Combine that body with a family fortune? It hardly seemed fair that one person could be so very blessed. Perhaps that was why I had been so keen to jump to the conclusion that Marco Donato couldn't possibly be intelligent, too.

But what if all those party pictures represented just a small part of his existence and Donato was frustrated at being portrayed as a playboy? Was it possible that he might really be interested in my academic research and – an inner voice so quiet I could barely hear it whispered the thought – by extension, in somebody like me?

14

13th November, 1752

I was sick with fear the whole of the following day. I tried my best to hide it but even Maria seemed concerned. She laid her hand on my forehead and suggested she call the doctor. I insisted I was fine but perhaps I should be allowed to stay home from church? To my surprise, Maria agreed. Then she added she would still attend church herself and make arrangements for the priest to visit the house later that evening. She knew I would not want to miss the opportunity to say mass altogether. Crafty witch. Still, for at least a few moments, she seemed to love me for having given her an excuse to have her holy man visit without waiting for darkness to fall.

The priest came right after celebrating mass. Maria stood at the door to my bedroom, wringing her hands and looking convincingly worried. Of course the priest was not a doctor, he said, but he could see God would not be requiring me soon. We said a couple of prayers together and he let me have a swig from his travelling sacrament. I wished I could have had the whole bottle. Anything to blot out my worries.

Maria, generous as ever with my father's money, told the priest she would like to give him lunch for his troubles. Perhaps it was best away from my sickroom, however.

The priest agreed. He blessed me, twice, then followed Maria down the corridor. Their progress was stately for two or three steps before I heard them chasing along like a couple of children in their haste to be private together.

Once again, I wondered why religion seems to outlaw everything that brings people happiness. Or perhaps it is because something is forbidden that it brings so much joy? Maria spent a lot of time sneering at all the poor, decent men who might have married her (for she certainly claimed to have her suitors). Had the priest been a respectable fishmonger instead of a fisher of men, I do not think she would have been even slightly interested.

Anyway, I didn't care about Maria and her soul. Leading a man of God astray had to be worth several lifetimes in purgatory. I cared about *my* soul, which was right then teetering on the edge of Hell itself. What had happened to my letter? Would I ever know?

All day long I counted the bells. Maria, thank goodness, didn't bother me all afternoon. She and the priest looked in on me together just before he went to celebrate evening mass. The priest kindly said he would return later on so we could pray together before bedtime.

I didn't need any prompting to pray that day. I prayed *all* day. I prayed that my correspondent would have read my letter in the spirit in which it was intended. I prayed he would understand I had not written to him lightly, but in trust and in confidence. I prayed he would be a gentleman and keep my secrets safe.

I dared not wait at the window that evening, for fear that if the gondola appeared, it would be crammed with young men come to laugh at me, but at half past midnight came a rap on my shutters. I pulled the covers up to my ears as a battle raged inside me. Answer the rap and risk humiliation? Ignore it and risk losing my one chance for freedom? My visitor was persistent. I took my chance. The visitor was my gondolier and he came bearing another letter.

Sad Madonna of the Open Window,

I read your letter with a sorrowful and heavy heart. How is it possible that a beauty such as yours should be hidden away? Not only your physical beauty, but your intellect too? For that is the far greater crime. To be allowed only to read the Bible – that book of contradictions – is a criminal waste of your young mind. How fortunate then that God, perhaps, has sent you the perfect correspondent . . .

You say you are burning for a proper education. You want to know about science, philosophy and commerce. I can help you with all of this. I myself was educated at the University of Padua. I benefitted from being taught by the very best minds in all of Europe. In addition, I have a fine selection of books in my house and I would be only too happy to tell you everything I know. But of course, the question is how we will arrange for you to have your lessons. If the only contact we are to have is an exchange of letters via gondoliere then it will take me many centuries to pass my knowledge on. You have already explained to me that your father disapproves of education in a girl, so it would not work for me to approach him directly and tell him he is allowing a fine mind to go to waste. Of course, I could still tell him exactly that, but I fear it would not be in your best interests to enrage your father now.

I will think of something, believe me. I have received your

call and from this moment on, your education will be my
vocation. I understand you are a member of the congregation
of Santa Maria dei Carmini. I shall be there for mass
tomorrow morning. Please be sure to take communion.

14th November, 1752

Maria was delighted at my insistence on going to church
this morning. Ordinarily, she would have had to drag
me. I would have done anything – sewn a thousand night-
shirts – to avoid a turgid sermon from the priest she loved
so much. But I told her I was keen to thank God for
having delivered me from sickness.

'Be sure to take communion,' my new friend had
told me.

My mind raced with possibilities. What would happen
next? While Maria ducked her head and began her
prayers, I scoured the faces of the congregation for someone I hadn't seen before – my correspondent must be a
stranger. There were very few people and I saw no one I
didn't already know. It struck me then, for one horrible
moment, that my correspondent was in fact someone I
already knew. Old Giorgio Cavatelli caught me looking at
him and returned my look with a most horrible smile.
Not him! Surely! I offered up a prayer of my own. His
initials were right. As he gurned in my direction, I felt my
whole body flush hot and cold with horror.

But then the organ struck up and the priest processed
down the aisle. He was followed by his two assistants. The
cross-eyed one with the slight limp I had known for many
years. The other . . .

I could barely concentrate on the service. There was

only one person I didn't know in the whole congregation and that was the priest's new assistant. 'Be sure to take communion.' Was that him? Had I been writing to a man of the Church?

I followed Maria up to the altar to take communion. First the terrible bread, then the wine to choke it down. The new assistant was offering the wine. As I sipped, he told me, 'As soon as mass is over, tell your chaperone you need to confess.'

And I did. Once again my body felt hot and cold but this time it was not from horror. Though my correspondent was a man of God, one look into his face had filled me with the most unholy ideas. He was handsome beyond my most hopeful imaginings, with his dark hair and long-lashed eyes. He was tall and broad-shouldered. When he looked at me, I could tell he was trying hard not to laugh, as was I. Though my urge to laugh was more from a strange nervousness than hilarity. To make things worse, he licked his lips and I felt a flutter deep inside me as I imagined the large hands that held the chalice somewhere altogether less holy. I told him I would be first in line to admit my sins. I had the feeling I would be first in line to commit them too, if he only asked.

Maria was more than happy to sit on the church steps in the sunshine while I went back inside to 'confess'. I slipped into the booth. The priest's mysterious new assistant opened the shutter between us.

'Forgive me, Father, for I have sinned.'

'You haven't even started yet,' said the voice on the other side of the grille.

'You're a priest,' I said.

81

'I certainly own the outfit,' said my friend. 'How else am I supposed to gain access to such a devout young girl? Besides, I look good in it.'

'Vanity is a sin,' I reminded him.

'Worse than pretending to be a man of God? I will be going to Hell either way. So, tell me, my dear. What are we to do with you? I was surprised to read your letter. Girls your age are usually only looking for a husband.'

'The last thing I want is a husband,' I exclaimed. 'I want access to the kind of education that my brother expects as his birthright. I want the ability to chart my own destiny.'

'Isn't that up to God?'

'I don't believe God would want me to be ignorant.'

'I believe you are right. Well, listen, dear Luciana. I can certainly help you. In fact, you can start right now. I have left a book for you beneath the chair you are sitting on. You will find a new book there whenever you come to confession. Tucked inside it will be my instructions.'

I groped beneath my seat for his first gift to me. I pulled out a common prayer book. 'What? But it's a prayer book!'

'At first glance. Look inside,' he said. I opened the book to find the content was altogether different from that I had expected.

'The cover is loose. I shall use it to contain each new volume. It will keep you from having to explain your choice of reading to your chaperone.'

'Of course.'

'Now, I think you must go. A girl of your age shouldn't have so much to say to a priest. People will start to be suspicious.'

I agreed. But before I left the confessional, I couldn't resist leaning closer to the grille in an attempt to get a better look at him. He was leaning close too. Our eyes met. His were a very dark grey. I was reminded of the bear I had once seen at a fair in Turin. Though it had been behind bars, to me its eyes spoke of the wilderness and the joy of true freedom. Remembering the bear, I put my hand up to the grille. My new teacher matched my palm with his own. I thought I could feel his skin's heat.

'Who are you?' I asked. 'What is your name?'

'You would be shocked to hear it,' he said. 'And since I do not wish you to be prejudiced against me, for now you may call me your teacher. Now go. Please, go.'

I thanked him and ran to find Maria.

The book he has given me is an introduction to philosophy. I feared at first I would not understand it but he has marked several passages with notes of his own, designed to make things clearer for the novice. What luck that providence has sent me such a teacher. I promise I will be a good student.

But tonight I find I am wishing for something more than access to great works. Every time I close my eyelids, I can feel his gaze upon me. I can see his smile through the confessional grille. I feel myself falling into the darkness of his eyes. I feel myself wanting him to look at me. More than that, I want him to *touch* me, in ways I'm sure are not appropriate. I had better confess again first thing in the morning.

15

Marco Donato had not been bored into retracting his invitation. His email in response to my explanation of how I came to be in Venice was kind and polite. He told me he wished he'd had more patience for study as a young man. He said he was in awe of those scholars who had the tenacity to bring the past back to life. His email encouraged me to think I really was welcome – in the library, at least.

My second day there, the same routine. The old retainer, bowed like a musical clef, opened the door to me at ten. We processed through the garden. I cast a guilty look at the denuded rose bush. So far as I could see, there were no new blossoms budding. Probably wouldn't be for some time. But the fountain was still dripping and the sparrows were still bathing. Across the path, the marble lovers still gazed into each other's eyes, adoring each other for all time.

Inside the library, I settled back down at the desk with my dictionary, my notepad and a magnifying glass. Some of Luciana's handwriting was incredibly tiny. She crammed twice as many words onto a page as one might have expected. Perhaps she thought she would run out of paper before she ran out of things to say.

I read on. It really was a test of my translation skills. Not for the first time, I wished I had more of a talent for languages, but I was glad all the same that I had persisted with my studies. Little did my teachers know the romantic root of my passion for Italian.

I was fifteen years old and spending a school holiday working as an orderly at St Vincent's, a private hospital near to my grandparents' house. You see, for a while I had ambitions to become a doctor rather than a historian and my parents thought it would be a good idea for me to see the realities of healthcare up close.

That summer, a young Italian man who had been badly injured in a car crash was recovering in the hospital. Rumour had it he was driving a Ferrari and lost control of it as he raced down a country lane. The crash had left him broken and burnt. He was also mute through shock and lay with his face turned to the wall day after day. He didn't speak to anyone but I developed a fantasy that if I spoke Italian to him, it would shake him from his stupor. One of the nurses told me I wouldn't harbour such romantic thoughts if I'd ever seen the mess beneath the bandages that covered the poor man's face. I assured her otherwise and every time I was sent in to fill the water jug in his room, I made sure to pause and mutter some banality about the weather in his native tongue.

For the first two weeks, he didn't seem to hear me. He did not react to my presence in the room at all. Eventually, however, I grew bolder. I decided I would force him to notice me. I walked around to the side of the room he always faced and inserted myself between the bed and the wall on the pretence of picking up a stray tissue. He couldn't avoid looking at me. Except he did. If I tried to get into his line of sight, he simply closed his eyes.

I don't know why I didn't give up. From my adult perspective, I can see that my determination to pull the poor man out of his well of unhappiness was nothing short of harassment. He'd been badly injured in a crash. He was thousands of miles from home. What reason did he have to feel appreciative when I bothered him with my appalling phrasebook Italian? But at the same time, I felt a strong, almost spiritual, urge to connect with him. Something fated. The nurses didn't seem to have a great deal of time for him. One of them went so far as to say the unfortunate guy's accident should be a lesson to us all. If he hadn't been able to afford a Ferrari, he wouldn't have been driving so fast. Sometimes, there were advantages to being ordinary.

I suppose the fact that he wasn't ordinary was a big part of my fantasy too. The Ferrari, the riches and the glamorous lifestyle were still part of the dream for me. Despite the nurses' gossip, it never occurred to me that my dream boy might really be facing a lifetime of pain. In my fantasy, he would recover fully. When the bandages came off, he would look like a model, with perhaps just one artful scar to remind him of how we had come to be together in our castle on a Tuscan hillside.

So I persisted and when he finally looked at me, five weeks into my campaign of kindness, his eyes, dark and sad, always swimming with tears, gave me enough encouragement upon which to build a dream of a whole life. When we were together, those eyes would swim with tears no more.

Naturally, when I went back to school in September, I transferred my teenage enthusiasm to a lad from the local boys' school who would actually talk back to me. Still, I thought about the poor Italian from time to time. When he was recovered enough to be moved, he went back to Italy, I suppose. Assuming he did recover. I don't even know which city he was from. The nurses had told me he would always be horribly scarred. He had suffered horrendous burns to much of his body. But at least he'd lived. Unlike his passenger.

Anyway, that's why I decided to take up Italian. Out of a crazy notion that I could save a rich young man's life with his mother tongue and he would shower me with gifts and love me for ever out of gratitude. It seemed especially poignant now that I found myself in a private Venetian library, translating an eighteenth-century teenager's diaries. How naïve I had been to believe in such a romantic fantasy. How naïve Luciana seemed, too.

I couldn't help but laugh at some of Luciana's diary entries. There is nothing more dangerous or determined than a bored teenage girl. Her decision to write back to the stranger in the gondola had been a risk by anyone's standards. I couldn't wait to read on and discover how the situation unravelled now they had met face to face – albeit on either side of a confessional screen. But as before, I had only a couple of hours. At midday, the old man returned to remind me my time was up.

'Excuse me,' I said in Italian. 'I feel so rude. I haven't asked your name.'

'I haven't offered it,' said the man. 'But you may call me Silvio.'

'Silvio,' I echoed. It was not a name I would have expected. Silvio spoke of a young man with glossy black hair, entrancing every girl in town with his patter. Well, perhaps that was the way it had once been. We all grow old. 'I'm Sarah.' I offered my hand. Silvio accepted a handshake.

'Have you worked here long?' I asked.

'All my working life,' Silvio confirmed. 'All my life. I was born here. My father was the boatman of this house.'

More and more interesting. What stories Silvio must be able to tell. 'Has . . . has the house changed much since you've worked here?' I dared to ask.

'I have to take something off the stove,' was Silvio's response. 'You know your own way to the door.'

★ ★ ★

Back at the office, I wrote an email to Donato as promised, paraphrasing the diary entry I had read that day. He wrote back to me, congratulating me on my translation skills. He asked how I had learned my Italian. I considered a fairly banal response but decided, for some reason, to tell him the truth.

I had a Florence Nightingale complex.

I regretted sending it. I hoped Donato would not think I was making light of the poor crash victim's suffering. For the time I'd worked at the hospital, I really had cared for that man. Or thought I'd cared. My feelings for him were as genuine as an unsophisticated teenager's feelings can be. I was relieved when I received a reply just a couple of hours later.

How lucky for that young driver you made such an effort to cheer him in his hour of need. You are obviously a woman of great sensitivity and I am sure he recalls your terrible accent with great fondness. Meanwhile, it sounds as though our Luciana is inviting trouble. What do we think of this 'teacher' of hers?

I wrote back:

For the moment, I think I will have to reserve judgment. He certainly seems serious about helping her gain access to the books she is unable to find at home.

Indeed, the next few pages of Luciana's diary were occupied solely with her new academic pursuits. Having managed to persuade Maria – and her father – that she was going through the sort of devout religious phase teenage girls sometimes go through, Luciana was easily able to find a reason to go to confession at least every other day. Though she didn't always find her own personal priest in the confessional, she always found something under the seat.

Luciana devoured the books her new friend sent to her.

History, philosophy, politics and economics, all of them carefully disguised in the prayer-book's cover so that she could read in front of Maria during the day. At night Luciana wrote in her diary, but she also wrote to her teacher, asking questions and questioning answers, passing messages inside the prayer book and by gondolier. Some of the letters were in the library's collection and I matched them to the diary pages. It struck me that Luciana was a far better student than I had been at her age. Perhaps there was something to be said for keeping teenage girls locked away.

Meanwhile, I was establishing something of a pattern in my new life. Each morning I went to the library. In the afternoon, I typed up my notes for my thesis and for Donato. He continued to write back to me. I was surprised but very pleased. I hadn't expected that he would really be interested in Luciana's diaries beyond his polite initial inquiries, but it seemed I was wrong. He was very interested. What's more, he claimed to have read many of the books Luciana ploughed through in between making her 'confessions'. In fact, in many ways, Donato was more interested in Luciana's studies than I was. What brought the papers to life for me was the domestic detail. Though Luciana's thirst for knowledge was being quenched at last, she was still the same girl who had sat dreaming at her bedroom window. Her chaperone still vexed her. And she was developing an interest in her scholarly friend that went beyond the possibilities for educational enlightenment.

I smiled in girlish recognition when I read of Luciana's annoyance that, on the one day her hair looked especially shiny, she had to give her confession to an old priest rather than her young friend. The matter was compounded by the fact that she hadn't practised her confession that day. In the end, she thought about her hair and plumped for 'vanity'. I wrote about it to Donato.

It's fascinating. Even though Luciana was writing in the eighteenth century, her diary entries sometimes read as though they were written by a 21st-century teenager. She has all the same concerns. The same conceits.

Donato quickly wrote back.

Your interpretations of Luciana make me laugh. As soon as I am able to find the time, I will have to read this secret diary myself. In the meantime, of course you must avail yourself of the library whenever you need to. I am very proud and happy to be supporting such a worthy academic cause. So long as you promise to keep me up to speed with our Luciana's adventures.

I agreed that I would.

Donato's next email arrived.

And one other thing. Perhaps you could tell me some more about yourself. Is there anything of the teenage Sarah Thomson in the diaries of Luciana Giordano?

I blushed with pleasure at his personal question and wrote back at once.

Oh, of course. I remember only too clearly what it was like to be that difficult age, feeling every inch a grown woman but still being treated like a child. My parents were probably not unduly strict for the time, but to me, as a teenager, they seemed positively Victorian. They sent me to an all girls' school, possibly hoping that without the distraction of male classmates, I would achieve my academic best with ease. But even if there were no boys in the classroom, they were a constant obsession. My friends and I spent hours discussing the exotic creatures at our brother school on the other side of town. All our free time was devoted to catching sight of one. Perhaps if we had been allowed to learn side by side, those young men would have had less mystique and we would have got a great deal more work done.

So, yes, I do see something of myself in Luciana. Not just in her obsession with love but in her need for excitement. At least I knew that as a reward for all those lonely years of study, I would be off to university, where I could spend as much time with the boys as I pleased. How frustrating it must have been to know that the world beyond her father's house might never be hers to roam? From her father's house to her husband's house without time to make a few mistakes in between? No time to explore. No time to fall hopelessly in love with the wrong person. I firmly believe that heartache is terribly important. How can we be kind lovers ourselves, if we don't know what it feels like to be hurt?

Where did that piece of cod philosophy come from? I asked myself when I reread the email before sending it. I almost cut the offending sentence out, but instead I took a deep breath and pressed send.

16

If being hurt makes kinder lovers, then I would be a world-class girlfriend next time round, because Steven Jones had made carpaccio of my heart.

I first met Steven when I was a final-year undergraduate. He had recently gained his doctorate and was teaching the odd tutorial to earn his keep in the history department. Though it wasn't love at first sight – Steven wasn't exactly your classic Prince Charming in his rumpled shirts and ancient faded jeans – he was so clever and funny that I quickly began to fall for him. I found I wanted to be in his company all the time, so I signed up for every tutorial group and seminar he offered. My essays improved immeasurably as I tried my best to impress him. As Luciana's diary was proving, every eager student should develop a crush on their teacher if they want to get ahead.

I was over the moon to discover that the feelings I had for my tutor were mutual. After a boozy Christmas dinner with Steven and my fellow students, he walked me back to the house I shared with my best friend and kissed me on the doorstep. He told me he had feelings for me that went beyond simply wanting my body. He told me he thought we might be soulmates. That, however, was as far as we went for a while.

He was so careful and courtly, taking his time, telling me it was important that we approached any potential sexual relationship as adults rather than as teacher and pupil. He reminded me he was ten years older. People would naturally think he was taking advantage. But he also said he had never been involved with a student before. What I should have reminded myself of at the time was that he was in his very first year as a teacher and I was his very first student.

Finally, we could not keep our hands off each other any longer. I went for a private tutorial. We started kissing in his office and ended the day in his bed. I was wild with desire for him. At twenty-one, I had never before experienced such mind-blowing passion. I had certainly never before had an orgasm. If I wasn't already lost to love for Steven when he kissed me, then the morning after we first made love, I would have given my life for him. Our sex life was a revelation. For at least four years, we made love every time we spent the night together. Then we moved into the same flat. But it was still good, if slightly less frantic, when we were under the same roof full time.

Over the seven years we were together, the dynamic between us changed. Though Steven had insisted we enter our relationship as equals, of course at first I had looked up to him, older and more experienced as he was. As I grew more confident of my own intellectual abilities, however, I was less in awe of his.

I remember vividly the first time I dared to argue with his opinion in front of other people. We'd been together for five years by this time. I was studying for a PhD and questioned one of his pet theories in a room full of undergraduates. He handled it with humour in the moment but later our disagreement spilled out of the seminar room and into our private life. When the seminar ended, he told me he was going for a drink with some friends. I sensed that I wasn't invited. He did not come home at all that night, though the following day he was contrite and we made love as passionately as ever. More passionately, in fact. When he kissed me it was as though he would rather have bitten me. Showing a dominant streak I had not noticed in him before, he dragged me around the bed, pulling my legs apart and roughly lifting them over his shoulders so that he could penetrate me more deeply. He penetrated me so deeply it almost crossed the line between pleasure and tear-jerking pain. On one level I definitely enjoyed it. I loved giving myself up to him. I loved the feeling of abandonment that came with submitting to whatever he wanted right then. But the coldness in his expression as he came that day was strange to me. It wasn't an expression I recognised, though I would come to see it far more frequently than I wanted to.

After that night when I didn't know where he'd gone to, I was more careful when it came to disagreeing with Steven in public. Officially, he had apologised for escalating an intellectual argument into a personal row and a night spent apart, but something had changed for ever. Indeed, while our sex life became more interesting as a result of the new tensions, our dealings with each other outside the bedroom were increasingly cautious.

When I mentioned to Steven that I was interested in making a study of Luciana Giordano, he told me I was wasting my time. No one would be interested in funding such a work. When I proved him wrong, getting funding from not one but two different foundations, he refused to be impressed and was grudging with his congratulations. A little later he went so far as to tell me that academic bodies were 'throwing money' at women's studies in order to comply with government quotas. I never would have believed he would belittle me like that.

And yet I continued to love him. I continued to try to make him feel that he was the centre of the universe. He was certainly the centre of mine. I talked up his research at every possible opportunity. Meanwhile, the angrily rekindled flame of our sex life guttered and dwindled. On more than one occasion, Steven came home late and slept on the sofa, telling me he hadn't wanted to wake me up by getting into our shared bed. I began to think back with nostalgia on the days when he would have woken me up whatever time he came home and insisted on trying to make love to me to boot. Proper love. Tender and caring. Now I tried to reignite our passion in every way I could dream of. I failed.

Of course what I should have realised is that eventually another Sarah would come along: younger, wide-eyed and ready to be impressed by anything. Steven chose easy adoration over the hard work of love.

Seven weeks after the end of our relationship, I still felt tears spring to my eyes on a daily basis. I was determined, however, not to be beaten by our break-up. This sabbatical in Venice was a chance for me to shine. It was important that I didn't waste my opportunity. The pain of heartbreak might eventually make me a kinder lover. In the meantime, the best way I could think of to show Steven that he hadn't beaten me was to produce a thesis worthy of long-lost Luciana.

17

Before I knew it I had been in Venice for a fortnight and I was starting to feel quite at home. I could make my way from the apartment to the university without getting lost. I flirted with the guy who owned the vegetable boat. I was even on sniffing terms with the fussy dog in the bar on the Campo Santa Margherita, the one who would only eat beef. My colleagues Nick and Bea were fast becoming good friends. Nick, especially, made sure I need never feel lonely. He invited me to join him for dinner almost every evening. He was wonderful company, full of anecdotes and tall tales.

Meanwhile, my correspondence with Marco Donato was becoming more and more informal. Alongside our continued discussion of Luciana's antics, Marco, as I now addressed him, and I exchanged more information about our own lives. I told him more about school and my home town and my summer job at the private hospital. He told me about his childhood in the city, about summers spent on the lagoon, winters half-drowned by the *acqua alta*. He told me about his flamboyant paternal grandfather and his grandmother, a loving, simple woman who was somewhat overwhelmed by the trappings of her husband's extraordinary success. Still, Marco's 'simple' grandmother seemed impossibly glamorous to me. I told him about my own grandmother, who had pronounced my mother a 'harlot' because she dyed her hair.

Then she wouldn't have liked my mother at all,

Marco confided.

Marco also told me about the moment he left Venice for high school in the United States and how the other students had mocked him for his name and his exotic accent, until he broke the school bully's nose. He joked about it:

> I inherited my skill as a boxer from my maternal grandmother. She was great at bedtime stories too.

I told him:

> My grandmother was a wonderful storyteller, too. Those nights when Gran was looking after me were the only ones when I actually looked forward to bedtime. She had a big old book of fairytales. My favourite was 'Beauty and the Beast'. I think that story might actually have been what inspired me to torture that poor guy in the hospital with my schoolgirl Italian. I loved the central theme of it. The notion that we can all be transformed by love.

Marco wrote back,

> It's a very nice notion. And I think the fact that you believed it says a great deal about the goodness of your soul. You are Beauty.

'And you are taking the mickey,' I responded. But though I had yet to lay eyes on him, Marco Donato was fast becoming my best friend in Venice. Surely I had to meet him soon?

Despite my professed approval of the moral behind Beauty's story – that looks don't really matter – I set off for the library each day with a sense of immense anticipation, dressed as carefully as someone going to a job interview. Or, more accurately, on a date. My colleagues back in London would not have recognised the smartly dressed woman setting out from

Ca' Scimietta to the Palazzo Donato. I certainly didn't bother to put on a full face of make-up to go in to the university back home. Mind you, some of my fellow academics in England looked as though they rarely washed.

On my third weekend in Venice, I spent more money than I could afford on skirts and dresses from a boutique recommended by Bea. She was only too happy to help me Italianise myself, insisting I dump the thick comforting jumpers that had been as much my signature look as that Danish detective's and wear two thinner layers instead.

'Italian style. Just as warm and much, much sexier,' she told me. She was right. Without my baggy jumper, I had a waist again. 'You've got an incredible figure!'

I hugged Bea's compliment closely. I hadn't felt as if anything about me was incredible for quite a while. My baggy jumper had become something akin to armour. What had changed? I suppose it was the possibility of Marco's attention that made me want to come out of hibernation again.

I was once your classic bluestocking, telling myself what was on the inside mattered most, but that had definitely changed. I wanted to be ready to impress Marco when I finally saw him, as I was certain must happen soon now that we were writing to each other so often. How could we not meet? We were exchanging up to twenty emails a day! And when we did, I wanted him at least not to look straight through me. Every morning, as I dressed, I remembered the photographs I had seen online. Marco, handsome and stylish and always surrounded by beautiful women: the kind of women who had nothing to do but prepare for the next party. I had neither the time nor the money for the sort of grooming those Côte d'Azur party girls could indulge in, but I didn't want to be the archetypal hopeless academic either. Just because I wanted to be taken seriously didn't mean I couldn't flick on a bit of mascara from time to time.

Meanwhile, I had my favourite photographs of Marco book-marked. There was a shot of him on top of a mountain, in ski gear, grinning at the camera with his ski goggles pushed back on his hair. I liked to think of him about to complete a black run back to the village. Of course, it went without saying he must be a great skier. He was a sailor, too. Another favourite was a shot of him on the deck of a beautiful old boat, perhaps one of his grandfather's, hauling in a sheet. His face was taut with concentration. His jaw was square and strong. His arms looked magnificent. What I loved most about both these photos, however, was the fact that Marco was, unusually for him, alone in both shots. He had no beautiful woman draped round his neck like a living, breathing scarf, so I could imagine that I was on the other side of the camera lens. And I could imagine more clearly what it would have been like to share those moments with him.

At the same time, my imagination was straying in other, more exotic directions too.

Perhaps it was because I was spending my nights alone, having shared a bed with Steven for so many years. Perhaps it was all the spritzes I drank in the bar with Nick and Bea. Perhaps it really was the spooky four-poster. Whatever the reason, my dream life had become full of sensuality and sex in a way I had never experienced before. Night after night, I woke up twisted in the sheets, hot and yet shivering with the last shudders of a tremendous orgasm. When I tried to remember the dreams, the details were a jumble, but more often than not they now took place at the Palazzo Donato and Steven's face was replaced increasingly often by that of the man in the mask, Steven's upper-class English voice by an Italian one, whispering urgent instructions, telling me how much he wanted me.

'You are so beautiful, Sarah. Your beauty is so pure it burns me.'

The stranger's hand would slip between my legs. I would press myself hard against him. I didn't care how greedy I seemed. I wanted him inside me. I grasped his buttocks, pulling him closer, closer, closer. I twisted my fingers in his jet-black hair. I begged him to put me out of my misery and fill me with his desire.

'You are so wet. You really want me. You need me,' the stranger murmured.

I definitely needed something. I was starting to go nuts. Three weeks in Italy and I had still heard nothing from Steven. It was now almost ten weeks since we broke up. Seven years can never be forgotten in the blink of an eye, of course, but perhaps it was time to start thinking more seriously about a life without him. About moving on.

But was I doing the right thing by transferring my affections on to Marco Donato? I was developing a full-blown teenage crush.

18

About three and a half weeks into my time in Venice, Marco sent me an email that started to alter the way we communicated with each other.

'These emails are OK,' he wrote. 'But they have some disadvantages compared to a real conversation.'

My heart leapt. He was going to suggest a meeting at last. But no . . .

'How do you feel about direct messaging?' he asked.

Direct messaging? It was hardly 'meet me at the station with a carnation in your buttonhole'. My heart did a bellyflop in disappointment. The best I could say was that it meant Marco wanted a conversation in real time.

I emailed him a response.

> I don't know. I can't say I've lain awake at night thinking about it. As far as most people are concerned, I'd prefer to email. Easier to say what you want to say without being interrupted. I suppose direct messaging is useful in some ways in that it's more like a conversation, but I worry it might be a distraction. Not that 33 emails a day aren't a distraction.

This referred to the thirty-three emails he had sent in the last twenty-four hours. Some about my work, some about my life in Venice, some about nothing much at all.

Marco replied. 'You're right. I should not be suggesting any distractions when you have such a short time to finish your important work. I know you are a very dedicated scholar. However, I do so enjoy our correspondence and it would be fun I think to "chat" in real time, don't you?'

'Real time is very different from reality,' I pointed out. 'Why don't we just email each other until we have a chance to meet in person?'

'Who knows when that will happen?'

'You're a very busy man, I know. Too busy for direct messaging, surely?'

'Indulge me,' Marco wrote back.

How could I not?

Minutes later, we were connected by direct message and I sent the first missive.

'Better?'

'Much.'

'Don't you have work to do?'

'Always, but it's boring. Amuse me, Sarah.'

'What about *my* work?'

'Should I let you get on?'

'I can give you five minutes.'

'In that case, let's make them count. Tell me about your first kiss.'

'What? I'm not sure I can remember.'

'Every girl remembers her first kiss.'

'OK. His name was Ben. We were at nursery school.'

'Your first *proper* kiss.'

'Why should I tell you? How do I know you're not really Marco's cat?'

'Speed of response. Cats are no good at touch-typing.'

'All right . . . My first kiss was Jamie Elwood. We were twelve. I think he did it for a dare. He tasted of Juicy Fruit chewing gum. You?'

'Today I am asking the questions.'

It felt as if that was always the case. Our sharing of

information was feeling a little lopsided. While I knew all about Marco's favourite childhood pasta dishes, I didn't know what he did with his life these days. Apart from email me. Likewise, I assumed he was in Venice but I didn't know for sure. I decided to try to draw him out.

'No more questions today, please. I've got work to do and I'm sure you have too. It can't be easy heading up the family business.'

Marco avoided giving me a straight answer.

'You're so dedicated to your work. I should not disturb you so often. But I so enjoy reading your emails. It amuses me to imagine you, the serious academic, as a flirtatious young girl, joining the choir so that you might be able to catch a glimpse of some undeserving boy.'

I replied, 'How do you know he was undeserving?'

'Trust me, all teenage boys are undeserving. I certainly was. There was a girl who once loved me. A friend of my cousin's. She sent me a love letter. It had clearly taken her a great deal of time. She illustrated every capital letter. I showed it to my friends. We laughed at her purple prose for days.'

'It was most unfair of you to share that love letter with your friends,' I responded. 'It makes me wonder if our correspondence is being read by strangers right now.'

'You haven't said anything you are ashamed of, surely?'

'Yet,' I responded, aware that it was a flirt.

'Believe me, Sarah. I am a changed man. These days I fully understand the value of another person's feelings. I would not betray any confidence you might decide to share with me. Should you ever decide to share a real secret, you would find me a very good confidante. As I am sure I would find the same of you.'

'For now I am happy sharing Luciana's confidences,' was my bloodless response.

'But I find I am just as eager to know more about *you* as I am Luciana,' was Marco's reply. 'Indulge me just a little longer. I know a good deal about your past, but what about your future, Ms Thomson? What happens after Venice? There must be someone back in London eagerly awaiting your return.'

'Alas,' I responded. 'There is not. Not any more.'

'That is the kind of answer that invites more questions.'

'You can't expect to ask me any further questions over direct message,' I wrote. 'I don't want to commit myself to print. But you guessed correctly. A recent break-up. Just six weeks before I came to Italy, in fact.'

'Whoever he is, he did not deserve you. Tell me about him.'

'There isn't much to tell.'

'There's always a great deal to tell. And I may have a useful perspective on your situation.'

'Who says I need a perspective? Perhaps it doesn't bother me in the least.'

'You'd be a very cold-hearted woman if that were the case. It's only been a couple of months. Why don't you try me?'

'I don't want to bore you.'

'Nothing you say could possibly bore me. I find I want to know you, Sarah. I want to know you properly.'

A curious sensation crept over me. It was not unlike the feeling I'd had when Steven first told me he was interested in me, after that boozy Christmas dinner. Did I dare to think Marco was telling the truth? Did he really want to know more? It was certainly unexpected, the way our email relationship had blossomed. I knew I looked forward to hearing from him. The number of times he wrote to me seemed to suggest he felt the same. He'd suggested direct messaging. And yet, why not move it forward properly? Why not meet face to face? I asked him.

'Confessions are easier when there's a hint of anonymity, don't you think?'

'I have nothing to confess.'

'Just tell me about your foolish ex-boyfriend, Miss Thomson. Consider it the price of your continued access to Luciana's letters.'

'That sounds like blackmail. But you asked for it. The man who just broke my heart . . .'

Broke my heart?

I found myself deleting those words and replacing them with, 'The man who turned out not to be good enough for me was called Steven.'

The cursor blinked with disbelief. Why wouldn't I admit to Marco that my heart had been broken? Was it because I didn't want him to think of me as 'taken'? Because even though Steven's continued silence was making it clear he didn't care whether I was waiting for him or not, I knew that to admit to Marco that my heart was broken was to admit there was still something tying me to another man. That might discourage Marco from continuing with our flirtation and our flirtation was something I did not want to have to do without.

For that reason, which I didn't fully understand at the time, I gave Marco a heavily abridged version of my doomed love affair. I gave names and places and talked about Steven's professional envy, but I definitely stopped short of telling Marco about the brief acrobatic renaissance of our love life that I now knew had only sprung from repressed disdain.

Marco responded.

'Ah yes. If there is one thing that a man finds hard to bear, it's a woman who is no longer impressed by him.'

'Then we're all doomed, aren't we? Isn't intimacy about showing our vulnerabilities and knowing that they won't be held against us? Shouldn't it be a relief to know the one you love has seen you as you truly are and yet still loves you?'

'Perhaps. But we men more often find it hard to forgive

our loved ones for uncovering those vulnerabilities in the first place. We don't want to know it's safe to be weak in your arms. We want to be the strong ones. We want to be perfect for you.'

'Kind and faithful will do.'

'You deserve that.'

'But what about you? If you'll forgive me saying so, you had quite the reputation as a party boy. In every photograph I've seen of you, you've had women draped over your shoulders the way other guys wear their jackets. You were obviously very popular with the girls. I can only assume it was one very special woman who persuaded you to take yourself off the market. Given the brace of supermodels you seem to have stepped out with, she must be an absolute stunner. Tell me more.'

There was no response. The DM window remained empty for far longer than I'd expected. The quickfire conversation that had taken up most of the afternoon had come to a halt. I reread my last message several times in an attempt to gauge just how badly I might have offended my correspondent. I couldn't find anything that seemed an obvious trigger. I hadn't said anything that wasn't true, after all. And the one interview I had read online had suggested Marco was proud of his reputation as a ladies' man.

I pulled myself up short for being so paranoid. Perhaps Marco hadn't stopped messaging me because he was offended. Perhaps he had just stepped away from his computer for a moment. Even billionaires need to pee. And the kind of money that funded a lifestyle such as his needed management. He was probably placing a call to a business associate somewhere, of moving stock from one account to another. A man like Marco Donato didn't have time to chat online all day long.

Of course that was the logical explanation, and goodness

knows the same applied to me. That morning I had probably written three thousand words, but none of them had been on the subject of my thesis. I needed to get on with my own work but I found I could not concentrate at all. The only thought in my mind was what I had said that would make Marco log off so suddenly after he had been pestering me to move to DM. There were a thousand possible reasons why, from computer failure to the palazzo having caught fire, but the only one that seemed real to me was that I had in some way upset him. It was foolish thinking. It was self-obsessed. But that was what I thought all the same.

19

After an hour or so, I let Bea persuade me to go for a coffee. I made the right noises while she told me about some inter-departmental gossip, but it didn't really help to distract me.

'Don't you think?' Bea asked at one point, soliciting my opinion. I realised to my horror that I had no idea what I was supposed to have an opinion about.

'You could look at it that way,' I said, taking a risk. 'Or perhaps there's another angle.'

'What angle?' Bea asked. She wrinkled her brow in confusion.

I had to admit I hadn't heard a word.

'You're very distracted,' Bea observed. 'What's it about? Have you heard from him? The old boyfriend back in London?'

'No,' I said. 'Nothing at all.'

'How long has it been now?'

'Since we split up? Almost three months.'

'The coward. You're better off without him,' Bea assured me. 'I know it may not feel like it now but this time next year you'll be kicking yourself for having wasted a moment think-ing about him when you could have been getting yourself an Italian stallion.'

I laughed, grateful that Bea was not offended by my disen-gagement but was instead concerned that I might be upset about Steven. She had such a sunny nature. She believed everything could be fixed with a dose of healthy flirtation.

With that in mind, she swiftly moved on to the various attributes of the men who frequented our floor in the university building. She confided she had a bit of a thing for one of the security guards.

'We have nothing in common, of course, and we would have nothing to talk about, but there's something about him. He's such a handsome brute.'

Like Marco Donato, I thought. A handsome brute. That was how I imagined him when we first started to write to one another but it seemed he was a sensitive one to boot. Bea and I went back to the office. Another two hours passed. I revised a single paragraph of translation six or seven times. I went for another coffee. I revised another paragraph. The sun started to go down. And then, like the sound of an angelic herald, I heard the ping of an arriving message. Marco.

> As I told you, I am a very different man from the one you
> see in those photographs online. I'm not entirely proud of
> the way I lived back then. My life was devoted to hedonism.
> I picked up many hangers-on and, at the same time, lost
> my most true friends. Though I didn't have a moment to
> myself and my days were full of frantic activity from dawn
> till dusk and beyond, I realised that, after all, I was building
> nothing real. When the party ended, I saw how empty my
> world had become. I had to change my life. So, you ask if
> there was a special woman who made me turn my back on
> the party lifestyle? In some ways, there was, though not in
> the way you imagine. Or in the way I imagined. You'll
> forgive me if I don't elaborate for now.

Oh, I would have forgiven him anything. I was simply glad he was writing to me again and had not cut me off. I resolved to be more careful from then on. Obviously, I had not yet quite earned the right to tease my new friend. This was the problem with an acquaintanceship confined to the written word. Had we been sitting face to face over a coffee, I might have seen his expression change as I strayed onto the subject of the women in his life. I might have realised I was about to make a transgression and wouldn't have probed too hard. Never mind, I told myself. I had another chance. Immediately, I replied and told Marco how much I was looking forward to getting to work the next day, which was a Saturday – I was allowed access to the library on weekends now, too. I felt daring.

If – seeing as it's the weekend – you had time to step away
from your office, I could show you what I'm working on.
The pages of the diary themselves are something worth
seeing. Luciana sometimes doodles in the margins. She's
got quite a talent for drawing.

'Alas,' said Marco. 'I will be out of town. But I look forward to hearing what you discover next.'

I sank back in my chair, feeling more rejected than I should have done. I googled Marco's name for the photographs I had come to know almost as well as my own reflection. I looked into his flirtatious brown eyes as though I might find an answer in the long-frozen images. He seemed keen to know about me and yet he was making no effort at all to bring our new friendship offline. What was the reason? If another girl had put the question to me, I would have told her Marco was hiding a wife or a girlfriend at the very least. That was certainly Bea's opinion when I asked her later that evening.

20

Friday night was party night. The bar was full of colleagues from the university. Nick and Bea were on fine form. By ten o'clock, however, people were drifting away and only we three remained huddled together on the bridge, our breath like smoke in the frigid sea air. It was time for ghost stories again. Bea announced that we were all to talk about the one that got away. She told the story of her first love, back in Rome, who broke her heart when he tried to seduce her younger sister.

'I say "tried" to seduce. I strongly suspect he succeeded.'

Nick told the story of Clare, a fellow undergraduate at Oxford, who had left him to take holy orders.

Bea and I spluttered in amused disbelief.

'I am not even slightly joking,' said Nick. 'It's one thing to be left for another man. It's quite interesting to be left for another woman. But to be left for a lifetime of celibacy? If that isn't the ultimate insult to a man's prowess in the sack . . .'

'You were young,' said Bea, rushing to his defence. 'You've improved a great deal since then, I'm sure.'

A look passed between them that suggested Bea knew that much first-hand.

'What about you, Sarah?' Bea asked.

'Do I have to?'

'You do.'

For the second time that day, I talked about my relationship with Steven and how he'd traded me in for a younger model.

'He's an idiot,' said Nick.

'Thank you. You don't have to say that.'

'No. I'm serious. He is an idiot and not just because he let you slip through his fingers. I've seen him at conferences. The man talks out of his arse. How he ever got that job, I simply do not know.'

'Oh, love! Love,' Bea mused as she waved a glass in the air. 'Such exquisite torture. Why do we bother? Let's drink to the people who broke our hearts.'

Nick and I clinked glasses with her.

'May they all die horribly,' Bea added.

Nick and I seconded that.

'A broken heart is the very worst pain you can imagine,' Nick opined. 'The birds stop singing. The sky goes black. You feel sure you'll never trust anyone again. Then suddenly, one day, everything changes. You stand on a quay in this wonderful city. You feel the sea air on your face. You see a certain someone step off a boat and she smiles at you and the sun comes out again.'

Bea looked at Nick with raised eyebrows. Then she looked at me. Nick was looking at me too.

'That's a nice thought,' I said. 'Poetic.'

Nick raised his glass in another toast and held my gaze for a little too long.

Not too much later, I made my excuses and went back to Ca' Scimmietta. Not only was I keen to avoid a hangover, I was eager to see if Marco had written again. He had. Unfortunately, it was not with a promise that he would come and meet me the following morning after all. But he did wish me pleasant dreams. Pleasant dreams? Ha! If only he had known about my nights in the monkey bed. I was beginning to think it was haunted by a sex-starved ghost or one of those incubi that medieval women blamed for their nocturnal misdemeanours.

As soon as I closed my eyes, I was back in the garden of the palazzo. I walked round the fountain in the centre, counting my footsteps as they crunched on the gravelled path. I was wearing a long white dress, like an old-fashioned nightgown. My feet were bare. My hair was loose around my shoulders. The neckline of the dress had slipped down over one shoulder. When the man in the mask appeared behind me, he lifted my hair out of the way and pressed a kiss to my bare skin.

'I've been waiting for you,' I said.

'I've been here all the time,' he assured me.

I turned to face him and looped my arms round his neck. I looked through the holes in the mask, deep into his eyes. I wasn't afraid of him any more, but there was still a distance between us that I couldn't seem to cross. I tried to bridge that distance when he made love to me.

When he pushed into me, I held his gaze. Though I didn't say the words out loud, every time he thrust into me I told him I loved him through the acceptance of his body in mine. Still he would not take off the mask. It seemed he would never trust me enough not to hold something back. Even as he orgasmed, he would try to look away from me. When I grasped his head with my hands and tried to force him to make eye contact, he simply closed his eyes. He continued to protect himself, hiding deep inside.

I was starting to be confused and frustrated by my dream visits to the palazzo. What did they mean? Were my dreams a metaphor for my broken relationship with Steven – who was adept at keeping secrets, it turned out? Or were they a metaphor for my half-blossoming relationship with Marco? In both cases, something was being held back from me. Who was the man in the mask?

21

If I do not venture this much, then all will be lost. I know it is just a matter of time before my father decides I should take a husband. I know also that I will have little choice in the decision. A suitable mate will be chosen for me. There is no room for romantic love where my future is concerned. It will be a disaster. Papà makes a point of surrounding himself with like minds and I cannot stand the idea of marrying a man who holds as little store by a woman's education as he does.

But if I can present my education as a fait accompli and convince him I would be just as big an asset as a business associate as married off to some ignorant merchant who would buy me much as he would buy a cow, how different life could be. I could work alongside my father. I could be a good businesswoman. I am every bit as intelligent as the men in my family and I know there are women in Venezia who run empires.

First I must complete my education. And for that I must find a way out of this house. The books alone are not enough.

Last time I made confession, I explained my frustration at length. I told my new friend about my mother's death and my father's fear that he should lose me too, and how that resulted in his going to the most ridiculous lengths to try to protect me. First with the plague mask and now by keeping me locked in the house with a painfully stupid chaperone. I told him about Maria and her nightly visits from the priest.

'What a devout woman she must be,' my new friend responded.

'Indeed,' I spat.

'But how fortunate for you that she is so regular with her confession too. While the priest is inside, his boat is outside the house, after all.'

I don't know why I'd never thought of it myself. How I've lamented the fact that our boatman takes our boat with him when he goes to see his girl out on Murano. I told myself if there had been so much as a seaworthy plank on our pontoon, I should have been away in a flash. But there has been a *barchetta* tied up outside our house. Night after night after night. The priest rows himself to see Maria in a *barchetta* that even I could control.

So I had my means of getaway, but I still needed my disguise.

The following day, I had an idea of my own. Apart from keeping me from mischief, Maria has been entrusted with teaching me to sew and make lace as beautifully as any of the *figlie* at the Pietà. After months and months with nothing to do but sew or read the boring bits of the Bible, I can make stitches so tiny they might have been made by a spider. I've made lace so light and delicate it floated in the air. My project for the moment is stitching my own trousseau.

I caught Maria trying on a veil I'd made, no doubt

imagining herself marrying the priest. She was embarrassed when she saw me and I knew of old that when Maria is feeling in the least bit humiliated she quickly turns it against me. She would find some reason to criticise me. Perhaps even make me unpick half the work I had done. I moved quickly to prevent this moment from becoming something I would have to suffer for days. Instead of asking what she was doing, I said, 'Oh Maria. What a beautiful bride you will make.' She looked suspicious of my friendliness, as well she might.

'I have been thinking lately of how very hard you work,' I said. 'When the priest read the story of the virtuous woman in church the other day, it was as though he was talking directly to you. You work so very hard to care for me and for my brother. I'd like to help you. It's my Christian duty.'

I saw a pile of my brother's clothes on a bench near the door.

'Are these for mending?' I asked.

Maria nodded.

'Then let me do it. It's all very well stitching a beautiful trousseau, but I'm sure God will send me a husband all the more quickly if I make myself useful to you first.'

Maria was only too pleased to let me take over her share of the mending, though she made me promise my brother should never know. I promised. After all, I told her, isn't it better to be humble and do good deeds in secret?

'And since it must be a secret,' I said, 'I must not do the mending here, in the day room, where my brother might walk in and catch me at any moment.'

Maria agreed. I retired to my bedroom to stitch.

What luck. My brother had sent for mending almost an entire outfit. There was a shirt, and trousers, and three stockings. Perfect. I would wear two of the stockings and stuff the spare one down the trousers to make my disguise more convincing.

My brother, though he is two years older than me, is not so very much bigger. I could complete the costume with my own shoes. Naturally, my father forbade me from wearing any shoes of a design one might mistake for fashionable. Likewise, my black cape is just the same as everybody else's, if slightly less well worn because I hardly go anywhere. All I needed was a tricorn and a mask. I knew my brother had several.

Getting my hands on them was easy. I told him I wanted to borrow them for drawing practice. After sewing, drawing was the only pastime I was permitted. My brother shrugged and let me have his oldest hat and a mask that smelled quite disgusting when I tried it on. How I would wear it for long enough to make my escape, I did not know.

Maria undressed me and helped me into my nightgown. Minutes after she left me, I dressed myself as a boy. For once I listened eagerly for the arrival of the priest. I heard him address himself to Maria, promising salvation for her soul. Heavens, how could anyone believe she had so much to confess when she never went anywhere but church? It seemed an awful lot of people were happy to turn a blind eye in Venezia. If they had but known I was right behind the door, with my eye to the keyhole! All I wanted was for them to fall into each other's arms and get on with their sighing. Having observed them for the best part of a week, I guessed that once Maria's door banged shut, I had three hours. Almost four.

Now for the part that had kept me anxious all day. It was easy enough to put on my disguise, but how would I get into the boat? I could see it, tied where it always was, but somehow the drop from my sill looked a great deal bigger and more intimidating than before. I leaned out of my window as far as I could, estimating the jump. At best I would end up in the water. At worst, I might well break my neck. I hesitated to see if my courage would build in me. It didn't, but I was determined I would not miss my rendezvous. Using a twisted sheet tied to the bed as a safety rope, I swung my leg over the windowsill.

The canal was silent. Someone was smiling on me from on high with regard to that at least. There was no one to see my escape. I brought my other leg out and sat on the sill like an acrobat, waiting to grab the trapeze. Alas, there was no trapeze; I had to somehow turn round and drop to the next level as gently as I was able. There was a sort of ridge, an architectural embellishment, about five feet below me. If I could let myself down onto that, perhaps I could drop to the landing raft from there.

How did cats do it? By knowing they would be landing on four feet rather than two, I supposed.

Carefully, as quietly as I could, I inched myself over the sill. Was I tall enough that I could hang on while I waited for my feet to make contact? Only just. My arms were stretched to their limits. I thought they might pop out of my sockets, like the arms of the doll I'd once had as a child.

But for that moment, I was dangling from the windowsill. Anticipation was totally blanked out by fear. What on earth was I thinking? I was half ready to call out for Maria and get her and the priest to haul me back into the house. I truly was between the devil and the deep blue sea. Maria and the priest might save my life, but they would exact a heavy price for their assistance. Could either of them be trusted not to mention the incident to my father? I had to let go and jump. I edged my way to the corner of the house and fell like a sack of grain into the priest's boat. I landed, thank God, if not like a cat then at least with all my limbs of a piece.

Such an adventure I had, getting to our rendezvous. How different Venezia is by lamplight. Normally, I should have been afraid, but my mission made me strong. I needed to see my teacher face to face without a grille between us. I had not time to continue my education in such a piecemeal fashion as I had been receiving it so far. Not if I wanted to pre-empt my father's attempts to marry me off.

My teacher told me an old friend had lent him a house for the purpose of our meeting, since his own abode was too far from my palazzo to make it a reasonable distance for me to travel alone. Certainly, it did not take me long to get to the street my teacher had scribbled on a scrap of paper, but the environs were an education in themselves.

I had heard Maria and the cook whisper about the prostitutes in the *Carampane*, who advertised their wares as boldly as the fishermen showed their mackerel. I had not expected Maria's whispers to be true. Some of them opened their dresses right down to the waist. It was difficult not to stare. They certainly stared at me and offered me all sorts of wicked distractions.

I had a further shock when I arrived at the address.

It was a poor sort of house. Half derelict. I wondered if I had taken a wrong turn. I hesitated to knock on the door, but no, it was the right place and he was there.

This was the first time I had seen him without a priestly garment. Though it was not warm that night, he was dressed merely in an undershirt and breeches. His feet were clad only in stockings. I immediately averted my eyes. I had not seen a man outside my own household in such a state of undress before. It made me embarrassed.

'I have surprised you,' I said.

'Not at all,' he said. 'I have been making myself comfortable in anticipation of your arrival. Come in.'

He relieved me of my hat and mask and we went straight upstairs to what I presume was the best room. The room for receiving guests. But it was unlike any kind of public room I had been in before. The whole was dominated by a bed – an enormous four-poster with thick velvet drapes. The blackened oak pillars of the bed were extravagantly carved. It was piled high with pillows. The coverlet was folded back, revealing the sheets beneath in a manner every bit as shocking to me as my teacher's decision not to put on a jacket.

'So you came,' my teacher said. 'You've passed the first test. You are clearly a woman of resources. And you look very good in trousers.'

I blushed. 'They are my brother's.'

'Won't he miss them when he goes gambling at the Ridotto?'

'He has other pairs,' I pointed out.

'Of course he does.'

I felt like an idiot for saying so.

'Sit down.'

I looked around me for a place to settle. There was nothing else in the room but a couple of leather-backed chairs and a small table. Nothing else in terms of furniture, that is. Everywhere I looked were books, piled as high as the windowsills. There were books on the table, beneath the table and under the bed. It was the room of someone who cared little for anything but reading and sleeping. As I perched upon one of the hard chairs, I wondered again to whom this little house belonged.

'I'll get you a glass of wine.'

'Don't you have servants to do that?' I asked him.

'Of course I have servants. You have met my gondolier. But I thought tonight you would prefer to have privacy. Just you and me alone. We have much to talk about. We won't wish to be interrupted.'

He was right. There was so much I wanted to tell him and so much I wanted to ask. I had brought the latest book he'd left in the confessional. It was a treatise on economic policy. I did not understand the half of it, but I wanted him to think otherwise. I had been trying to come up with intelligent questions all day.

'This was very interesting,' I said.

'Oh that,' he said. 'I couldn't get on with it. I don't think the author has a clue.'

'I thought you gave me this book because you believed in the theories inside?'

'Perhaps I just wanted to see if you could spot horse-shit too.'

I put the book down on the table.

'I must admit I didn't agree with everything the author said,' I said carefully.

'Good. Then you really are learning.'

'I think so. In fact, at dinner the other evening, I had to try very hard not to interrupt my brother,' I explained. 'He was telling my father about a deal he struck with a Spanish silver merchant and I saw at once it did not work in my brother's favour. But he would not listen to me. What man will?'

'I will listen to you.'

'You have already changed my life,' I told him. 'Though I have not moved from my tiny world between the palazzo and the church, I feel as though I have sprouted wings.'

'You are very much outside your tiny world now, are you not?'

'Indeed.' I let my gaze wander around the room, but dropped my eyes to my hands again when my teacher and I both looked at the bed at the same time.

'I have something a little different for you today.'

'You do?'

'Philosophy, politics and economics, while they may make the world go round, could leave one rather lacking. What the politicians and businessmen of our day fail to understand, time and again, is the effect of emotion on all things. For that reason, we should also read poetry. Luciana, this book is entirely for your pleasure.'

He handed me a slim volume. I peered at the title. It was a book of poems by Veronica Franco, the most notorious woman ever to have lived in our city. I had heard of her of course. If only as the heroine of a cautionary tale. She had lived wildly. She was a courtesan. She charmed the great and the good and counted dukes and kings among her lovers. But she died in unhappy circumstances, of the plague, which robbed her of her looks before it sent her to her grave.

'That is what happens if you are beautiful and vain,' Maria had concluded.

I opened the book.

'Why don't you read some to me now?' my teacher asked.

'Shall I start at the beginning?'

'Perhaps. Come closer. That way we can move the candles together and you will be better able to see what you are reading.'

I did as I was instructed.

'Read aloud. Read this one.'

Blushing, I began.

So sweet and delicious do I become when I am in bed
with a man who, I sense, loves and enjoys me, that
the pleasure I bring excels all delight, so the knot
of love, however tight it seemed before, is tied tighter
still.

The mention of bed brought great heat to my cheeks, but it was not just the poem that affected me. I had been feeling most strange from the moment I moved to sit next to him. Though we were not touching, I could feel the warmth of his body flowing into me. The fire in the grate was low and needed stoking but I was suddenly getting so hot I had to loosen the cravat at my neck. I couldn't do it. I had tied it badly – in an approximation of the way my brother did – and now that I tried to untie it, the damn thing became thoroughly knotted. My teacher noticed my struggle. It made him smile.

'I'm feeling a little constricted,' I said helplessly.

'Here,' he said. 'Let me help you. Turn towards me.'

I turned so we were face to face. Our eyes met and he regarded me with such an intensity I had to drop my own eyes to my lap again for fear of crying out. I sat very still. His hands, with their long fingers, were at the knot in my cravat for quite some time. It seemed I was well and truly bound. But eventually he was able to free the knot and slide the silk from my neck. He did it slowly, so that I felt every inch of the material glide across my flesh, awakening my senses and making me hotter still. I closed my eyes and let out a little moan. Next thing: I must have fainted. When I came to, we were on the floor and I was lying across his lap. He had his arms round me to keep me from the dirty wooden boards. He brushed my hair back from my face.

'My poor dear,' he said. 'It's too hot for you. Perhaps you ought to lie down on the bed.'

The bed. That bed! I had been determined I should stay away from it, but right then it seemed a far better choice than staying in his arms. I thanked him and got to my feet. I would lie on the bed for just a moment to recover myself. After that, I would ask to read some more economics. But he stood just as I did and caught me again.

This time he kissed me.

★ ★ ★

I did not resist him. I knew I should, but I did not. Before he took me, I had already been possessed by a spirit so daring and devilish I wanted everything he promised to give. Now I found myself opening my mouth to him so that his tongue could roam deep inside. Meanwhile, he removed my boy's shirt with far greater alacrity than he had removed the cravat. I was wearing nothing underneath. At the same time, he took off his own shirt, so that suddenly his bare flesh was pressed against mine.

I had never been naked before except in the presence of women. I did not know whether my body would be considered beautiful by a man such as I stood before now. He was certainly beautiful to me. Though he had shown himself to be a man of letters, his body was that of a man used to vigorous exercise. His muscles were well-formed and spoke to me of strength and agility. Of power and domination. I tried to read the truth of my own beauty or lack of it in his eyes. He walked me backwards to the bed and pushed me down onto the mattress. He stood above me, looking down on me. His eyes were different from any time before. There was a curious distance in them. Unfocused but desiring.

I grasped up a piece of sheet to cover my nakedness.

'Stop,' he said, tugging the fabric away from me. 'I want to see you in your full glory.'

He pulled down the trousers I had stolen from my brother. Underneath, I wore my girlish undergarments. He removed those too. I should have resisted him. I know I should. But I did not. I could not. I found I wanted to be naked in his presence. I wanted to see him naked too.

He obliged me. He stepped out of his breeches. He

wore nothing beneath them. And thus I saw my first human penis. I had studied statues and frescoes, of course. I thought I knew what I would find. But oh! Either the sculptors were too modest or my dear teacher was absolutely monstrous! His penis stood straight out from his body. It was as long as my forearm. I could not help but cry out.

'You see what you have done to me,' he said.

He laughed when I asked if it was painful.

'It feels quite wonderful,' he assured me, lying down beside me at last.

We were as naked as Adam and Eve before the fall. He drew me to him. His smell was so enticing. As he pulled me hard against him, I buried my face in his neck and breathed him in. His hands roamed all over my body. He kissed me on my neck and my breastbone. He kissed my nipples. It was the most tremendous sensation. I could not have imagined how wonderful it would feel. My body vibrated with delight.

'Are you . . . ?' he started to ask. 'Oh, of course you are, my darling girl. I must stop. I must not do this to you. You have not asked for it.'

'Don't stop,' I told him. 'Don't stop. This is exactly what I want.'

His fingers caressed the hidden part of me. He pressed at the opening where secretly I had touched myself before. I braced myself for the pressure of his finger on my hymen. I expected to be torn in two, but his finger slipped in easily.

'You are aroused,' he said with a hint of amusement. 'But we must arouse you further to ensure you do not feel any pain.'

He touched the most private piece of me gently. I found myself pressing hard against his hand. My body was vibrant with desire for him. I knew that whatever he asked of me, I would give it. He could have my richest treasure. He moved so he was between my legs. I felt something else press against me. Against me and suddenly into me. I gasped with surprise. Without a moment's notice, I had given him my all.

There was pain, but not as much pain as I had expected. It was brief and it was quickly overwhelmed by a sort of animal desire to have him in me. I wanted him to melt into my body. He held my face and studied me intently as he began to move.

'You must tell me if I am to stop,' he said.

Nodding, I returned his gaze, hoping that my eyes communicated my trust in him. I was surprised to find I had no fear of what would come. I wanted it. I embraced my fate. I felt every moment he was in me more vividly than I had ever felt anything before. Slowly, slowly he moved inside me, watching me for the slightest signal that all was not well. His concern gave me great confidence that what we were doing was right.

'You can move too,' he told me. 'Push upwards.'

I did so and suddenly he was in me to the hilt. I gasped.

'I am hurting you,' my teacher exclaimed.

'I am not hurt,' I assured him.

He kissed me on the tip of my nose.

Not quite knowing what to do with them, I let my hands wander down towards his bottom. I found myself using them to pull him further into me still. I closed my eyes. I even wrapped my legs round him. I tried to match his rhythm until . . .

'Ah!' he cried out.

Suddenly he was struggling to be away from me. I tried to hold him tighter.

'Don't. Don't!' He pulled out. His penis, still hard, was jerking upwards towards his belly, white liquid spewing from its tip.

When the spasms subsided, he fell onto his stomach beside me, burying his face in a pillow. I sat up.

'Is that it?' I asked. 'Have I lost my maidenhead?'

He rolled over onto his back. He was laughing.

'Yes. That's it,' he said. 'Now I imagine you're wondering what all the fuss is about? Don't worry. It will get very much better.'

It already seemed something quite wonderful to me. As I considered what had just passed between us, he pulled me closer to him and looked into my eyes.

'Thank you,' he said. 'You have given me a gift I will always remember. I hope you will let me show my gratitude in a hundred different ways from now on.'

As I dressed, he explained to me why he had pulled himself from me so abruptly and, at last, I properly understood the story of Onan. I agreed, of course, that it would not help my cause at all if I found myself with child. But when he asked me if I would be back, I promised him I would. I knew I could not stay away. I had given him the most precious part of me and I wanted to be his for ever. I told him so.

He nodded and pulled my chin like I was a child to him. 'For now, you do,' he said.

I bristled. 'Do you doubt my capacity for love?'

'Not at all,' he said. 'I feel sure you will always find space in your heart for more love, my dear.'

But it was getting late.

'We must return you to your own bed before anyone notices you are gone.'

He walked with me back to the place where I had left the priest's boat. The prostitutes called out to him. They seemed to know him well.

'Hey! How about your little brother? How about we show him something new?' they asked him, referring to me.

'I think he has learned enough for one night,' was my teacher's response.

He lifted me down into the boat and clambered in beside me. He rowed me back along the Grand Canal, right to the watergate of my father's house. As he tied the priest's boat to a mooring pole, I looked up at my bedroom window in despair. It looked far further up than down. I would never be able to get back in.

'Come on.' My teacher braced himself and lifted me up to the window as though I were a bale of hay. I tumbled over the sill and looked down at him.

'How will you get back?' I whispered. 'You can't take the priest's boat again.'

'I will find my way,' he said. 'And tomorrow I will leave you a rope in the confessional.' He tipped his hat at me and off he went, jumping from boat to boat like a thief until he reached an alleyway and disappeared.

He still had not told me his name. Why was he being so secretive when he'd had every part of me? For a moment, his capacity for plots and intrigue and his fellowship with the prostitutes of the *Carampane* unnerved me. Perhaps he was a notorious thief? Even a murderer! But my worries soon abated. I knew he would reveal his name to me eventually. I knew I already trusted him. I loved him.

22

Having read about Luciana's deflowering, I was all but convinced. I was delighted to be able to tell Marco in my next email that I was now ninety per cent certain I had found *The Lover's Lessons'* anonymous author. The circumstances in which Luciana had lost her virginity were so similar to those described in the novel. It was too big a coincidence to mean anything else. She had to be the writer.

Marco replied that he was very pleased my research had brought me to the right conclusion. Later, he sent me a direct message.

'Does this mean you don't need to visit the library any more?' he asked.

'Oh no,' I assured him. 'I need to get all the proof I possibly can. I have to know everything.'

'So do I,' was Marco's response. 'And not just about Luciana.'

I didn't take too much notice of his last sentence. I was so excited to be able to tell him that I even thought I might be staying in the very house where Luciana lost her virginity. The door-knocker and the enormous carved bed both suggested as much. That had been an odd thing to discover and only added to the growing sense I had that my visit to Venice was somehow fated. It was as though Luciana herself was willing me to reveal the truth, guiding me from wherever it is we go after death.

'It seems too great a coincidence,' I wrote. 'Can you imagine? You have to come and see it.'

'Is she haunting your dreams?' Marco asked me.

I didn't tell Marco the half of it – about the strange dreams and the times I'd felt far from alone when I woke up in the night. Neither did I tell him about the sensation I often had in the Palazzo Donato, that some benign spirit was with me there too and that was why so many of my erotic dreams began with a meeting in his garden. He'd have thought I'd gone nuts. He decided to up the ante anyhow.

'What about you? Tell me how you lost your virginity, Sarah Thomson.'

This was certainly a change of direction.

I leaned back in my chair. I blinked my eyes tightly shut as though imagining that when I opened them again, Marco's message would say something different. But there it was. He really was asking me how I had lost my virginity. I snorted as I wrote my off-the-cuff reply, 'I think this would have to be a case of I'll show you mine, if you show me yours.'

Two minutes passed before he replied.

'All right. Let's both set down our stories and exchange them in an hour.'

'Are you serious?'

'Deadly serious. Why not?'

'How can I tell you something so personal? We've never met. We hardly know each other.'

'I don't think never having met in the flesh means we don't know each other, do you? We've shared quite a few things already. I know the names of all your childhood pets. Your favourite fairytale. About your dislike of Marmite. I know the name of the first boy you kissed. I feel, after these few weeks of correspondence, that we are beginning to know each other rather well.'

'I suppose we are.'

'Good. And I've told you I think you would make a good

confidante. In that case, it's time we shared some real secrets. Here is my suggestion. We will write candid accounts of the day we lost our virginities. You may be assured that your story will be seen by no one but me and I hope I can expect the same discretion in response. But spare me no details. I want to know everything. Are you prepared to accept my challenge?'

I thought about it for far less time than I had expected to.

'You'll have to settle for everything I can remember.'

'Done. Start writing, Sarah Thomson.'

But I didn't start writing. I sat and stared at my screen. This was the most ridiculous thing I had ever agreed to do. I started to type an email saying I had changed my mind. I wasn't going to tell anyone I hadn't met face to face such a personal tale. I'd barely discussed the moment with my best friends at the time. It seemed, however, that Marco had pre-empted my cowardice. After ten minutes, a direct message appeared.

'I suspect you have not started to write. You are still worried you can't trust me.'

'What reason do I have to think otherwise?'

'I have shown my absolute trust in you. You know, I hope, that no one apart from my staff has been allowed access to the Donato library since 1999.'

'Then why did you decide to let me in?'

This was the question that had been on my mind for a long time. As I waited for his answer, I realised I had more invested in Marco's reasons than I dared admit. Please, I begged him silently, don't say it's because you wanted a free translation.

His answer came at last.

'I could tell you are kind.'

'From my letter?'

'From your photograph. The one on the university website.'

I cringed at the thought of it, but I replied.
'That was recommendation enough?'

Of course. Don't you think we all end up with the faces we
deserve? Your face reveals that you smile a great deal. It's
open and honest. In fact, I have opened your department's
website and I am looking at your photograph right now. Of
course, you know the very first time you wrote to me, I
went straight to my computer to find out more. What man
wouldn't? You had written to me so beautifully, I was
certain your face would match your turn of phrase, if not
your handwriting. Were my suspicions confirmed? Not at
first.

I admit upon first inspection you were not what I might
call 'my type'. Your hair. Why did you wear it at such an
unflattering length? What was that sweater you were
wearing? And why hadn't you taken a moment to put on
some make-up? I wondered if you were too much of an
intellectual for such things. Were you the kind of firebrand
feminist who thinks that making the best of oneself is in
some way demeaning? Is it chauvinistic of me to suggest
such a thing? But you see, these thoughts possessed me for
only a couple of seconds, because I could tell that behind
the bad hair, and the sweater even a recently shorn sheep
would be reluctant to wear, you had a transcendent beauty.
Your best efforts with that knife-cut fringe could not hide
your beautiful cheekbones. Michelangelo might have
carved your generous mouth and your perfectly straight
nose. Your chin is feminine yet determined. You have the
face of a mythical heroine. A goddess. No amount of bad
lighting and ill-chosen costume could conceal your
beautiful bones.

Or your eyes. Who was behind the camera that day?
What had he said to make your eyes crinkle at the corners

like that? You were trying not to laugh – I can tell – but
your happiness still radiates from you like sunbeams.
There is mischief in those perfect blue irises. Blue like a
pair of old Levi's. That is a great compliment, I hope you
know.

As I read those paragraphs, I remembered the day the photograph had been taken. Steven had been the cameraman, of
course.

Marco continued.

Why did I let you come here? Why you and not any
number of young women eager to learn more about the
romantic past of my house? It was your eyes, dear Sarah.
They are full of kindness and trust. You have the eyes of
someone who would feel guilty if she so much as stole a
flower. I hope.

I blushed at that last line. Marco's dissection of my photograph had been enough to disconcert me, but the idea that he
knew about the rose completely threw me. Thank goodness
he couldn't see me as I sat at my desk. Perhaps it was a coincidence but it was such a random accusation to make, I was
sure he must know about my petty theft. How did he know?
Had Silvio seen me? Had he seen me himself? Was his the
shadow that lurked in the gallery? The idea that it might be
excited me. Especially now that he had told me he liked the
way I looked. Things were definitely warming up.

'I'm sorry about the rose,' I wrote. 'It was so beautiful.'

'It was waiting just for you,' he said. 'But what will you give
me in return for my most precious possession?'

I started at the appearance of the words from my dream,
which were in turn words from the version of 'Beauty and the
Beast' I had loved and treasured as a child. I did not answer
them quickly enough for Marco. He continued.

'I think the story of your virginity is a small price to pay for my forgiveness. Particularly given I'll be sharing my story with you too.'

'How can I refuse?' I typed back.

'Good. We'll talk some more about my garden later.'

23

Though Marco's email explaining why I had been allowed into the library had gone some way to unlocking my inhibitions, I still felt a little unsure that describing the day I lost my virginity to him could be a good idea. But I knew that my tale – even if I included every detail I could remember – would hardly be *The Story of O*. There was none of the intrigue or danger that surrounded Luciana's first experience of love. The day I lost my virginity was all very ordinary. I looked out of the window at the grey, late January day and tried to remember a summer day some twelve years earlier, somewhere far less glamorous than Venice.

I started to write.

Where shall I start with my story? A girl and her virginity should not be easily parted and I like to think I stuck by that maxim. Compared to Luciana, I was a late starter.

That's as far as I got before Nick wandered into the office, looking for someone to accompany him to the café on the corner for the second time that morning.

'Important email,' I responded, quickly closing my open computer window in case Nick was minded to take a peek over my shoulder.

'So important you can't spare five minutes to have a coffee?' Nick pleaded. 'It's always much less fun alone.'

'Funding,' I lied.

137

'Ah.' That was an excuse any academic would understand.

When I was sure I was alone again, I reopened my email to Marco and continued to type.

I still can't believe I'm actually writing this down. It feels quite strange to think about how I lost my virginity. Though in the years running up to it, losing your virginity seems like quite the most important thing that could ever happen to a girl, all these years later on, I remember the event itself far less clearly than I would have imagined. I can, at least, tell you exactly with whom I shared this coming of age. His name was Jason Edward Greening. He was one of the boys from the grammar school on the other side of town.

He was two months older than me and we met, in a sweetly romantic way, at rehearsals for the harvest festival service at the cathedral. One of the perks of being in the choir was getting to escape from school for a while. We were singing something by Handel, as I recall. Jason and I were seated directly across the nave from one another. Whenever I looked up from my hymn book, he was looking straight back at me. When the time came for us girls to get back on the bus and be driven back to school for the last lesson of the day, Jason tucked a piece of notepaper into my pocket. It had his phone number on it. Neither of us had a mobile, of course. I called him from the telephone box near the post office to avoid having to explain things to my parents.

It was a very romantic courtship, beginning the very next weekend with a midday Saturday rendezvous in the town centre, where we went for fish and chips. His friend was working behind the counter. He gave us extra chips for free.

For the next few months, we spent every spare moment together. Revising for my A-levels was so much easier with Jason on the other side of the kitchen table, equally absorbed in his books. Though my parents expressed concern that I might let my first romance take precedence over my studies, my exams actually felt more important than ever, as they suddenly symbolised the beginning of a bright and beautiful future with this boy I now loved. While my parents probably worried that we were ripping each other's clothes off in the privacy of my girlhood bedroom, Jason and I really were testing each other on important treaties of the sixteenth century.

So when our results were published in August, we had both done far better than we ever imagined. I was euphoric for a short time, until it dawned on me properly that we were going to university on different sides of the country: me to UCL and him to Cambridge. Though we promised that it wouldn't have any effect on our love for each other, I lived in dread of the girls Jason would meet at his new college. I imagined them sexy and sophisticated and ready to seduce him. I thought that if we shared our virginity with each other, it would be a sign of our commitment.

We planned it so carefully. The week after I told Jason I was ready, his parents were going out of town for the weekend to celebrate their wedding anniversary at a country hotel. They would be leaving him alone in the house for the very first time.

Jason's mother joked that he would organise a huge party and she'd come back to find her beautiful home completely trashed. She needn't have panicked. Jason and I had only one thing in mind and it didn't involve hundreds of teenagers. We were planning a celebration just for two.

I had been working at two jobs to save money for my first year at university, but suddenly I had something I wanted to spend my cash on far more than I wanted textbooks. After finishing my Saturday job in the electrical goods department of the store where I worked, I went upstairs to lingerie and rigged myself out with what I hoped was the ideal ensemble in which to cross the threshold from young girl to fully fledged woman.

I suppose I should tell you what it was like. I sincerely hope, as I write this, that you are good to your word, Marco Donato, and will keep this entirely to yourself. This revelation could ruin my reputation for ever. I bought a rather naff polyester all-in-one. It was supposed to look like cream-coloured silk. The gusset was fastened by poppers. Remembering the garment now, I can't believe I ever thought it would be sexy. I also bought a pair of white hold-up stockings. I couldn't afford a suspender belt but didn't think about going bare-legged. I was trying to achieve a look as momentous as the occasion but I looked less like a beautiful virgin than a dancer from a 1980s pop show. Especially when I accessorised the ensemble with a pair of chunky navy-blue court shoes, bought for me by my mother to wear to my cousin's wedding. They were the closest thing I had to 'killer heels'. And I suppose they would have killed, had I thrown them at anyone's head.

Anyway, I wouldn't have given a Victoria's Secret model a run for her money, but when I unveiled the ensemble that evening, Jason seemed to appreciate the effort I had made. He too had splashed out on some new underwear: a pair of dark-green silk boxer shorts. My first thought was what his mother would say when she saw them. He couldn't just throw them in the laundry basket.

We put on some appropriate music. Our favourite album, containing 'our song'. Actually, it was more Jason's favourite album than mine. He was big into Joy Division. I pretended I felt the same way about the music, so I lost my virginity to a dirge and recovered to 'Love Will Tear Us Apart'.

We decided we would use his parents' bed. To get round the possibility of any awful mess, we covered the fitted sheet with brightly coloured beach towels that would be less likely to show a stain. Though I was eighteen years old, I was still very naïve about the mechanics of making love for the first time and part of me expected a dreadful flood of blood we would never be able to stop.

It's because of that fear that we actually ended up making love for the first time on the bare floorboards, with a pile of towels to protect my back and Jason's knees.

So, the music was on. Jason lit a candle. We opened a bottle of wine: screwtop, Australian Chardonnay. We drank a large glass each, quickly. A glass of wine was all I needed to start to feel quite tipsy in those days.

It was strange how, given we had been unable to keep our lips off each other since we first met in the town centre, that day we were full of nerves. We kissed awkwardly, noses bumping, teeth clashing. Though Jason had seen me naked before – we'd done everything but full-on sex – he seemed nervous as he slid the straps of the teddy from my shoulders to reveal my breasts. He kissed them so reverently I'm afraid I actually laughed. I don't think that helped the situation.

The whole thing was so tense. It was painful. Even if Jason had been better at foreplay – even if I had known how to ask him for more – I don't think I would have been properly turned on that night. I just wanted to get it over with. Once he was inside me, I think I actually gritted my teeth. The condom didn't help to make things easier but thankfully, Jason was so excited by the fact he was losing his virginity at last, the whole experience did not take very long. I had seen him come before of course but when he came inside me, he seemed to have an out-of-body experience. He was quite embarrassed about it. I didn't come at all.

Afterwards, we got up from the floor and lay together for a while on his parents' bed. We didn't say much to each other. We were both a little awed by the fact that we were no longer virgins. Perhaps we were a little disappointed too that there had been no real fireworks. Of course, we would start working on improving that the following day.

By the time his parents came back from their anniversary celebration, Jason and I considered ourselves positive experts in the act of love. I think we must have had sex at least eight times in twenty-four hours. Such is the stamina of teenagers! After that, we seized upon every opportunity we could find to explore each other further. Though we didn't get another chance to spend the night together, we made very good use of the car Jason's parents had bought him for his eighteenth birthday. I still feel nostalgic when I see a red Fiat Panda.

And then, of course, we were off to university, where we would be utterly free from the constraints imposed by living at home. I couldn't wait to spend whole days in bed with my love. We agreed we would not see each other for the first couple of weeks, as we settled in to our respective colleges, but I was expecting us to visit each other every weekend after that. We were, after all, destined to be together for ever. But Jason wrote to me two weeks into that first term to tell me that he thought it was best we downgraded our relationship to a friendship. He told me his course required far more effort and attention than he had ever imagined. He would not have time to come to London to meet me at weekends. I knew it wasn't the whole truth. I was devastated. It took me a whole term to get over him and be ready to date someone new.

And here I admitted the worst of it.

I told my new university boyfriend that I was still a virgin. In some ways I still felt like one.

24

I sent my story exactly on the hour, as we had agreed. When I found no corresponding message in my inbox for the next fifteen minutes, I was ready to be furious. All that stuff about my honest face and then the flower and then . . . nothing. I was an idiot.

I was drafting an angry email in my head when Marco's own finally arrived. He prefaced his story with an apology.

> It is very strange. I have not thought about this subject for years. I did not expect to have many clear memories, but they have been almost unstoppable. I could have written for another half an hour but I imagine you sitting at your desk thinking you've been tricked and I do not like the thought of you cursing me for getting you to show your hand first. So, here it is. My own terrible story.

I clicked on the attached Word document.

> Her name was Chiara. She was my father's mistress.

His father's mistress! Already Marco's story had trumped mine.

> Someone once told her she looked like a young Sophia Loren and she played up the similarities at every opportunity she could. To me, she was certainly the most exotic creature I had ever seen. To my father, alas, she was but one of a string of similarly exotic creatures and as such he soon became bored of her.

Chiara was not impressed to be discarded. I think she thought my father would marry her but though my parents had lived separately for many years by this time, there was no way they would ever get a divorce. The love may have gone out of their marriage, but neither one of them was in a hurry to embrace the lower standard of living a division of their fortunes would ensure.

So, after a couple of years, Chiara was dispatched. My father took her to one side and explained that he would not be augmenting the collection of jewels he had already given her with a ring, so she should start looking for someone who would give her everything she deserved. She seemed to take it well. He assured her if she ever needed his help she should not hesitate to call on him. Likewise, he hoped they would be able to move in the same social circles without any embarrassment. Indeed, Chiara turned up at a restaurant where my father and I were having dinner to celebrate my sixteenth birthday just a week later. She was with another man, but she came across to greet us as if nothing had happened. Little did my father know that Chiara was plotting a revenge of sorts and that her revenge would be the making of me.

That night in the restaurant, Chiara asked my father if it would be OK if she borrowed me for a couple of days. She'd decided it was time to redecorate her apartment. Surely a young boy like me would appreciate a little paid work in his school holidays?

I didn't need paid work. My allowance was enough to support the average Italian family including all the grandparents and unmarried aunts. However, my father very much liked the idea of my doing some manual labour. At my grandfather's insistence, he himself had spent a summer working as a labourer on the family's boats. He claimed that long summer had changed his perspective and made him understand the value of true graft. He would have had me do exactly the same, except a labourer had been killed in an accident at the boatyard a couple of years earlier and my mother made him promise never to put me in that position. A little bit of house-painting, though. That wouldn't hurt me.

'Marco will be with you first thing in the morning,' my father promised his former mistress. She rewarded him with a glittering smile before she turned to me with a look so predatory, I felt my prick stand to attention at once.

When I arrived at Chiara's apartment the following day, she did not look as though she was waiting for the labour to arrive. Or perhaps she looked exactly as a certain kind of woman does when she is waiting for the labour to arrive. When she opened the door to me, she was wearing a negligee that barely skimmed the tops of her thighs. Over that, she wore a dressing gown, but it was so see-through and diaphanous as to be perfectly pointless as a cover-up. Her hair was dishevelled. Artfully so, I now understand. But her make-up was perfect. Her lips were painted a sinful cherry-red. Slick and very kissable.

'It's such a hot day,' she said. 'You look as though you could use a drink.'

She cracked open a beer for me. I hadn't even taken my jacket off, let alone earned a drink. Plus it was only just eleven in the morning. Still, I accepted it gratefully. I needed Dutch courage and wanted to seem mature.

'I think we should start in the bedroom,' she said. I followed her in there. If I had not suspected before that the decorating job was a ruse, I knew for certain now. Chiara had not made any effort to prepare the room for a fresh coat of paint. She had not packed anything away or covered the elegant furniture with dustsheets. On the contrary, she had filled vases with fresh flowers and the bed was neatly made with beautiful linen. She immediately lay down upon the bed and patted the mattress beside her.

'I have been thinking about a light green for the walls,' she said. 'And a slightly darker shade for the ceiling. If you come here, you'll get a better view of the room and be able to tell me what you think.'

Oh Chiara. It was the most ham-fisted seduction I would ever experience. She left nothing at all for me to do. As soon as I lay down beside her, she rolled so she was right on top of me. She smoothed my hair away from my face and looked deep into my eyes. I knew she was going to kiss me.

'Just like your father,' she said. 'If he weren't sixty-five years old with a paunch.'

Chiara's revenge was to let me take my father's place and make damn sure I knew I was an upgrade. She took it upon herself to teach me everything I could possibly want to know and a great deal more besides.

Ten minutes after arriving at Chiara's house, I was naked and so was she. I saw at once why my father had been so enamoured of her. If she looked wonderful in her designer clothes, she looked magnificent without them. Like most guys my age, I had pored over the *Sports Illustrated* calendar and ogled the ads for Victoria's Secret. But Chiara was something else. She made those models look scrawny and hard. The best way to describe Chiara's flesh was that it was luxurious. I could not get enough of her.

It seemed she could not get enough of me either. She covered every part of my body with kisses. She poured oil into her hands and massaged me until I felt as though every part of me apart from my prick was turning into jelly. When it came to my prick she acted as though she had never seen such a fine one. Her expression of delight is not one I shall ever forget. She was the perfect lover for a shy young boy who, like all young boys, worried that he would not measure up.

When she breathed, 'It's so big!' I was inclined to believe her.

I have wondered since that day how many other Italian boys Chiara relieved of their virginity. Having kissed and caressed me into submission, she arranged herself upon the pillows and invited me to climb between her legs. I was overly eager and clumsy but she bore it all with smiles.

Of course, I had experienced an orgasm before. I spent much more time in the bathroom than I cared to admit between the ages of fourteen and sixteen. But to come inside a woman was truly something else. It was transcendent. I had never experienced such a powerful feeling. It was as though my orgasm was being ripped from me. I shouted out. I think I may even have cried.

For the whole of that day, Chiara kept me metaphorically chained to her bed, letting me out of her sight only when she went to the kitchen to fetch another drink.

Her body was a marvel to me. I had, of course, seen naked women before, but they were girls at my high school in America, who were insecure about their feminine charms. They were always concerned about how they compared to their contemporaries. They were worried about being too fat or too hairy. Chiara had no such hang-ups. Of course, she had a wonderful body. Her legs were long and her breasts were as full as honeydew melons, but it was the relish with which she displayed herself that made her truly beautiful.

When I was with her, she made herself utterly available to me. She allowed me to explore and experiment. She was effusive in her praise when I got something right but gentle in her criticism too, so I was never afraid to try something new. She would have made the perfect schoolteacher. I learned so much with Chiara. She said it was her duty to give me a proper education so that the poor girl who eventually pinned me down would know the meaning of marital bliss.

I was the keenest of students. When Chiara suggested that I spend the summer helping her to 'paint the whole house', I leapt at the excuse to be with her. I wanted to be better than my father in every way and that included as a lover of women. When Chiara had finished with me – eventually she found herself a Greek shipping magnate whose vast wealth demanded exclusivity and she moved to Athens to be with him – she was kind enough to praise my skills in the bedroom to all of her friends. That summer, she told me, I had truly become a man. I promised her I would continue to practise everything she had taught me and by the time I was eighteen – when my father presented me with a visit to a prostitute as a birthday gift – I had already bedded most of my mother's friends, all of my father's friends' wives and my father's current girlfriend. The prostitute and I spent the evening playing cards.

25

I shook my head as I reread Marco's confession. I wasn't sure what I had expected. Something similar to my own story perhaps? Sweet first love and adolescent fumblings? Instead, Marco had lost his virginity to a professional femme fatale. A woman who had already been his father's lover? A woman who might even be justifiably called a courtesan? Likewise, the idea that Marco's own father would have sent him to a prostitute was way outside my experience.

I had a friend from university who defended the practice of sending young men to lose their virginities with a prostitute. It might not be so romantic, but it would definitely be more informative. How many men might have become great lovers had they been given just a little more instruction at a time when they might have been grateful to accept it?

I thought again about my own early experiences of sex. Though once we got going he was an enthusiastic shagger, Jason had barely touched me beyond the perfunctory. A kiss for each of my nipples. A few moments rubbing at me through my underwear. What would I have done if he had dipped his head between my legs and sought out my clitoris with his tongue? Possibly I would have protested, but what if he had persisted? Would I have enjoyed it? My first university boyfriend was similarly averse to using anything other than his prick and his fingers. What if he had experienced Marco's education? I might not have had to wait until I was twenty-one for my first orgasm.

'A very interesting story,' I wrote in response to Marco's tale.

'I am glad you think so. I hope you were not shocked.'

'Of course not,' I lied. I didn't want to betray my provincial feelings. 'But what became of your first love? Mine got his first at Cambridge and went on to law school. I heard he married a woman he met there and they now have a handful of daughters. I saw a photograph of him on Facebook. He's got rather fat.'

Marco responded, 'It sounds as though you had a lucky escape. As for me: after that crazy summer as her apprentice, I didn't see Chiara again until my father's funeral. She joined a whole row of his former mistresses at the back of the church. What a beautiful set of mourners they made. They were like a United Nations of beauty. My father had had wonderful lovers from all corners of the world. The most amazing thing was, they all seemed to know and like each other. Chiara was a particular favourite with everyone. Even my mother gave Chiara a nod as we walked out of the church.'

A United Nations of beauty. I was suddenly reminded of the girls in all those photographs online. Marco's girls might have warranted a similar description. I felt another little stab of jealousy. I wondered whether he had felt the same when he read about Jason. A suburban lawyer run to fat? Probably not.

I kept the tone light.

'Did Chiara marry the shipping magnate?'

'Unfortunately, he died before Chiara was able to snag him. In fact, rumour has it she rode him to his death on the day they got engaged. Silly girl. Talk about a compelling argument for no sex before marriage. After that, she left Athens and came back to Italy. I understand she still lives in Venice. Though we don't move in the same circles any more.'

'She's still here? Wouldn't you like to see her again?'

'It would be amusing. But I am not sure she would be

quite so keen to spend time with me these days. You see, I'm rather different from the young man she once took to bed.'

'More experienced and sophisticated? I can only imagine you've improved. Certainly physically. Men with faces like yours always age rather well.'

'Perhaps.'

'Or perhaps not. Which is why there are no pictures of you online taken this century. Haven't you been out since 1999?'

'I haven't been photographed. It's not the same thing.'

'Afraid someone will steal your soul?'

'I told you, I decided my playboy image wasn't doing me any favours. I'm a businessman. Who wants to invest with someone who looks like he spends all his time skiing?'

'Surely the fact that you can spend all your time skiing only shows what a successful businessman you are?'

'A good point, but I still think people prefer to think of me in my office rather than on the slopes. If it were possible, I would have all those old photographs taken down. There's nothing worse than being judged on your looks.'

'We can't help it though, can we? It's a natural human reaction and, as you said, we all end up with the faces we deserve.'

'Yes.'

The word hovered on my screen. I waited for the rest of the sentence. Nothing came.

'Are you still there?' I asked eventually.

No response came.

After that, I found myself on the receiving end of another prolonged bout of silence. Did I deserve it? Perhaps. I had been a little spiteful, if the truth were told. Childish. So Marco had lost his virginity years before I even heard his name. Why should it have mattered to me in the least who relieved him of the troublesome burden? But I was jealous. Stupidly so. Swapping our tales of virginities lost had taken the edge off Marco's compliments on my photograph.

I was reading back through that morning's emails and torturing myself with the idea I'd said something wrong again when Nick appeared and leaned against the doorframe of my office.

'Productive morning?' he asked.

'Sort of.'

'Sounded like one to me. Your fingers have been flying. It's been like sitting next door to a nineteen-fifties typing pool. I hope you get your funding after all that hard work.'

I blushed.

'Want some lunch?' he asked.

I decided I would. It was unfair of Marco to disappear on me again when we'd shared such important stories. I would give him a taste of his own medicine. Lunch with Nick was always a long affair. If Marco responded now, he would have to do some waiting of his own.

But when we came back from lunch, Marco still hadn't written. He didn't write to me for the rest of the day. It made me crazy. I had only just got over the habit of checking my email fifty times an hour for news from Steven and now I was equally obsessed with my new Italian friend.

I was determined not to let Marco's sudden lack of communication get to me. In the scheme of things, a day was nothing. I should try to be cooler. He'd flattered me. So what? However, I couldn't help but study every woman of a certain age I saw that day. I wanted to know more about Marco's first love. My competitor, as I now rather ridiculously considered her. A young Sophia Loren, Marco said. That was when?

Twenty years ago? She wouldn't have changed so much. I looked closely at the faces of the dark-haired beauties who clipped through the misty streets on their improbable heels. Any one of them could be Chiara. Would the kind of experiences the beauty had been able to pass on to Marco show on someone's face? Would they show as wrinkles? More likely as a glow, I thought.

Joining Nick and Bea at the bar for an *aperitivo*, I was convinced I had found Marco's first love among my fellow customers. A woman who looked strikingly like Sophia Loren perched upon a stool at the bar. She was immaculately coiffed and had a full-length black fur coat draped over her elegant shoulders. On her lap was a small white dog. Despite her age, which I guessed to be at least sixty, the woman was in the company of three much younger men, all of whom seemed desperate for her attention. When she laughed, she threw back her head and stroked her own throat in such a carelessly sensual gesture that even Nick's attention soon drifted in her direction.

Yes, I decided. That's the kind of woman who takes the virginity of a man like Marco Donato. He'd never have lost it to a girl like me. Plain and naïve. Flat-chested. With an unflattering haircut and a nasty sweater. I soon forgot the 'transcendent' part.

Bea left early. She had a date with the security guard. The 'handsome brute'.

'I don't expect there to be much conversation,' she assured us.

Nick and I were alone again. He bought me another drink and some *cichetti*. A good idea, though the bruschetta was as stale as ever.

'Tell me. What's he like, that Marco Donato?' Nick asked, when we lapsed into silence. 'You've been spending so much time at his house.'

154

'And I still haven't met him,' I said. 'But on email he seems very charming. He writes to me rather often,' I added.

I blushed despite myself. It was though I'd wanted to stake a claim on Marco by talking up our connection. Nick must have thought I was daft.

'I bet he does. I don't see how any man could fail to be charming to you. Or rather, be charmed *by* you.'

'Nick. You say that to all the girls.' I gave him a playful shove.

'Not at all,' he said. 'But you should know how lovely you are. I can imagine how hard it's been for you to come to Venice, leaving that rat of an ex behind. I got a sense of that when we did our truth or dare about heartbreak. But you are better off without him. The best girls never believe in their own worth.'

'Thank you, Nick. It's kind of you to say so.'

'Not kind. Just truthful. You seem like you need cheering up tonight.'

'Really, it's fine. I'm suffering from a slightly bruised heart, not general low self-esteem.'

'That's good to hear,' said Nick. 'I suppose flirting with Marco Donato must help.'

'How do you know we've been flirting?' I asked.

'Haven't you?'

'We just write about my research,' I insisted, wondering what Bea had told him.

'Too many people set their sights on the wrong person when they're trying to get over a break-up. Being rejected makes one vulnerable. And before you know it, you've ended up playing into the hands of another charming git. Out of the frying pan . . .'

Sensing he was still referring to Marco, I dropped my eyes.

'I see it all the time,' said Nick.

'I ought to go back to the flat,' I said. 'There's no need for you to walk me back. It's not far.'

'I know. But I'd like to anyway, and I understand that you're not extending an invitation if you accept.'

'OK,' I said. 'In that case.'

Nick was true to his word. He walked me to my door but did not try to get beyond it. Instead, he cocked an imaginary hat at me and disappeared into the fog. The strange thing was, though I had dreaded the idea of having to discourage him from coming in, I was a little sad to see him go. The flat felt emptier for his not having asked to come in. He was such a gentleman.

That curious emptiness turned to something approaching real happiness, however, when I saw that Marco had sent me a new email since I'd been out with my friends. He didn't respond to my last tease but I didn't care.

> I hope you have had a lovely evening. I must admit, I do wonder what you do when you're not in the office. Which Venetian haunts have you made your own? Who takes you there? A girl like you should not spend her evenings alone. You should be taken to the best restaurants and plied with the finest wine. You should be waltzed around the smartest dancefloors. You should be feted and adored.

Adored? That one word made the room seem suddenly brighter. I went to bed happily and dreamed of him. I was sure it was him, now. Even with the mask. Did he dream about me?

26

10th March, 1753

Did I look any different? I was certain I must. Back in my chamber, I was unable to sleep. My mind whirred as I tried to remember the events of the evening as clearly as I could. I wanted to write them down before I forgot even the smallest detail.

What a surprise the whole evening had been! It was not at all as I had expected. My education in such things was lacking, I suppose. It comes of not having a mother. I had heard Maria and the girls in the kitchen talking about wedding nights but the unmarried girls were all aflutter whenever such things were mentioned. For the most part, they were full of terror at the prospect. They spoke of a horror so awful it was enough to make the less robust take holy orders. The older women, women who had been married for many years, shook their heads in amusement but did not say anything to allay the twittering virgins' fears. Or mine.

So what was it like? What would I tell any frightened girl who asked me? Don't be afraid, I would say. If you love him, it will all happen as it is meant to. I felt, when he took me in his arms, as though I was in some way opening out towards him. When he kissed me, I felt a rush of warmth throughout my body, beginning from the

157

places where his hands lay upon me. He made me put my fingers between my own legs and feel myself wet with desire. My body did everything it could to welcome him.

It hurt a little. He had warned me it would, despite his best efforts to ensure otherwise. But it did not hurt as much as the girls in the kitchen claimed. In fact, it was a joyful kind of pain. And later, when he held me and kissed me and thanked me for letting him be the one, I started to feel more happy and alive than I have ever done. My skin tingled. It was tingling still when I climbed into bed.

After such an exciting evening, I thought I would never sleep again but I must have done, because one moment I was writing in my diary and the next Maria was throwing open the curtains and the diary was open on the floor beside my bed. I snatched it up and hid it under the covers. If she suspected I was in the habit of keeping a diary, she would certainly try to find it next time she was in my room alone. Thankfully, she was too busy looking out of the window to notice my scramble to retrieve the secret book. She was in some sort of dream of her own. She leaned on the windowsill, rested her chin on her hands and sighed.

'It's a beautiful day,' she observed. 'One of God's days.'

'Aren't they all God's days?' I asked.

Maria turned from the window at last. Her dreamy expression disappeared as she put her hands on her hips and regarded me sternly. 'Well, you seem to be determined to waste it. What's the matter with you? Why are you still in bed at this time?'

As she began to tie back the curtains around my bed,

she was her usual grumpy self. I decided that meant she had not noticed anything unusual. Good.

'I was having such a strange dream,' I said.

She nodded her head in the direction of the warm water in the jug.

'Well, you can stop dreaming now. Your father wishes to breakfast with you.'

'He does?'

I was nervous then, because if anyone other than Maria might notice a subtle change in my state of being, it was my father, who had known me my whole life. I stared at myself in the mirror, but not out of any vanity.

'Yes, yes,' said Maria, growing impatient as she held out my chemise. 'You're just as lovely as you were yesterday.' Sarcasm dripped from every word, but that morning I embraced Maria's spite. She would have not thought twice about telling me if I looked worse than before. That was certain.

So I had breakfast with my father. I walked into the room full of anxiety, sure my guilt must be written all over me, but he merely smiled briefly when I kissed him 'good morning' before he went back to reading his papers. Half an hour later, he left to visit a cargo boat newly arrived in the docks. He kissed me on the top of the head in passing. He had barely spoken to me. I don't suppose he could have reliably recalled the colour of the dress I was wearing. He had noticed nothing.

But oh, I am changed inside! I cannot stop thinking about my teacher. I am not interested in reading any more. I am not even interested in eavesdropping at the kitchen door. All I can think of is how I will escape my room again tonight and when I can be back in his arms.

He told me there is much to learn and know about the art of love. I want to continue my education now.

11th March, 1753

As promised, the next time I went to church I found a silken rope beneath the confessional stool. I wrapped it round my waist and covered it with my cloak. With the rope to help me, I escaped the palazzo even more easily than before and was with my teacher by the time the bells chimed ten. Once again, he was waiting for me, dressed only in his undershirt and breeches. He opened the door with a gallant gesture but as soon as I was inside, he wasted no time in pulling me into his embrace like a proper rascal.

I did not pretend to be coy this time. His kiss was too delicious and the feelings it aroused in me were far too strong. I didn't want to pretend. I wanted to do exactly what we'd done before. No. I wanted to go further. I wanted to feel him inside me again. I moaned licentiously as he slipped his hands inside my soft white shirt and cupped my longing breasts.

'Today has been so long,' I said. 'I could not wait to be with you again.'

'Nor I you,' he assured me. 'You have never been far from my mind. How is a man supposed to go about his business when all he can think of is your soft young skin?'

His hands roamed my body. I loosened my borrowed trousers and he tucked his fingers into the waist of my undergarments. He slid them down until he held my buttocks. He gave them a teasing squeeze that made me giggle.

'How I have longed to have a good view of this pair,' he said. 'And these.' He moved his hands up to my breasts again. 'You really are the most exquisite creature.'

With that compliment in my ears, how could I not oblige him with a closer look? Quickly, I stripped off the rest of my clothes and arranged myself on the bed in a pose I had seen in a painting by Tiziano. He stood at the end of the bed and observed me with an indulgent smile.

'If only Tiziano were still around to paint you,' he said. 'Though even he could not improve on God's work in your case.'

He regarded me for a moment longer before he stripped off his own shirt and breeches. If he thought I was beautiful, then I thought the same of him. I had not seen many naked men, of course. At least, not in life. Apart from in paintings, I could only think of the year the *acqua alta* came and all the men in the house stripped to the waist while they were shifting furniture from the lower rooms of the palazzo to safety on the upper floors. But there was no comparison between my father's old retainer Alberto, or Fabio the boatman, and my teacher as he stood before me now. His was a body that might have illustrated a textbook. His sinews were so well-defined, I was able to pick out the muscles I had seen described in the book of anatomy by Albinus. I felt fortunate to be able to gaze upon him and count the differences between his body and mine.

Where my skin was white and softer than a pair of lambskin gloves, his was tanned dark and felt hot beneath my fingers. Where my breast was smooth, his chest was sprinkled with fine black hair. The hair followed the contours of his muscles, making them seem even more pronounced. Another trail of hair led from his stomach to where his manhood sprang forwards. It was hard again.

'He has been bothering me all day,' my teacher laughed. 'It is like being in the control of another brain.'

'I am glad to see him so happy,' I said.

'Oh, he's very happy, all right.'

My teacher sat down on the edge of the bed. I raised myself on my elbow to look into his lap. His manhood seemed to twitch in my direction, as though encouraging me to touch him. I ran a gentle finger along its length.

'Are we . . . can we do what we did yesterday, again?' I asked.

'No. What you experienced yesterday was just the beginning. If you will submit to my expertise then I will teach you things about your body that will fill you with delight.'

'You filled me with delight yesterday,' I assured him.

'Trust me,' he said. 'There will be more.'

I lay back upon the pillows. Smiling at me all the while, he drew a finger down the centre of my body, making me shiver. Then he slid down the bed so that his face was level with my mound of Venus. I squirmed. His hot breath on my hair was more than a little ticklish.

'Lay still,' he instructed. 'Open your legs.'

I did not question him. But then he moved closer still, putting his face right in my mound, and I felt so full of sensation that I tried to push his face away. I tried to close my legs.

'I can see you are going to make this difficult,' he observed. He held my thighs firmly. Still I resisted.

'Are you going to kiss me there?' I asked him. I was horrified.

162

'I'm going to do more than kiss you,' he said.

I couldn't help it. I was suddenly very shy.

'This is no good,' he said. 'If you are going to refuse to accept your pleasure like a good girl, then I shall have to find another way.'

He raised himself up, still holding both my hands, and reached for the scarf I had tied around my hair before I tucked it beneath my brother's hat.

'This is for your own good,' he informed me, as he bound my wrists together and then bound them in turn to one of the bedposts. With my arms thus restrained, I tried to preserve my modesty by pressing my legs together, but my teacher made swift work of pulling them apart.

'I thought you wanted to know everything?'

'I do, but . . .'

'Just close your mouth and listen. A woman's organs of pleasure are not unlike a man's,' he informed me. 'Feel how when I apply my lips to your tiny bud, it begins to throb and swell just like my manhood. If I lick the tip, like this, then the sensation will only increase in intensity.'

I writhed in my bonds. I wanted him to continue to lick me and at the same time, I simply could not stand his ministrations. I felt a curious sensation throughout my whole body. It was as though someone had held pepper under my nose and my whole body was going to sneeze at it.

'Please, please,' I begged him. 'You must stop. I am afraid I won't be able to control myself.'

'I am afraid of exactly the opposite,' he told me. Then he disappeared between my legs again.

What a feeling! It made me long to take him inside me. I begged him to cure the ticklish intensity with a thrust. But no matter how I begged and struggled, he shook his head and refused me, holding my legs more firmly. There was nothing I could do but lie still.

But I could not be still. I bit my lip and strained against the scarf that held me. As the feeling became more intense, my body bucked upwards. I pressed myself against his mouth. I told him to lick faster. I was entirely wanton. I was possessed.

And then there came the moment when I could control myself no longer. I cried out. Powerful waves of feeling flooded through me. My very insides were undulating. I could hardly breathe. I gasped for air. I wanted only to press harder, harder against him still, though at the same time I begged him to release me. I begged him to stop. And when he wouldn't answer my pleas, I begged God and the saints to deliver me.

I kept my eyes tightly closed as the feeling exploded. Stars danced behind my eyelids. I felt exhausted and yet entirely renewed. I sank into the bed, with my hands still tied above my head. And then I started laughing. I couldn't stop myself. There was nothing to laugh at but my body was no longer in the control of my mind. I began to think I had gone mad.

My teacher sat up between my legs and smiled down on me. He untied my hands and I sat up. He wrapped his arms around me.

'Now, my little goose, tell me how silly you were to try to stop me? Tell me that was not the most delicious sensation you have experienced in your short sweet life. See?' He made me look towards the mirror. 'Your eyes are glittering. Your cheeks are perfectly flushed. You have never looked so lovely.'

'Or felt so well loved,' I murmured.

He kissed me on the top of my head. 'Sweet girl.'

'Now will you tell me your name?' I asked. 'Since you have seen parts of me that no other living being has seen since I was last bathed by a nurse.'

My teacher laughed. 'My first name is Giacomo.'

'A very common title. And your family name?'

'I need to know you better before I can tell you that.'

Then, tickling me like a fiend, he rolled me over onto the mattress and bit me on the bottom.

This time I knew the pleasure he had given me could be read all over my face. Every time I thought about the events that took place in his shabby room, I blushed with girlish shame, even as I wanted to laugh out loud at the deliciousness of it all. And he had assured me there was still much more to come. Much better! If I was going to Hell then it would be a wonderful journey.

I made it back into the palazzo without disturbing anyone, despite knocking over a bucket that had been left upon the dock. But I knew I had to be more discreet. I had to try to control my excitement. Lying in bed, I pressed a cold glass against my forehead to calm my passions. But it did no good and the following morning, Maria suggested I'd caught the *scarlatina*!

I have to be more careful, though I have never wanted to be more reckless in my life.

27

Soon, my account of losing my virginity began to seem very tame indeed. As did Marco's! Dear Luciana's entries in her diary were growing more explicit by the day. Her introduction to oral sex was just the start of it. Within a week, her teacher had persuaded her to let him put a finger in her arse. You can easily guess what came soon after. Had those critics who decided a young girl could not go from losing her virginity to testing the deeper waters of depravity so quickly been but able to read the pages I held in my hand, they would soon have altered their opinion. The pages were a gift to me. I was able to tell Bea without fear of contradiction that her theory about Casanova was wrong. Luciana Giordano was definitely the author of *The Lover's Lessons*. Some of the passages corresponded exactly with passages in the novel. They used the same phrases.

It was slightly embarrassing, however, to have to paraphrase them for Marco. Though I had shared the story of my virginity, telling him that Luciana was becoming a big fan of anal sex was something else. I felt oddly shy on her behalf. It didn't help that Marco remained so elusive. He was never in Venice, he claimed, though Silvio had once told me he was 'always there' and he had seen me steal the rose. And crazy as it sounds, whenever I was in the library at the Palazzo Donato, I felt that Marco was nearby. What was the real story? I was determined to find out more.

* * *

I had been visiting the Donato library every day for more than a month now, and not only had I yet to meet Marco, I still hadn't seen any more of the palazzo than the dark corridors that led from the front door or the watergate to the secret courtyard and the library beyond. Though in Luciana's diaries I had plenty to absorb my interest, I could not help but be curious about what lay beyond the one room I was permitted to explore at my leisure.

Of course, I had tried to find more hints to the real Marco on the library shelves, but there weren't many clues there. As far as I could tell, no books had been added to the library for several decades. At least, no new books. Every tome on the shelves was of academic interest. It might have been a university library. There were no stray paperbacks. No Harold Robbins. Not even a copy of *The Da Vinci Code*. Didn't everybody have a copy of *The Da Vinci Code*? Marco Donato's grandfather certainly looked like the kind who might have enjoyed the odd thriller.

But no. There was nothing that suggested the library existed in the twenty-first century. No modern books. No family photographs on the mantelpiece above the fireplace that might have filled in the gaps since 1999. The only thing in the room other than the books and the furniture was that painting of the eighteenth-century lady. Whenever I paused in my reading, I found my eyes drawn to that portrait. The woman therein seemed to gaze back at me. Her smile was every bit as enigmatic as the Mona Lisa's. It seemed to challenge me to find out more. Who was she, for a start?

For a short while, I thought she might be Luciana, but she was too old. Luciana had entered a convent as a teenager. Also, the painted woman's hair was too fair. Luciana had described her own hair as dark. Who was the mysterious blonde?

★ ★ ★

I got my answer as to the identity of the woman in the portrait a few days later. I'd been tempted for a long while by the thought of what lay further down the corridor, beyond the library. Naturally, I dared not ask for permission to roam but I decided I would stray regardless, using the need to visit a bathroom as an excuse if caught by Silvio.

The next time I was in the library, I waited only a few minutes before I made my escape. Since it was icy on the streets outside, I had worn rubber-soled boots that Silvio made me discard in the hall, so it was easy for me to make my way down the corridor in my socks without making too much noise. I knew exactly where I wanted to go.

The doors I was most intrigued by were at least eighteen feet high, made of heavy well-waxed wood that would not open easily. The centre of each door panel was decorated with a carved monkey's head remarkably similar to the door-knocker monkey at Ca' Scimmietta. There was an identical double door on the other side of the corridor. Again, it was decorated with monkeys' heads. Each of the monkeys' faces bore a different expression. I wondered what they represented. If they represented anything at all.

Horribly aware of how great a liberty I was taking, I glanced down the long corridor in either direction to make sure I wasn't being watched. I listened carefully to the silence around me, to make sure it really was silent. I could hear nothing other than my own breathing. I imagined Silvio somewhere on the other side of the house, in the kitchen perhaps, stirring the pot he always claimed he'd left on the stove. Well, I thought, here's hoping it's a risotto.

I grasped the handle of the first door firmly and twisted it. I did not expect it to let me pass without protest, but the door opened easily and without the slightest noise. The hinges must have been recently oiled. Though the Donato house had a strange air of desertion, it was clear a great deal of energy still went into its upkeep. As in the library, where there was not a speck of dust to be found, the intricately carved doors were free of dirt and recently polished, scented with good old-fashioned beeswax. It was still more mausoleum or museum than family home, though. I found it hard to imagine Marco relaxing in this room, kicking off his shoes and lying back on the sofa. With the door open, I remained in the corridor, looking in, until I was certain I would not be disturbing anyone.

I knew a little about Venetian architecture. I knew these rooms at the front of the house, overlooking the canal, were the rooms where the family would entertain guests. As such, they were likely to be the most sumptuously decorated rooms of all, while the rest of the house could be quite plain. When I first arrived in Venice, I had been overawed by the four-poster bed in my apartment, but what I saw now made a mockery of those few sticks of furniture in my borrowed flat.

What a beautiful room lay beyond the smiling monkeys! It was dark – the shutters remained closed against the weak February sun – yet in some strange way the room seemed to glow. Such light as did enter the room was reflected in a thousand small ways by the gilded edges of furniture and frames and what appeared to be an enormous mirror. While the rest of the furniture was uncovered, the mirror above the huge stone mantelpiece was shrouded in a pristine white sheet, with a tear that offered just a glimpse of the glass behind. There was another mirror on the opposite wall. That too was covered. How strange, when everything else was exposed.

I tiptoed round the room, looking for more clues as to Marco and his family's life. Once again, I found no photographs, no stray paperback novels or invitations on the mantelpiece, but there was another painting of the woman depicted in the library portrait. This painting was by a different artist though; I could tell without even looking at the name on the tiny plaque on the frame. I wondered if this was a better likeness. Certainly, the sitter looked more relaxed for this painter. She held a half-closed fan in her right hand. With her other hand, she reached up to hold the tail of a monkey that was sitting on her shoulder. The monkey, in turn, had a paw on top of the woman's head in a manner that suggested it was not always entirely clear which of them was mistress and which was pet. I looked at the monkey more closely. I wondered if it had been the model for the carved heads on all the doors.

Ernesta and her monkey was the title of the portrait. This Ernesta looked to be on the verge of laughter. I wondered how long it had taken to paint the portrait. It could not have been easy to persuade a monkey to stay in place for long enough to get such a good likeness. And how the monkey was decked out! No ordinary collar for this pampered creature. It was wearing a long string of pearls with one huge drop-shaped pearl as a pendant. What was all the more striking was that Ernesta was wearing nothing at all round her creamy neck. I understood at once what sort of statement this was supposed to make. 'Look at me. I am so beautiful I do not need adornment. I am so wealthy that my pets are dressed in pearls.' What a woman this Ernesta must have been.

While I was gazing at the painting, I heard the myriad bells of Venice begin to strike the quarter-hour. In fifteen minutes, Silvio would come to the library door and escort me to the exit. Perhaps Silvio had heard the quarter-hour chimes and already started to make his slow way through the house. I was thrilled by my secret moment in the grand salon but knew I should not risk staying there. I crept back to the door and into the corridor. I pulled the door shut behind me, giving the smiling monkey an affectionate rub on the nose as I did so. Then I tiptoed back to the library and by the time Silvio arrived, it was as though I had not strayed from my desk at all.

Silvio was as unfriendly as usual, but that day I bestowed upon the old man my most winning smile. My secret and the motivation behind it was a little bit like being in love.

Luciana was falling in love too. That much was obvious. As she spent more and more time with her teacher, the familiar cursive of her handwriting seemed more exuberant, some-how, as though she was writing more quickly than usual, so keen was she to share all her thoughts and feelings on the page. I recognised that craziness from the days when Jason and I were first exploring sex with each other. Such energy. Hormones raging. As I read on, I hoped Luciana would not be as disappointed by her first love as I had ultimately been by mine.

Perhaps she would be more disappointed, as her first lover was obviously a man of skill and generosity when it came to making love. Sometimes, when I read Luciana's diary entries, I was uncomfortably reminded of the early days with Steven. How sophisticated he had seemed to me compared to my previous lovers. Sex – lust – can be so blinding. When the blood is rushing from your head to your heart, it's easy to overlook the harder truths about the object of your desire.

I thought back to the very last time Steven and I touched each other. How in the flash of heat between our bodies, it had seemed possible that we would try once more to stitch the rest of our relationship back together. And then I thought about him wrapped around another girl. The girl behind the mask.

28

I had not been entirely honest with Nick, Bea or Marco about the end of my relationship. It had been a great humiliation to me. A humiliation more complicated than the obvious embarrassment one feels on losing out to a younger, more attractive, more malleable model. That happens every day, doesn't it? The old is replaced by the new. What was humiliating to me was that I could not help but feel I was in some way responsible for the way our relationship ended. You see, I thought introducing other people into our love life might somehow make us stronger.

Ever since that day at the seminar, when I first dared disagree with him, Steven had been drifting away from me. That much was obvious. He was making more excuses to stay late at the office and when he wasn't, we shared the once happy space of our home like a couple of flatmates rather than the devoted lovers we once were. At night, we slept with a chaste gap between us like two medieval monarchs on a tomb.

Still, I was desperate to save our relationship. I was sure there must be a way to reignite our passion. We – who had been so hot for each other – couldn't possibly be destined to become one of those couples that doesn't speak over dinner and eventually drifts apart. There had to be a way to bring the good times back. While I was supposed to be working, I spent way too much time online, looking at the advice on relationship forums, trying to figure out how to talk to Steven about my fears.

I tried all the usual things. I cooked nice meals, I wore nice underwear, and I tried to show more interest in his work. But actually, it wasn't as though I had slipped with those things in the first place. The growing chill between us was about something other than having let ourselves go. Doing more baking wasn't going to fix it.

Then I read an article in a magazine about a woman who claimed she had saved her marriage by agreeing to accompany her husband to a sex club. He was delighted at the prospect. She was terrified, imagining she might have to have sex with strange men in front of him or – somehow worse – might have to watch him making love to someone else. In the end, the lucky woman's husband only wanted to watch. They went to a club but they didn't join in, and having a naughty little secret to share in the bedroom when they got home strengthened their bond.

Until I read that article, I had always assumed that sex clubs were impossibly seedy: full of desperate women and dirty old men; but the club the writer described was entirely different from the places of my imagination. She said it wasn't so different from an ordinary nightclub. People wore fewer clothes, that was all.

So, crazy as it sounds, I decided to try the same thing. When Steven and I were together that evening, I told him I wanted to go to a sex club. He blinked at me. Then he laughed. He obviously thought I was joking. He said as much. I insisted. I told him I had always been curious.

'Really?' he said.

'Yes. Really.'

'I wouldn't have guessed.' His expression grew serious for a moment. 'I didn't think it was your kind of thing.'

'Perhaps you don't know everything about me after all,' I said. 'Perhaps I have hidden depths.'

I hoped he would be tantalised by the hint.

'You really want to go to a sex club?'

I nodded. My heart was beating so hard. My face was burning hot. I longed for him to tell me he found the idea repulsive. But he called my bluff.

'OK,' he said. 'If you want to. If you *really* want to?'

What could I say but that I did?

Steven smiled. His expression was a cross between amused and confused.

'When?'

We agreed to go the following Friday. Now that I mentioned it, said Steven, he had heard about a good place in King's Cross. It was called 'L'Enfer' – the French word for Hell. Perhaps we could start our adventure there.

I didn't ask Steven how he knew about this club. I plastered on a grin and told him I couldn't wait.

29

I spent the next week in a state of sick anticipation. I'd made a terrible mistake. I didn't want to go to a sex club. But I wanted to hold on to Steven so badly, I would have done anything. Anything at all. The way he whistled as he went around the flat in the run-up to our big night out told me he was experiencing none of my anxiety. The weekend held nothing but promise for him. In the meantime, he was kinder to me than he had been in a while. When we woke up in the mornings, he rolled over to kiss me, like he used to. He was tender again. If this was what the promise of a night in a club could do for our relationship, then what would things be like afterwards when we had a new secret to share? I tried to be optimistic.

On Friday evening, Steven came home with a gift for me. I opened the black tissue-wrapped package to find a set of underwear. It was unlike any lingerie I would have chosen for myself. I pulled it out and stared at it. Though the red silk bra was my size, it had no cups to hide my nipples. The panties could be more accurately described as string. Not even a G-string. Just a piece of string, threaded with cold red beads, which were supposed to slide over my clitoris as I walked, as Steven helpfully explained.

'That's what the girl in the shop said.'

I hated the girl in the shop.

'You want me to wear this tonight?' I asked him.

'You might feel underdressed if you don't,' was Steven's reply. 'Just try it. See how you feel.'

I went into the bedroom, stripped and put on the new underwear. It's possible I felt even more naked once I donned the flimsy scraps. I regarded my reflection in the mirror. The bra lifted my breasts so my nipples, which had hardened in the cold, seemed to point forwards like missiles. The beaded G-string was strange and uncomfortable. I felt as though Steven had chosen the underwear for someone else.

Steven crept into the room behind me. I watched his reflection in the mirror as he in turn regarded me from the door.

'I like it,' he said. 'Perhaps we shouldn't go out after all.'

I seized upon that throwaway line.

'We could have a club night all of our own.' I thrust a hip in his direction, playing along.

Steven crossed the room and slipped his hands around my bare waist. He cupped my cupless bosom and pressed his crotch against my buttocks, grinding so that the beaded string pulled taut against my clit.

'Much as I am reluctant to share this wonderful sight,' he murmured, 'I think it would be a shame to stay home.'

Much as I wanted to, I couldn't disagree. I had started this adventure, after all.

'There's just one finishing touch,' he said then.

He pulled another small black bag from beneath the bed and proffered it to me.

'Cupless bra. Crotchless knickers. Footless tights?' I joked.

It was a mask. A plain white half-mask of the kind the Venetians used to wear every day. I think the style was called a Colombina Punta.

'Everyone has to wear one. Club rules.'

Steven had a black version. He held it to his face and I shivered to see him made so anonymous. With the mask in place, he pulled me towards him again and crushed my mouth against his own.

'You'd better put something over that kit before I fuck you here and now.'

So I covered the thong and the cupless bra with a little black dress that was extremely demure by comparison. Before visiting the club that night, Steven and I had to attend a cocktail party thrown by one of his colleagues. I knew most of the people there – I'd known many of them for years – and yet I felt extremely shy and awkward in their presence. Steven assured me no one but him would know what I was wearing beneath the knee-length black dress with its high neckline, but I felt sure they must. Every move I made had the pearls on the G-string rubbing against me obscenely. I could not help glancing down at myself to see whether they were pressing outwards against the fabric of the dress too. It was not warm in that room and my nipples puckered and strained to be seen, without cups to hide behind. I felt sure they were obvious.

Several times, Steven caught my eye across the crowd and smiled. But his smile suddenly seemed wolfish and unkind. Once, having smiled at me, he turned back to the man he was talking to and when they suddenly burst into laughter I had the awful feeling they were laughing at my expense. Had Steven told him where we were going next? Had he told him what I was wearing beneath my plain black frock?

I spent another half-hour talking to Rod, the party host, who was so deaf I practically had to shout in his ear. In my state of paranoia, I began to think that was exactly what he wanted, so he could get a better look at what was going on beneath my dress. I folded my arms tightly over my chest, shielding myself from his eyes. He asked if he should turn the heating on. I blushed so hard I needed air conditioning.

Eventually, Steven came to fetch me. I would have said 'rescue' but it didn't feel like that at the time. He told the old academic, 'I must take this poor girl home.'

'But it's only ten o'clock,' Rod complained.

Steven batted the protests away.

'You're going on somewhere else, I know it,' Rod pressed. 'Where are you heading to? Had a better offer?'

'That would be telling,' said Steven. And then he winked, making it obvious once and for all that we weren't heading home to have cocoa.

Outside the party, I told Steven how uncomfortable I'd felt.

'Everyone was looking at me. Everyone knows I've got something weird on under my dress.'

'Don't be ridiculous,' said Steven. 'They don't have that much imagination.'

'The way Rod was looking at me . . .' I continued.

Steven silenced me with a kiss. He put his hands underneath my coat and squeezed my right breast hard. I winced. He'd never touched me like that before, with the intention of causing me pain, however playfully.

'I liked the way he was looking at you,' Steven told me. 'It made me hard to think he wanted you, knowing I'm going to have you later on.'

I prayed he would tell me then that we should go straight home. I prayed that the idea of me trussed up like a stripper beneath my demure dress while his colleagues ogled me would have been enough of a turn-on for now. In the course of our relationship, I had never before tried to make him jealous. Would the envy of his friends have made a difference? Steven hailed a taxi. Gallantly, he opened the door so I could step inside first, then leaned in through the window to tell the driver we were going to King's Cross. The opposite direction from home in every sense.

30

Ten minutes later, the taxi driver pulled his cab up to the kerb and clicked the off button on his meter. I was sure he was watching me in the rear-view mirror as Steven found the change to pay our fare. When Steven told the driver where we wanted to go that night, he said he knew the address well. Did he know what went on inside there as well? The way he looked at me seemed to suggest he did. My black dress didn't feel much like protection any more.

As gallantly as he had helped me into the cab, Steven now helped me out. I wobbled in my heels. I was unaccustomed to wearing them. Steven put his arm out to steady me.

'Who told you about this place?' I asked at last.

'I overheard some of my students talking,' he said.

'Your students?'

'They're a wild bunch. Just like your cohort were.'

I thought about my undergraduate friends. They'd liked to drink and party, but swing? I didn't think so.

'Stop worrying, Sarah. You were the one who suggested we try this in the first place.'

He was right. But now that we were at the club, I wanted to turn and run.

'If you hate it, we'll leave.'

'Is that a promise?' I asked. He nodded distractedly.

'You need to put the mask on,' Steven reminded me as he pressed the doorbell. I snapped the white mask into place. Despite this gesture to anonymity, I had never felt more vulnerable in my life. I felt so obvious. As if the eyes of the world were upon me.

Behind the plain wooden door – as anonymous as that belonging to any other warehouse on the street – stood a bouncer the size of a tree. He was flanked by a small woman dressed in a patent-leather corset. A gold half-mask hid her distinguishing features. Her jet-black hair was pulled back in a ponytail. She was wearing high-heeled boots that added an extra five inches to her height. So far, so stereotypical. She gave us the once-over and waved us inside.

The shabby exterior of the building had not given any clues as to what was hidden inside. Once, the warehouse had contained sacks of grain. Now the plain brick walls were hung with black velvet drapes. A central dancefloor was ringed with gilded tables and chairs. The lighting was low and dramatic. Each table had its own candelabra, for the most flattering glow.

'And the hot wax,' Steven pointed out. I shivered at the thought of wax on bare skin.

We went straight to the bar. When I told Steven I would need plenty of Dutch courage, he bought me a triple vodka tonic. I drank half of it quickly, longing for the alcohol's disinhibiting qualities to get to work as soon as possible. Steven sipped his own drink thoughtfully.

'Thirsty?' he remarked, when he saw I had drained mine in minutes.

I asked myself what I was so afraid of. It was just as the magazine article had suggested. At first, looking around the room, it didn't seem all that different from an ordinary night-club. A little more Gothic perhaps but not frighteningly so. The other people at the bar seemed pretty ordinary too, apart from the fact that their faces were hidden. They were dressed for the most part in normal clothes. No one was naked. Most people were standing or sitting and talking. There were a couple of girls on the dancefloor, dancing with each other around their clutch bags. It was just like an ordinary club in that respect too. The men would have to drink a hell of a lot more before they felt emboldened enough to trip the light fantastic. Was this it?

'Where does everything happen?' I asked.

'There are rooms off the dancefloor, dedicated to whatever you fancy. We could take a look.'

'Give me another minute. And perhaps another drink too.' Steven obliged.

'What if some guy comes on to me and I don't like him?' I asked as I sipped my new vodka.

I think I wanted Steven to say he would make sure no guys got near me at all, but instead he said, 'The rules of the club are that no man can touch a woman without her express permission. If you don't like the look of someone, you don't have to get involved. You'll be all right.'

'They'll probably be scared off when they see how big and strong you are,' I teased, hoping to jolt him into protective mode. He didn't rise to it. 'But if anything happens here,' I continued, 'it stays here, right?'

'Of course,' said Steven.

'And it doesn't make any difference to us. To our relationship,' I added, though of course that night was all about making a difference.

From behind my mask, I stared at the other clubbers. They didn't look too threatening, but I knew I didn't want any of these strangers to touch me. I had never been attracted to the idea of anonymous sex. For me, sex had always been about the context and that context was always a relationship. It's not that I was prudish. It's just that I felt sex was something I only wanted to share with someone I knew I could trust. Not some random man – or woman – in a mask. I assumed, wrongly as it turned out, that Steven ultimately felt the same.

'Come on,' he said. 'Let's explore.'

He took my hand and together we did a circuit of the club. Around the dancefloor, in a horseshoe shape, were several curtained-off cabanas. Steven pulled back the curtain of the first one. Inside, a couple reclined on a pile of colourful cushions. They were both more or less dressed. The man was stroking the girl's thigh. They were laughing. It didn't seem any more outrageous than the kind of behaviour you'd see in any nightclub up and down the country. Her tight leather skirt was lifted a little higher perhaps. His hand ventured a little further. But there was nothing that made me feel especially voyeuristic.

It should have been obvious which rooms contained the most outrageous action from the number of people who were trying to get in to watch. Steven led me towards a room on the other side of the dancefloor. Here the velvet curtain bulged outwards, thanks to the crowds trying to cram their way inside. Steven went in ahead of me. He was tall. He could see over the people in front of him. I had to content myself with glimpses between other people's limbs, until a man, with somewhat misguided chivalry, motioned that I should step in front of him for a better view.

In contrast to the rather demure petting scene in the first room, the three people at the centre of attention in this room – two men and a woman – were all naked. Naked apart from a glittering collar around the woman's neck, that is. The sight of the collar made me shudder and put my hands to my own neck involuntarily. I couldn't imagine wearing a collar in a million years. In fact I felt tense at the thought. Steven looked back towards me. His eyes shone black behind his mask.

I stared at the threesome. At first, I couldn't make out what was really going on. On the bottom of the pile was a man. The girl was sitting on his lap and he had his hands around her narrow waist, holding her tightly against him. Meanwhile, a second man knelt between the girl's legs. When he pressed himself away from her, on his arms, I could see they were still very much connected.

It was double penetration. The guy on the bottom had his cock in the woman's anus. The guy on top was screwing her missionary style. And she seemed to be enjoying every minute of it. She threw her head back and gave a little grunt with every thrust. She had her arms raised above her head. It was only now I noticed that her wrists were bound together.

'Oh, oh, oh,' she sighed.

I was mesmerised. I fixed my gaze on the girl's open mouth, which seemed, somehow, the most erotic point of the picture. Then I felt something knock against the small of my back and turned to see that the man who had so gallantly let me past him to get a better view was now pleasuring himself. He had undone the front of his leather trousers and set his penis free. With each upward stroke of his hand, the glistening head of his penis knocked against me. I turned to glare at him, but he wasn't even looking at me. Like everyone else in the room, he was staring at the threesome on the bed. He was bringing himself off like an automaton.

Steven glanced over to see how I was doing. He saw the look on my face, looked towards the object of my horror and, thankfully, pulled me straight out of there.

'He was . . .' I started to form my complaint.

'You can't blame him. I was ready to do some of that myself.'

'You were?'

'It was crazy, wasn't it?'

'I suppose.'

'Didn't you find it in the least bit arousing?'

Though I didn't want to, I had to admit I did. I could still picture the woman's expression of abandon as she opened herself up in every way. I told Steven it was the first time I had ever seen live sex. To start with a threesome like that was more than I had ever imagined.

'Really?' said Steven. 'It's really your first time?'

'Yes,' I said. 'When else would I have seen it? *Where* else? You've known me since I was twenty-one.'

'I don't know. Didn't you ever watch your friends at school? Your friends at college?'

I shook my head. 'Did *you*?'

'Clearly, I had the wrong sort of friends,' Steven smiled. 'But you enjoyed it, yes? It wasn't so bad?'

He smoothed back my hair.

'Doesn't it feel liberating to be free to watch something like that? No one is judging you here. No one knows who you are. No one cares.'

'I don't feel as anonymous as I thought I would,' I told him.

'Nonsense,' he said. 'Besides, who do we know who would come here? All our friends are too square. Want to see some more?'

I wasn't sure I did but I nodded. Since he had glanced over to see me under siege from the self-pleasurer in the three-some room, Steven had not taken his arm from around my waist. I'd worried that the sight of seeing other people having sex would make him disconnected, but right then, he seemed to want to be closer to me than he had in a long while. However that affection had been come by, I decided to make the most of it. I took his closeness to mean that underneath the bravado, he was actually finding the whole experience a little discomfiting too and wanted me beside him because I represented safety. I hoped I represented love.

31

We entered another cabana. Here, two women sat on a sofa. One of them was dressed like Sally Bowles in *Cabaret*, in a waistcoat, bowler hat and fishnets. It seemed to be a popular look. There were at least three Sally Bowles lookalikes in the club that evening. This one was a particularly good facsimile. Beneath her mask, she had a mouth just like Liza Minnelli's. I wondered if anyone had ever told her that. Perhaps that was why she chose the costume.

Right now, Liza's lookalike lay back with her eyes closed. The other woman, who was dressed in a tattered white basque that brought to mind a zombie bride, was gently caressing the space between her legs. She merely stroked the Liza double through her knickers for a while, before she hooked a single finger beneath the knicker elastic and started to take things further. I could not help but stare as the zombie bride started to slide her finger in and out of her friend's vagina. Perhaps the alcohol was working at last; I was starting to feel, if not comfortable, then at least a good deal less anxious.

'Have you ever thought about making love with a girl?' Steven whispered into my hair.

'Yes,' I told him.

It seemed like the right thing to say.

'Tell me about it.'

'It was a long time ago. I was a teenager. We all have crushes on more sophisticated girls at school. I fancied a girl who was two years ahead of me. She was house captain.'

185

His smile widened. 'That really turns me on.'

He kissed the side of my face. I turned to meet his lips and we shared as passionate a kiss as we had ever done. I felt a flutter of the old arousal in my chest. I wondered if he felt the same. He squeezed one of my breasts. Hard, like before. I flinched and tried not to show it.

'You are so hot tonight. Did you ever tell her how you felt?' he asked.

'No. I didn't have the guts. She would have laughed, I'm sure.'

'I wish you'd asked her. I wish you'd done it.'

We watched the women on the sofa for a while. Eventually, the girl dressed as Sally Bowles came in great shuddering gasps that looked and sounded like death throes. Her companion spent some time smoothing her hair as though to soothe her, then the two women changed places and the Sally Bowles lookalike set about making the zombie bride come in exchange for the pleasure she had just received. Quid pro quo.

She slid to the floor and knelt between her companion's open legs. She took off the bowler hat she had been wearing the whole time and moved closer, bringing her mouth level with her friend's clitoris. Steven gripped my arm to make sure I wasn't going anywhere. I pressed myself against his side.

'Was this what you thought about?' he asked me.

'I didn't even know such things were possible. I was an innocent.'

'So you never acted on your crushes, is what you're telling me?'

'No,' I said. 'I never did.'

'There's always a first time,' said Steven.

I persuaded him we should go back to the bar to get another drink, leaving the two Sapphic lovers alone (apart from a dozen voyeurs). The club was starting to fill up now and there were some more interesting-looking people around: people with serious costumes, some of which looked painful, like the studded corset that squeezed one man's waist as small as a Victorian girl's. I saw my first pair of nipple clamps on a woman who stood beside me to order a drink. I wished I had the guts to ask whether they turned her on.

Steven bought me another vodka tonic, heavy on the vodka. I sipped it slowly as I watched the comings and goings on beneath the glittering lights. There were many more people dancing now. Or perhaps strutting is a more accurate term. A statuesque redhead was leading a small, shaven-headed man around the dancefloor on a lead. Who were these people? What did they do in the daytime? What jobs did they hold down while they dreamed of spending their nights dressed in straps and chains? The shaven-headed man clambered up the redhead's leg like an unruly puppy begging for attention. She kissed him on the top of the head. It was an affectionate kiss. I wondered if they were together outside the club. Would they share tea and toast at the breakfast table in the morning? Did they talk about their outfits over lunch?

Just then a woman strode by in a rubber suit that covered every part of her, with just holes for her eyes, her mouth and her ponytail, which bounced like the tail of a dressage horse. I felt very suburban and unsophisticated by comparison. I must have looked it. The rubber woman's eyes slid over me, dismissive and disdainful.

However, I seemed to have caught the fancy of someone else.

32

The girl was dressed in black leather shorts with a matching leather basque and a small red velvet cape. Her hair was short and spiky. Bottle blonde. Her felted mask, cut in the shape of a cat's face, didn't cover her full, glossy lips in their red glitter paint. She came up to stand beside me and Steven at the bar. She grinned as she stroked her hand across the side of my cheek. I started at the unexpected contact.

'Hello, beautiful,' she said.

I said hello in return. Steven nodded in her direction. He was playing it very cool.

'You look a little uncomfortable,' she continued. 'Is this your first time in the club?'

'Is it that obvious?' I asked.

The girl laughed. 'It's OK. I remember my first time too. It's quite a scene if you're not used to it.'

I had to agree.

'But everyone is very friendly. No one's here to judge you. And no man can touch you without your say-so,' she reminded me. She curled her way around my body like a real cat, so that suddenly she was standing between my man and me.

'You could definitely have my say-so,' she told Steven, as she thrust her breasts in his direction.

I felt myself grow hot with jealousy at the thought. But then she turned back to me.

'Tonight, however, I'm looking for something a little bit different,' she said. 'A little softer.'

She held my gaze with her own.

'Care to come and sit down?' she asked me.

I looked to Steven. He nodded encouragingly.

'You can come too,' cat-girl said, tucking a finger into his belt.

'What's your name?' I asked.

'Ah,' said the girl. 'We don't deal in names here. At least not in real names. But if you want something to call me, you can call me Kitty.'

She indicated her cat mask and made a corresponding mewing sound.

'OK, Kitty,' I said. 'You can call me Jane. Like Jane Doe.'

'That works,' she said. 'It even suits you.'

Because it was so dull? I wondered. It didn't occur to me until much later that she didn't ask Steven what his name was.

Steven and I both followed Kitty into one of the velvet-curtained booths. It wasn't empty. None of the rooms were empty now that the club was in full swing, crammed with Londoners in search of the exotic. But we found ourselves a corner and settled onto a deep, cushion-filled sofa with our drinks. Kitty somehow made her way in between us.

That said, her attention was all on me. While I talked a bit about how I was finding my first ever experience of a swingers' club, she stroked my shin and tiptoed her fingers all the way up to my thigh. She caressed my face and twisted my hair into ringlets.

'You have very pretty hair,' she observed.

'Thank you. I like your hair too.'

I ran my hand over her blonde spikes experimentally. They were stiff and brittle with some kind of gel.

'Aren't you hot in that dress?' she asked me. 'I can't help thinking you'd be more comfortable if you just took it off.'

'I – I don't know.'

Once again I sought out Steven's eyes, to take my cue from him. He nodded. It was almost imperceptible, but I could tell from the set of his mouth – a sly smile – that he was enjoying this, enjoying watching me being seduced. He wanted me to carry on. Still, I was nervous about taking the dress off, knowing what was underneath. But was it any more outrageous than Kitty's outfit?

'I'll go first,' she said.

She untied the ribbon holding her little cape in place and revealed that her leather basque did not have cups either. Without the cape, her generous breasts were fully on show. They were like a pair of perfect pink snowballs, tipped with impossibly rosy nipples. I wondered if she had rouged them. She pointed them in my direction.

'You can touch them if you like.'

I was nervous as hell as I reached out and traced the curve of her right breast. Her skin there was soft and warm and dry. It felt like a young girl's cheek. I did the same to the left breast. Steven sipped his drink, never taking his eyes off us but, thankfully, not trying to join in the touching. For now. Kitty moaned as I gently squeezed her nipples.

'Let's see yours,' she said.

Kitty helped me out of my dress. She smiled broadly when she saw what I was wearing underneath. I felt incredibly exposed. I tried to preserve my modesty with the discarded dress. Kitty pulled it out of the way.

'Beautiful,' she murmured.

I started to protest. She put her finger to my lips to prevent me from throwing back her compliment. She had incredible confidence, though I guessed from her flawless figure that she must be very young.

Certainly, she was not in the least bit shy about touching me. She immediately reached out and cupped my naked breasts. She grabbed them. She circled my nipples with her thumbs, bringing them to hard peaks. A shiver ran through me. I looked down and saw that however hard my mind was trying to resist her, my body was giving in. She dipped her face towards me and replaced her fingers with her tongue, which flickered like a snake tasting the air. I couldn't help moaning a little with pleasure. I looked at Steven. He nodded at me. He smiled.

'Go ahead,' he mouthed.

Meanwhile, Kitty's hand moved down towards my beaded G-string. She placed her palm over my mons veneris, pressing the beads so that they were hard against my clitoris. She moved her hand backwards and forwards, increasing the friction. I found myself lifting my pelvis towards her, pushing back so that I could feel even more.

'Is that good?' she murmured.

I told her it was. I wasn't lying. Despite myself, I was growing incredibly aroused. I felt a fluttering sensation deep inside me – a combination of nerves and excitement – and soon it was as though I had allowed another creature to take over my body. When Kitty went to kiss me again, I took her face in both my hands. I was no longer passive. I kissed her as hotly as she kissed me. She continued to press the beads against me all the time, moving them backwards and forwards over my clitoris in a tantalising rhythm. When she pushed a finger into me, I felt myself tighten around her, pulling her in. While the sensations intensified, I scratched at Kitty's back, drawing a groan of pleasure from her that made me proud to hear it.

'Is this good?' she asked again.

This time I couldn't form the words. I just pressed harder against her while an unmistakable orgasm grew inside me. I couldn't stop it. I didn't want to. Steven stood above us now with his penis in his hand. My eyes drifted towards him. He stared at me as his hand moved rhythmically.

'I'm coming,' I cried out.

Then Steven came too. His penis jerked wildly as his sperm traced an ecstatic arc in the air, landing with an artistic splatter all over Kitty's magnificent bosom. When he had finished, Steven collapsed onto the sofa beside us, laughing. Kitty laughed too. I stayed still and caught my breath. I had not experienced such a strong climax in a long time.

'Tissue?' Kitty passed me the box. 'You were magnificent. You really let go. I can't believe you're a first-timer.'

'Believe it,' I said.

'In that case, I can only imagine how good you'd be with a bit of practice. Any time you want another go . . .' she winked.

I looked at Steven. He was still panting from his exertions but he was looking at Kitty with something approaching adoration. He caught me staring at him. He kissed me on the forehead, as a sort of peace offering, I suppose.

'I think I'd like to go home now,' I whispered.

'OK,' he agreed.

I was flooded with relief. We were leaving. I found my dress and pulled it on over my head. The beaded G-string I left where it had fallen. It wasn't any use to me now. I didn't care if I never saw it again.

Steven pulled up his trousers and buckled his belt. He hadn't taken anything else off.

Kitty did not have much to do to rearrange her outfit either. She was almost completely unruffled by our tangle. Just like a real cat. I half expected her to lick her hand and use it to paw down a single unruly curl. I did not expect what she *did* do next. Having kissed me one more time, she turned to Steven.

'I'll see you on Monday,' she said.

33

'Monday?' I asked.

'Yes,' said Kitty. 'In the seminar room.' She said it as though I should know.

I realised then that Kitty was not a stranger to Steven after all. When he spoke about having overheard his students talking about the club, what he actually meant was that he had heard about the club from this girl. This one girl who was grinning at us now from behind her stupid cat mask. I also realised with a flash of anger that this was almost certainly not the first time Steven had seen this girl without her clothes on. As she sashayed away and Steven and I headed for the exit, I tackled him with my suspicions.

'I've seen her before, yes. Outside college, I mean.'

'You've had sex with her.'

Steven didn't answer me. I tugged on his arm. 'Tell me. Please.'

'I haven't. Not yet. But you have.'

Steven pulled me close to him. He tried to kiss me. I pushed him away.

'You said "not yet". You want to, don't you?'

'Come on, Sarah. I thought you wanted to experiment. I thought we were coming to a new understanding. What does it matter whether I've seen her before?'

'I didn't know she was your potential *lover*.'

'Sarah, please,' Steven pleaded. 'She's not. Don't ruin this. You had a good time. We've had a good night. Haven't we?'

It was way, way too much for me. I had opened myself up to the new and exotic in an attempt to prove to Steven that I was still worthy of his interest. He had used my eagerness to hold on to his love against me. I thought that night would be a one-off. He'd had me make out with a girl he already knew. Was he interested in a long-term share?

'Seriously, what does it matter?' he asked. 'It's just sex.'

He made it sound so tacky. And in my heart I felt I was tacky too. It was worse than I had feared.

'It was your idea to go to the club in the first place,' he pressed on.

'Not that specific club. Not where your *friend* goes. You set me up. I would never have agreed to getting naked with one of your students.'

'And that's precisely why I didn't ask you. But you expressed an interest in doing this thing. And right up until Kitty let on she already knew me, you seemed pretty happy with the way things were going.'

'It's different. It was meant to be just sex. Now I know there's a connection. You've been having an affair.'

I ran down the road.

'I have not been having an affair,' Steven called after me.

Semantics. Though we slept in the same bed that night and though Steven made an effort to talk me round, I could not be consoled. He reminded me that the club visit was all my idea. He said that even if he had fucked Kitty – which he swore he hadn't – physical infidelity was not the same as falling in love with someone new. It was just about satisfying an appetite. Not in my view.

We argued all weekend. I could not get past my anger that Steven had let me get involved with a woman he knew, with the intention of making our relationship a threesome. On Monday morning I knew what I had to do. The trip to Venice was already organised. I would spend the time left until my departure date sleeping on the sofa at a friend's house. I wouldn't tell her anything other than that Steven and I were taking a break.

Of course, I couldn't resist finding out more about the mysterious Kitty when I was next in the office. I trawled through the university's student profiles online until I found someone who fitted what I remembered about her. Though I had not seen her whole face, I would have recognised her smile anywhere. Her slightly crooked teeth. Her glittering red lipstick. I bet she thought of that as her 'signature' look. Her passionate pout.

Her full name was Catherine Adams. 'Kat' was the nickname she more usually used. She was in Steven's tutor group. She was only nineteen years old. She had an exemplary academic record and was clearly going to be something of a star. But for now, she was in awe of Steven and was willing to follow wherever he led her. I wondered whether she had been amused by the idea of seducing his partner or whether, like me, she had done it only because she wanted to please him. I felt sick as I remembered how similarly young and naïve I had once been. How naïve I still was.

I closed my laptop and started packing. By the time Steven came back from his office that evening, I was gone.

Did I expect Steven to try to save our relationship? Of course that's what I hoped for. In the time I had left in London, however, he didn't attempt to find me and talk things through again, though I'd left a note on the kitchen table telling him where I would be. I declined to go out with my friend to drown my sorrows because I was hoping that Steven might come round. He didn't. And instead of leaning on my friend over a bottle of wine and some chocolate dessert like I was supposed to, I tortured myself with the idea that Steven had gone straight to his Kitty Kat. Now I wasn't standing in his way, the fling could become something more serious.

I can't tell you how much worse it is to be replaced by a younger model when you know exactly what it is your lover sees in his new girl. Every time I closed my eyes, I saw her luscious red mouth. I heard her infectious loud laugh. I saw her domed white breasts peeking over the top of her shiny leather basque. I even began to wonder if Steven had bought that basque for her, from the same place he bought that hateful beaded G-string for me. The events of our night in the sex club were on constant replay in my mind.

When my friend asked what had gone wrong, I told her that the break-up had been coming for a long time. I didn't want to tell anyone the truth. And now I was trying to soothe my broken heart with an email flirtation that would probably never be anything more. Why did that bother me so much? Why did it hurt me that Marco didn't want to meet in person, when Steven had betrayed me far more spectacularly?

Maybe Nick was right and I was more vulnerable than I cared to admit. I was nowhere near ready to forget about the girl behind the mask.

34

10th April, 1753

How I looked forward to nightfall! After a month, I had my routine well-practised. The moment Maria left my room, I crept from my bed and pulled out the boys' clothes, which Maria thought had gone in a bundle to the church.

The prostitutes from the *Carampane* greeted me like an old friend, no longer bothering to ask whether I wanted to feel their tits. Instead, they asked me when they could expect to see me give my first sermon. My teacher had told them I was studying to be a priest.

'Such a waste!' one of them sighed.

'The best-looking ones are always that way,' said her friend.

I had my own key to the monkey house now and would often let myself in to find my teacher already at his desk. He would tell me about developments in the city's politics, about business deals and wars brewing on the farthest reaches of the city's jurisdiction. He showed me his accounts and explained to me the concept of interest. There are ways of making money even if you don't have something to sell.

Then we read together. We read history and philosophy but I still enjoyed poetry best. Veronica Franco was my favourite, of course. I soon knew her poetry by heart.

I decided that Veronica Franco's life was far from unhappy. She wrote so beautifully of passion. How could she have written so wonderfully had she not experienced true love's highs and lows? And while the plague may have taken her corporeal body, she had left behind her a body of work that would live for ever. As I read the poems out loud and watched my teacher drift into a reverie, wasn't Veronica in some way living through me? Still charming. Still disarming. I felt I had many reasons to be grateful to Veronica. I wished I might have spent time with her.

Sometimes it struck me that to be born rich could be a misfortune. To be born wealthy is to spend your life under observation. Had I, like Veronica, come from nowhere, no one would have cared about the 'seemliness' of my actions. I would have been able to move freely about the city. I would have been able to laugh when I wanted, love where I wanted, learn whatever I cared to. My life could have truly become my own creation.

I wanted to be able to be like Veronica Franco. She was bold and she was challenging and she was loved. In the bedroom at least.

'That's the paradox of men,' my teacher explained. 'We all admire a woman like Veronica Franco. We all long for her to pay us just the slightest bit of attention. But do we want our wives and daughters to model themselves on her ways? Absolutely not. Veronica Franco was a rare creature.'

I wanted to be a rare creature too.

25th April, 1753

The Festa di San Marco was one of the rare occasions of the year when I was allowed to don anything remotely resembling finery and join my father on his boat. The Doge would be making an offering at the Basilica followed by a fine regatta and our family must be represented.

From the discreet comfort of our boat, I watched the other people on the lagoon. Not far from us, an enormous gondola was moored. The people on board seemed to be having a wonderful time. A small orchestra serenaded them while they lolled on velvet cushions and laughed. While my father was watching the ceremony, I made a study of that gondola. There were five people on board but only one of them was a woman. A single woman entertaining four men! Who was she? How was she able to flaunt herself in such a free and unfettered way?

Maria caught me staring. 'A courtesan,' she spat. 'Surrounding herself with her lovers. It's a disgrace.'

'Oh. I thought the men must be her brothers. How do you know she's a courtesan?'

'Tchuh,' Maria turned away from the spectacle. As if she could answer a question like that while we floated on the lagoon with my father within earshot!

Of course, I continued to watch the courtesan whenever Maria's attention was elsewhere. Which it often was, because her priest had rowed into sight with his choirboys. Poor pious Maria was trying desperately hard not to stare at him. Meanwhile, I tried to imagine the conversation on the courtesan's boat. The four men I claimed to have taken for her brothers were taking it in turns to amuse the mysterious woman, while she indulged them with the occasional laugh that rang out across the lagoon as clearly as a bell. The men all looked well born. They were dressed in the kind of fashions favoured by my brother. The courtesan – well, she was in an altogether different class. Though I would not have said she was beneath her companions. Not a bit of it.

The courtesan was luminous. She was like the heroine of a love poem. It was more than her sumptuous clothing, which was as fine as any I had ever seen. It was the elegance of her gestures and the music of her laughter. It was in her daring. Out on the lagoon in broad daylight with four men. And a monkey. Oh, when I saw the monkey, how I longed to turn to Maria and ask if I had imagined the little creature. Then it hopped up from the courtesan's lap to sit on her shoulder. She held its tail to keep it there while the young men passed the animal morsels of fruit to keep it amused. I had never seen a monkey before except in pictures.

I could not tear my eyes away from the courtesan and her pet. There was no sight more interesting to me than the way she indulged those four men on her boat and the manner in which they fell over themselves like circus clowns to amuse her. I wanted that power. I wanted to know how she had it.

I was sure that, at one point, the courtesan looked back at me. A smile played across her lips. It was a smile that told me she was very happy indeed with the way she was living and dared me to suggest otherwise. I looked down at my hands. Then, when I was sure neither Maria nor my father was looking, I lifted my face towards the courtesan and smiled right back at her.

★　★　★

That very same afternoon, Maria accompanied me to the Chapel of the Mendicanti to hear the choir give a concert of new works by their choirmaster. Such a pleasant way to spend the afternoon. Those girls certainly had angelic voices, as befitted their mythical status as God's divine human instruments. But how much more interesting I found the curious creatures now I knew they were not so pure as they would have us believe. My teacher had told me a most interesting story. To help raise money for their lavish convent, the young ladies of the Mendicanti choir occasionally gave concerts at the houses of their most generous benefactors.

'And after they've finished singing,' my teacher went on, 'a couple of them can usually be persuaded to give a private demonstration of their proficiency in playing a pipe.'

By 'pipe' he meant 'penis', of course. I did not believe it but he swears it is true. He said my naivety about such matters made me far more innocent than most convent girls he's known.

'They haven't ended up in a convent because they believe in serving God. They ended up there because they were orphaned or impoverished. They are every bit as red-blooded and keen to know more about the world as you are. And they live in hope that they will demonstrate such ability, a smitten admirer will marry them out of their misery.'

So, while Maria professed to be transported by the miraculous nature of their music, I studied the girls in the brief moment when they crossed the transept in an attempt to guess which ones were best on the wind instruments.

'Oh, to be able to sing that well,' I said to Maria as we filed out into the sunshine.

'To be able to sing that well takes immaculate purity of heart and soul,' Maria sighed.

Well, my soul was well and truly blackened. Every night I could, I spent with my lover. I no longer even cared if my father was in the house. I would escape and see my teacher or die.

Some nights, we spent very little time on formal teachings. Our discussions on such matters were curtailed to the length of time it took for me to get out of my shirt and boots. The hard chairs remained unoccupied as we jumped straight into the bed and I continued my education in matters far more interesting than Sophocles. Suffice to say, I could play the pipe as well as the good girls at the house of the Mendicanti.

Oh, how delicious were the hours we spent together. I thought I would need nothing more than my teacher's company in that sparsely furnished room to be happy for the rest of my life, but a few nights after the Festa di San Marco he surprised me by telling me we were going out. He was taking me to the Ridotto, the gambling house.

35

Another day in the library. The pieces of the jigsaw were coming together quickly now. Having read about Luciana's visit to the Festa di San Marco, I wondered if the woman who held the monkey in the painting at the Palazzo Donato was the same woman Luciana described as a courtesan. Then I spent the morning reading a passage in which Luciana described her first experience of giving a blowjob and her teacher's attempts to turn her into an expert. It corresponded exactly with a passage in *The Lover's Lessons*. When I had finished translating the passage, I sat for a long while gazing out of the library window at nothing in particular, until my mind inevitably drifted towards my own love life. I thought about Steven and Kat, and then Marco.

I was still emailing or direct-messaging Marco every day, though he continued to dodge my request to meet to talk about the diaries face to face. He claimed that business kept him away from the palazzo and me. And yet he still seemed to have time to respond to my messages. I had tried to find out a little more by casually observing to Silvio, 'Signor Donato must be a very busy man.' He gave his usual head-tossing nod and carried on polishing a banister.

I sensed there was little point in asking him where Marco's office was. A couple of times, I thought about sneaking upstairs to see if Marco had a desk in the house, but I could think of no plausible excuse were I to be found straying so far from the library, and the potential for embarrassment kept me on the ground floor. I had to content myself with browsing the stacks, hoping that perhaps a love letter might drop out of the pages of one of the books.

Marco's elusiveness was beginning to feel like a personal insult, but still I continued to write to him. The only difference was that perhaps I was a little less open than I had been if he ever asked a personal question. However, that was to change.

One Thursday afternoon, I sent Marco my latest transcript. I'd translated a passage in which Luciana described a narrow escape on her way to her lover's house. She'd crossed paths with her brother on the Rialto Bridge. The adrenaline engendered by such a close shave had made the sex she had with her teacher that night better than ever. They'd wrestled with each other for hours on end, going through their entire sexual repertoire until Luciana's teacher collapsed exhausted – midway through taking her up the backside – and told Luciana she would have to look for a younger man if she was going to be so voracious.

Luciana wasn't the only one feeling voracious. I'd felt distinctly turned on as I read about her latest adventures. So much so that I felt self-conscious as I left the library after reading them. But as I had been doing ever since I started visiting the Donato library, I transcribed Luciana's diary faithfully and without abridgement. I wrote in the attached email to Marco, 'I feel a little embarrassed sending you such a dirty document. The shy bluestocking in me is slightly appalled. But you asked to know absolutely everything.'

I sent the email, then I went for a coffee with Bea. She was full of stories about her security-guard lover that would have been worthy of Luciana. I let myself be distracted by tales of her guy.

When I got back to the university there was something in my inbox. I hoped that it would be Marco's response to my last email, but to my surprise, it was from Steven. He'd sent it from his personal email address, I noted at once, not the office one.

Dear Sarah,

I imagine you've given up expecting this email. How long has it been since you walked out on me? Almost three months, I think. That doesn't mean to say I haven't thought about you every day. It's more the case that I've been stuck for words to describe how I feel about what happened between us. And Kat.

My heart contracted at the name of the girl in the mask but I read on.

Sarah, I understand why you jumped to the conclusion you did. I suppose I would have done the same. If you had waited long enough to hear the truth – stopped shouting and really heard it – perhaps you wouldn't have run away as you did. I was not lying when I said that Kat and I were not having an affair. We're still not. I could never be in love with a girl like her. My feelings for you were, and still are, too strong to make any space for another woman in my heart.

Sarah, no other woman could ever compare to you. Your intelligence and your humour captivated me from the moment you walked into my class seven years ago. I remember so clearly the first time you smiled at me. The love in your eyes! It felt like coming home. I knew at once that I wanted to be with you. There was no one I would rather talk to, share ideas with, share dreams with. I loved you from the very beginning. Our relationship was never just about physical desire.

However, the fact is that I am a very physical man and, you have to admit that after seven years, a physical relationship can't help but go stale. Remember how we used to laugh at some of the couples we knew? The ones who had clearly stopped fancying each other? Perhaps we shouldn't have laughed at them so heartily, because losing your lust for a partner is agony when the love doesn't disappear at the same time.

That night, after we went to the club, you accused me of trying to force you to leave me by flaunting my relationship with Kat. On the contrary, Sarah, I was trying to save us. The question of what might become of us as our physical desire for each other waned had been preying on my mind for months. We were drifting. The distance between us was growing by the day. We hardly touched one another any more. I didn't want to break up with you but I was feeling like a steam kettle about to explode. I didn't want that pent-up desire to explode as a full-on affair, so when you suggested the night at the sex club, I was relieved beyond imagining. I thought it was your way of telling me you wanted to experiment too. I thought we might be saved.

The evening, I thought, was a revelation to us both. I felt closer to you than ever as I watched you explore your desires. I thought we had reached a new understanding. But when you found out I already knew Kat, that changed. I realised from your anger that you had only suggested going to the club to please me. There was no hope that we could rediscover our passion through exploring that world after all.

I have thought about you endlessly, dear Sarah. I miss you terribly and I don't know what to do about it. Perhaps I didn't write to you before because it seemed there was no hope you would ever forgive me. We were right for each other in so many ways, I hate to think that is the case.

I would like to be with you again. If you feel the same way, let's end this stand-off. I love you and I want you in my world, but I have to tell you that we will need to do something about our sex life. Something to bring the excitement back. If you're not prepared to do that, then you were right to walk away. I've never wanted a vanilla sort of love. If, however, you think back on that night in the club and can admit you found it exciting too, then for God's sake let's be together. I got that post at the Sorbonne that we talked about. I leave for Paris in a month. Come with me.

Yours always,
Steven

I couldn't believe my eyes. I read the email again, looking for the punchline. 'A vanilla sort of love' certainly delivered a punch of one kind. I felt my soul curl up with shame as I remembered the night in the club, the release I had felt in Kat's arms and my subsequent fury at the idea that Steven might want her too. My hand hovered over the delete button. To think I thought I had come through the worst. And yet Steven said that he loved me and missed me. He wanted me back by his side. My soul leapt at that. Wasn't that what I had dreamed of? If there was still love left at the heart of us, couldn't I bear everything else?

'A vanilla sort of love.'

The words were still echoing in my brain when another email came through. Perhaps if I hadn't just read Steven's attempt to win me back, perhaps if his email hadn't left me feeling dull and naïve and horribly provincial, I would have responded differently. This second email was from Marco.

'I have an important question to ask,' he began. 'You must answer me with absolute honesty. Do you ever find yourself aroused when you read about Luciana's adventures?'

'Yes,' I wrote back. 'Yes, I do.'

36

My response to Marco was followed by a period of silence. It was early evening. Nick and Bea had left for the bar. I remained behind, claiming I had work to do. That much was true. I did have a lot of work to finish, but what I was really intending to do was reply to Steven's email. How I would reply, I still did not really know.

I sat at my desk with my head in my hands, weighing Steven's offer of reconciliation. He thought about me every day. Didn't I do the same? Think of him, that is. I thought about the specific things I missed about him. His laugh, his smile, his warm hug on a winter's day. The way he made scrambled eggs on a Sunday morning. If we could get the sex part right, I could have all that back. That was what he was promising. But getting the sex right was now a whole different game from upping the ante with expensive lingerie and whipped cream. Whenever I thought about sex with Steven now, the girl in the mask was not far behind. Her cat's eyes. Her perfect pout and her childlike crooked teeth. Her breasts like two scoops of ice cream. Would I have to share everything with women like her from now on?

I started my email to Steven a dozen times but didn't finish it.

Then I heard from Marco again.

Thank you for being so candid. I don't think I expected such a straight answer. But now I am intrigued. Have you ever touched yourself while sorting through her letters or reading a passage in her diary? I have to tell you, Sarah, I like the idea of you being in my library, all alone, with your hand between your legs as you read about the sexual awakening of our heroine. In fact, that is all I am able to think about when I know you are in my house. I picture you in that dusty room, sitting at the antique desk. I see you leaning forward in concentration, with your hair twisted into a bun to show off the nape of your neck. I long to place my lips on your neck and breathe in the sweet scent of you.

What was this? I shivered before I read on.

When I close my eyes, I see your slender fingers on the paper, carefully tracing the words in that faded, swirling hand. I long to take your hand and kiss your wrist. I long to place your cool palm against my face and feel you soothe all my cares away.

Then I would take both your hands and lift you to your feet and ask you to come with me, to one of the comfortable chairs. Would we fit in there together, do you think? How closely we would have to hold each other to squeeze into one seat together. I want to be close to you. I want to feel your heartbeat fluttering against mine.

I think about what it would be like to peel off your clothes, slowly, and reveal the woman beneath. I want to press my lips against your naked flesh. I want to feel your warmth and breathe in the perfect smell of you. I want you to sigh in my arms.

Will you touch yourself for me, next time you are in my library? I want you to imagine I am with you. Imagine that your hand is my hand. Please tell me how it feels when you think of your skin against mine.

How did it feel? I was hot and cold all over. Without really thinking about it, my hand had drifted between my legs while I read Marco's email. Of course, I had already imagined what it would be like to have Marco make love to me in the library. To know that he was thinking about it too was electrifying. For the moment, all thoughts of Steven left my mind.

I wrote back to Marco.

'Where are you? This is ridiculous. Can't you come back to Venice and help me make this fantasy a reality?'

'I wish I could. But for now you will have to make do with the fantasy. If you like, however, I could be with you virtually, in real time. You take your laptop with you into the library, don't you? All you need to do is go online. I will give you the pass-code to the house Wi-Fi.'

I don't know what surprised me more. That Marco was suggesting virtual sex or that the Palazzo Donato had Wi-Fi.

'You want to have cybersex?'

'If that's what you want to call it. Will you do it?'

I couldn't help but draw parallels between what he was asking me now and the way I had tried to bust through my prejudices to keep Steven by my side. Was this any different? Marco was certainly asking me to do something I hadn't done before. It wasn't high on my list of 'must do's. But I didn't want to be hung up any more. I didn't want to be 'vanilla'.

Marco seemed to sense my hesitation.

'I want only for you to be happy. I didn't expect you to be so blunt in your answer to my question about the diaries. I would never have revealed my own fantasies otherwise. This is for your pleasure, Sarah. If you don't think it will please you, then you must tell me "no".'

I told him I would think about it. He sent me the login details for Palazzo Donato's network.

* * *

Back at my apartment, I stayed awake until late, going over my relationship with Steven in my mind, trying to come to a decision as to whether there was something worth saving. Or perhaps I should put him behind me once and for all and go after something more than emails with Marco.

37

The following morning I set off for the library as usual, but this time I was nervous. I had my laptop with me, fully charged and ready. Of course, that wasn't unusual. I often took my laptop to the library. That morning, however, it seemed conspicuous. Was I really planning to have a virtual assignation? Had I got so desperate? I hoped that Marco would have forgotten his proposal. I soon realised he hadn't.

Silvio opened the door to the house as usual.

'You will be here on your own for the morning,' he informed me. 'Signor Donato has asked me to collect some papers from his lawyers. I will be gone until midday at least. They always take their time.'

I had wondered how Marco would guarantee Silvio would be unable to interrupt me at my 'work'. Here was my answer.

'Oh,' I said. 'How frustrating.'

'I will go to the market on my way back,' he added.

I nodded.

'I hope you are worthy of my employer's trust.'

'Believe me,' I said to myself. 'I hope the same of him.'

So Marco had arranged everything. I let myself into the library. The fire was lit. Luciana's papers were on the desk. So far, no different from any other day. I unwound my scarf and took off my coat. I sat down. Still, I waited for an extra ten minutes after I heard Silvio leave the house, to make sure he didn't come back for a forgotten umbrella or scarf, before

I dared log in to Palazzo Donato's private network. When I did, Marco was waiting for me on DM.

'You're late to your desk today.'

'I've been at my desk for the past ten minutes, but wanted to be absolutely sure that Silvio wasn't going to come back before I dared go online.'

'He won't be back for at least an hour. I've sent him to the other side of town and, as I'm sure you've noticed, he doesn't approach anything with a particular sense of urgency. Thank goodness. So . . .'

The ellipsis blinked.

'So . . . ?' I typed back.

'Are we going to do it?'

'Yes,' I responded, after a moment. 'If you like.'

'If *you* like, Sarah. You can still say no.'

'I don't want to say no.'

'OK. But let's not read from Luciana's diary after all. I want you to tell me what you think it would be like if we made love. You and I. Tell me how to make you happy. Tell me what you imagine when you think about me.'

'I don't know where to start.'

'Then maybe you should open the top left-hand drawer of the desk.'

I did as I was instructed. Inside the drawer I found a small vibrator, shiny black and the size and shape of a pebble. I picked it up and held it in the palm of my hand. It was smooth to the touch. Expensive. I pressed the on button and felt the buzz, which could be varied in intensity from a faint throb to something far wilder.

Marco messaged me.

'You've stopped typing. I imagine you are holding your gift.'

'Yes.'

'Good. I hope you don't mind that I took the liberty.'

'I mind the idea of Silvio putting it there.'

'He didn't.'

I paused.

'You said you were away.'

'I was.'

'You're in the house?'

He didn't respond to that.

'What do you think of your present?'

'Romantic,' I typed. I added a sarcastic emoticon.

'I thought it would make things more interesting.'

'Having you in the room would make things more interesting.'

'Alas, not today. Today we are going to make love with our minds.'

'And a vibrator.'

'And a vibrator . . . I assume this won't be the first time you've used one.'

'No,' I wrote. 'Not the first.'

I hoped he would not ask me when the first time had been. It was with Steven. How daring it had seemed at the time. Compared to a threesome in a sex club, however . . . I breathed deeply to put the girl behind the mask out of my mind.

'Am I alone in the house? I don't want to be disturbed by another servant. Or your wife.'

Wife. I'd said it at last.

'I don't have a wife, Sarah. There is no woman in my life except you.'

I was about to type something sarcastic but before I could, he carried on.

'I would not put you in a position to be humiliated. You will not be disturbed. No one ever enters this house except me and Silvio, and Silvio, as you know, will not be back for a while.'

'Then come and join me.'

'Indulge me, Sarah. Let things happen this way.'

I sat back in the chair with the vibrator still in my hand.

'Are you ready?' Marco asked.

I typed 'Yes' with my free hand.

'Then let us begin.'

I felt ridiculously self-conscious as I waited for Marco's instructions to appear on the screen. The hesitation with which the first message appeared seemed to suggest that this was a new experience for him too. I wondered if it was. I certainly hoped so. The idea that he was practised at the art of virtual seduction made me feel ugly and small. I had to push that from my mind, if there was to be any chance this would work.

'Sarah,' Marco wrote. 'Please tell me what you are wearing.'

I almost laughed. I typed back, 'I'm wearing a dress. It's a shirt dress, with buttons all the way down the front.'

'And underneath?'

'Underneath it I'm wearing a black slip with lace round the edges, over a bra and a pair of knickers. Both also black. And some stockings. Hold-ups. Not really warm enough for the weather.'

'But very sexy,' was Marco's response.

'I'm glad you think so.'

'I think we should get you undressed,' Marco continued. 'Would you please start to unbutton your clothes?'

'All the way?'

'Yes. Please.'

I set the vibrator down on the desk for a moment and unbuttoned my dress. I wondered if Marco was going to have me strip to my underwear. Thankfully, with the fire blazing the library was very warm, despite the weather outside. While

I was safely cocooned in the library, rain spattered against the tall windows. I hoped that meant that Silvio would take his time at his errands, staying in a café somewhere to keep out of the downpour.

'Is the dress undone?' Marco typed.

'Yes.'

'Then slide your hands over the front of your slip. I hope it's silk.'

'Of course.'

'Do it slowly. Imagine I am standing in front of you and seeing you for the first time. Imagine my smile. I have never seen anything so beautiful. Let your dress fall. I am pushing it off, revealing your beautiful shoulders. I am tracing one with my finger. Please do that for me. Imagine your finger is mine.'

I did as he suggested. It felt a little strange.

'Have you shrugged the dress off yet? Do so.'

I did.

'Look to your left. Behind that curtain is a mirror. Uncover it.'

I got up and pulled the curtain aside. There was a full-length mirror behind it. It hung from a pair of hooks hammered into one of the shelves. I wondered how I had not noticed it before. Marco must have put it there for me. Or did Silvio? I felt horribly self-conscious again, imagining the old retainer following Marco's instructions.

I returned to the laptop on the desk. I read the next instruction.

'Can you see your reflection from where you are sitting? Look at yourself in the mirror, Sarah, and see what I imagine seeing myself. See how beautiful you are in your simple under-clothes. Your black slip suits you so well. It skims across your curves, not clinging but caressing. When you move, it moves with you and echoes your movements. Cross your legs.'

I crossed my right thigh over the left.

'Let the slip ride up to show the top of a stocking. You have beautiful legs.'

I wanted to ask how he knew.

'Your ankles are so fine. Your feet, with their high arches, are so pretty and erotic. I want to take them in my hands and feel their delicate strength. I want to kiss them.'

'I might be ticklish,' I typed.

'Then I would enjoy hearing you beg for mercy,' wrote Marco.

I glanced from the screen to my reflection. The soft light of the fire cast a flattering glow on the little flesh I had so far revealed. It shimmered on my hair, which was where Marco turned his attention next.

'How are you wearing your hair today?' he asked.

'In a twist,' I told him. 'Held in place with a single clip.'

'Undo the clip and let your hair fall loose. It's such a beautiful colour. It shines coppery in the firelight. I imagine running my fingers through it and loosening it further still. Imagine me burying my face in the waves and breathing in your perfume. The delicious scent of May rose and jasmine that lingers in the library long after you have gone.'

'How do you know?' I interrupted.

'Don't interrupt me. Be seduced, Sarah. I want you to feel desired. Unfasten your hair now.'

I undid the clip and let my hair fall.

'Look at yourself in the mirror again. Imagine my hands on your bare arms. Tip your head back so that I may see your hair tumble over your shoulder blades. Expose your throat so that I may kiss you there. Look in the mirror. See how your eyes are darkening. Your pupils are dilating with desire. Hitch up your slip to show more of your elegant legs. Uncross them. Run your hands up the inside of your thighs. Rest your hands over the front of your knickers.'

'OK.'

'Then slide them to one side.'

'Shouldn't I take them off?'

'No. Just move them so that your pussy is exposed.'

I held the fabric of the gusset out of the way.

'Stroke yourself,' wrote Marco.

'How?'

'How you usually do. How you like it.'

Tentatively, I ran my fingers over my soft pubic hair.

'Are you wet?' he asked.

My fingers reached the opening of my vagina. Carefully, I touched myself.

'Not yet.'

'Pick up the vibrator,' was the next instruction. 'Turn it on. Gently. Touch it to your clitoris.'

Suddenly, the room felt very warm indeed.

38

Of course this was not the first time I had used a vibrator, either alone or in the presence of someone else. However, there was something about using the sex toy at Marco's behest that made me aroused before I even touched the shiny black pebble to my clitoris.

As when I masturbated on my own, I used my left hand to part my labia so that my clit was more exposed. I had turned the vibe on at its lowest setting but still, when it made contact with my flesh, it felt as though I had been given an electric shock. I turned it off.

'How does it feel?' Marco's question appeared on the screen.

'Smooth,' I told him. 'Slightly cold. On lowest setting and the sensation is already too much for me.'

'I hope not,' wrote Marco. 'Turn it on again. Hold it against you.'

I obliged.

'Imagine, if you will, that my hand is where your hand is now. Imagine I am stroking the vibrator over your clit. Gently. Teasing. I'm barely touching you at all.'

I let the vibrator slide backwards and forwards across that naughty nub of nerve endings. As I got used to the pace of the toy's oscillations, I was able to bear it more easily.

'Now hold it in one place. Find the sweet spot.'

I pressed the vibrator against the left side of my clit. For some reason, it had always been slightly more sensitive on that side.

'Press a little harder.'

I already had.

'Move it very slightly, just enough to fool yourself that the feeling is going away.'

I did.

'Move it in tiny circles. Imagine it is my tongue that caresses you now. Just tickling the tip of you.'

I had a strong vision of Marco's face.

'Now put a finger inside you. You're wet. You're such a bad girl.'

He was right. My finger slid inside easily.

'Fuck yourself with your finger while you imagine my mouth on your clit. Keep going. Keep going. Keep going. Don't stop . . .'

I couldn't have stopped if I wanted to. Fortunately, I definitely didn't want to. My body had taken control.

I threw my head back and let my orgasm overtake me. It was glorious. It shook my body so violently that I had to cling to the edge of the desk to keep from falling onto the floor. Afterwards, I flopped forward onto the desk, with my head on my arms. I started laughing. I couldn't help myself. The ridiculousness of the situation combined with the exhilaration of my orgasm overtook me.

'Was that good?' Marco's question blinked from the screen.

'It was very good,' I typed, still shaking with small aftershocks. I looked at my reflection. I was flushed from my climax. My eyes glittered. I didn't think I had ever looked so pleased with myself.

'I knew it would be,' Marco's words appeared.

'Then imagine what it would be like if we were in the same room,' I dared to write. 'Can you come and see me?'

'I can't.'

'You're here in the house, aren't you?'

'I'm not.'

'Marco, we have to meet. We have to. This is insane. You've brought me to an orgasm and I don't even know what your voice sounds like.'

'It sounds exactly as you imagine, in your heart.'

'I'd rather hear it for real.' I felt daring enough to ask him to meet me again.

'I have to go,' said Marco. 'You should probably get ready to leave yourself. I will write to you later, I promise.'

He logged off.

I stared at the screen, stunned that he'd pulled the disappearing trick again. But he had. There was nothing I could do but get dressed. I picked up my dress and shook it out. As I put it on, I watched myself in the mirror again. I felt exhilarated and wicked. Vanilla no more.

Silvio arrived just as I was closing my laptop.

'Everything has been OK?' he asked me.

I assured him that it had.

'Good,' he said, looking at me with his head slightly to one side. A little quizzical. I smoothed back my hair and gave him my brightest smile.

'I'll see you tomorrow,' I said.

'Yes,' said Silvio. 'Perhaps.'

I left the library before I burst into laughter again. I almost slid down the corridor in my haste to be out in the courtyard so that I could take a breath of cold winter air and attempt to take control of myself. It was while I was rushing to get outside that I heard the distinct sound of a door being closed on the floor above me.

The sound brought me up short. Silvio was still in the library, I was sure, or at least in that part of the house. He could not have moved fast enough to get upstairs in time.

Given that I was supposed to have been in the palazzo on my own, who was closing the door on the first floor?

Standing by the fountain, I looked up at each of the gallery windows in turn. Who was up there? The windows looked back at me like blinded eyes. I continued to stare upwards, shielding my eyes from the sun to get a proper look. I hadn't imagined that door slamming, I knew it. There was only one explanation. Marco must in the house. He was watching me. Perhaps he had been watching me all along. Had the mirror concealed some sort of camera? My exhilaration turned to anger and the uncomfortable feeling that I had been used.

I pulled my coat tightly round me and left the house as quickly as I could.

Back at the university, I direct-messaged Marco at once.

'I'm beginning to feel like a bit of a fool. I know you were in the house today. Please don't deny it again. You said I should be wined and dined and adored. You said you would like to see me dressed up for a night on the town. Cybersex isn't quite the same thing. Why won't you come to me?'

'It isn't possible.'

'Why isn't it possible?'

'I can't tell you.'

'You're ridiculous. Don't expect to hear from me again.'

39

28th April, 1753

My teacher kept his promise. We were going to the Ridotto di San Moisè. And, it seemed, as he had also promised, he would make sure I was the most beautiful woman in the room. When I arrived at his poor house, dressed in my brother's clothes as usual, I found a trunk waiting for my attention. It contained the most beautiful dress I had ever seen.

Oh, I had never seen anything quite so lovely. I clapped my hands together in delight as the frills spilled out. I snatched it up. Oh, oh, oh! It was just like the dresses I had admired from my bedroom window. So extravagant. Like the blossom of an exotic flower. Red and orange and all edged with gold lace.

'It's perfect,' I said. I threw my arms around my teacher's neck and smothered him with kisses of gratitude. 'It will suit me wonderfully.'

'It will suit me better,' he said.

'What?'

I was already slipping off my cloak, eager to get into these more colourful swags, when he picked up the dress himself.

'Yes. It is just right for me.'

And with that, he stripped off his own shirt and stepped

into the gown before I had a chance to protest.

'Help me,' he said. 'I don't have the faintest idea how I'm supposed to do this up.'

I was dumbfounded.

'Don't just stand there. We're going out. Show me where this part goes.'

He was serious. I was not going to be wearing the red dress.

'Then what am I supposed to wear?'

'You keep reminding me how important it is that you must not be recognised. You'll wear your brother's clothes. If anyone is looking for you at all, my dear, they will be looking for a beautiful young woman, not a skinny boy who's struggling to grow his first beard.'

He plucked at imaginary hairs on my chin and I gave him a clout for his trouble.

'My love,' he said. 'You are more beautiful than the sun. Even in a boy's clothes, you will outshine every woman at the Ridotto tonight. The danger is that you will burn so brightly that your identity will be the subject of gossip from the Giudecca to the Ghetto before the real sun rises tomorrow morning. People who know your father may be in attendance. We must be careful. Have this.'

He handed me a new mask. It was a hateful *servetta muta* with a button for my mouth.

'Why have I got to wear this thing?'

'Because your voice is as easily recognised as the nightingale's song.'

'But it doesn't go with a boy's costume,' I countered. 'A man would never wear such a thing.'

'You have a point,' said my teacher. 'You may wear this instead.'

This time he handed me a *medico della peste*. A plague mask. I got it within an inch of my face before the smell of the herbs that must have been left in the beak since the last time the plague swept through the city made me feel nauseated. I handed it back.

'I am *not* wearing that.'

'Then the *servetta muta* it must be,' he said.

Anything was preferable to the awful smell of long-dead roses and valerian. Ugh. Valerian. The smell of feet. It was bad enough on its own, but the association with those months when my mother was dying made it too much for me. I felt my eyes begin to water.

My teacher reached out to touch my hand. He let me put on the plain white half-mask I normally wore. 'I'll wear the *servetta*. I don't need to eat tonight. Just don't say anything stupid.'

The Ridotto di San Moisè was the last place on earth that my father would have wanted me to visit. As far as he was concerned, the gambling house in a wing of the old San Moisè Palace was a short step from Hell. But I was very excited to be going there. To me, the Ridotto was a place of unsurpassable glamour.

My teacher's gondolier brought us to the watergate. We were both of us, my teacher and I, confused by our swapped garments, me waiting for a hand to help me from the gondola, my teacher jumping to his feet, only to be scuppered by his voluminous skirts. Fortunately, there was such a hubbub going on, I don't think anyone noticed. The front of the house blazed with torches. Liveried footmen helped fine ladies from their boats. There was much excited chatter. A quartet played us into the hall. A glass of wine was pressed into my hand. I took one for my teacher too, but of course he could not drink it, wearing the hateful *servetta muta* as he was.

I offered him my arm and we made our way into the main room and the tables. We would not be gambling that night as between us we had precisely no money, so we took a couple of chairs at the side of the room and watched proceedings from there.

I was entranced by the Ridotto's habitués. The many-layered skirts of the masked ladies flounced like the tail feathers of exotic birds. One woman in particular held my attention. Catching me looking at her, she pirouetted across the room to come to a graceful halt on the seat beside me, with her skirts deflating around her like sails without wind. She turned to me and smiled, warm and friendly.

'I don't believe we've met,' she said. 'Aren't you going to introduce yourself, young man?'

My teacher had warned me not to talk but how could I not respond to the woman's polite enquiry? She would have thought it strange. I considered for a moment pretending I was mute, like the servant girl at my aunt's house in Turin, but that would be ridiculous. So, I tried instead to keep my voice down in my boots as I gave her my brother's name. It was the first male name that popped into my head. I'd have to sort out the damage to his reputation later.

The woman shook her head. 'No. I know Amadeo Giordano. He's taller than you. He's broader here.'

The woman laid her hand on my bound chest (my teacher had insisted I be bound for this excursion even though, he said, I was so flat no one would normally

227

notice). As she did so, her mouth widened into another smile and I remembered all at once where I had seen her before. She was the courtesan on the boat that sunny feast day. I blushed.

'Your secret is safe with me,' she murmured. 'As is your friend's.' In a louder voice she continued. 'Your "mother" and I are great friends, young man. Signora,' the courtesan addressed my teacher, 'It is getting very hot in here and I should like to step outside. Will you accompany us for the sake of propriety?'

My teacher nodded, and though he kept his mask firmly in place, I could tell from what little I could see of his cheekbones that he thought the idea of doing anything for propriety's sake very funny indeed. I did my best to play my part and bowed low, as I had seen my brother do, sweeping both of the 'ladies' ahead of me with my three-cornered hat. The courtesan giggled and swatted my shoulder with her fan as she passed.

The party was very grand and well-populated and there were plenty of people in the garden that evening, but eventually we found a space well away from the rest of the crowd. The courtesan laid her mask in her lap and my teacher unmasked himself too. He gasped for air.

'That thing!' He flung the *servetta muta* to the floor. 'I don't know how you women cope with them.'

'Exactly,' said the courtesan. 'It is a cruel punishment to inflict upon the creatures you profess to love, don't you think?'

I agreed with her. 'Terribly cruel.'

'This young man would never expect such a thing of

his companion,' she continued. I nodded enthusiastically, keeping up with the game.

'If that young man had any balls,' said my teacher, 'I'm sure he would.'

We all laughed. The courtesan smiled at me encouragingly but still I kept my mask on. I would do so until my teacher told me it was safe. The courtesan turned back to him and tapped him upon the knee with her fan.

'Madam,' she continued the charade. 'You have been most remiss. I have not seen you in my salon these past six months.'

'Not since that filthy Duke tried to run me through with a sword. The company you keep, dear Ernesta, really has been going downhill. I'll come back when you get rid of that clown. He's an absolute idiot.'

'But the Duke is a very generous man.' The courtesan fingered the string of pearls around her neck. I noticed my master's mouth twitch in disapproval as the courtesan tugged the string out of the bodice of her dress to reveal at the end of it a single pearl the size of a blackbird's egg. I had never seen anything quite so magnificent. No wonder she didn't want to send the Duke away.

The courtesan saw me admiring her jewellery.

'You may try it on if you like,' she said.

'I don't think it will match his costume,' said my teacher.

'It is indeed a very modest outfit he's wearing. He must be from the north.'

Did she know I was from Turin?

'Aren't you going to introduce us?'

'Take your mask off, little brother,' he said to me.

I obeyed.

The courtesan smiled widely.

'Oh well done. Well done indeed. What a clever disguise. But I think I know where you found this one. You have your brother's nose, my dear. And your name?' she persisted.

'Luciana Giordano.'

'And I am Ernesta Donato.'

It was a name I had heard spoken in whispers.

I had never seen my master quite so nervous as he was in the presence of Ernesta Donato. There was something about her that seemed to bring out the little boy in him. I could not imagine ever teasing him quite as wickedly as she did. I could never have imagined him accepting it. It was like seeing a big cat, which has just torn a rabbit into pieces as a game, curling up in the lap of its mistress and agreeing to be treated like a kitten. She persuaded him that we should leave the Ridotto and accompany her back to her house.

When we arrived, I was absolutely dumbfounded. Raised as I was in the bosom of the church, I'd lost count of how many times I'd been told that the wages of sin is death. The Palazzo Donato suggested otherwise. In Ernesta's case, the wages of sin were keeping her very nicely indeed. Oh, what a beautiful house. It was lit so brightly. In anticipation of her return, every lamp in the house was blazing and the light was made brighter still as it bounced off gilt frames and magnificent mirrors and even a string of diamonds that hung from the back of a chair, where Ernesta had obviously tossed it as she left the house as a child might discard a string of clay beads.

Ernesta saw me looking at them.

'They were in competition with my new pearl,' she explained, as she picked up the diamonds and held them towards me. 'Try them,' she said.

I had heard it was possible for courtesans to amass a certain degree of wealth thanks to their generous patrons, but how rich must Ernesta's patrons have been to lavish her with such incredible gifts? And the house! Even the most successful merchant my father knew could not have afforded a house as wonderful as this. And Ernesta had earned all this while lying on her back.

'Heavens, no,' she said, when I was bold enough to ask. 'I earned all this precisely because I don't just lie on my back. And because every gold coin, every pearl that is pressed into my hand, I can make into two.'

'When Venezia next goes to war, they'll come to Ernesta to fill the war chest,' said my teacher.

'And I shall lend them everything they need at a ruinous interest rate. A woman needs to know about money,' she told me. 'When your natural assets finally fade, you must be certain you have less ephemeral assets to keep you warm at night. Wine?'

Ernesta rang a small golden bell and a manservant appeared, before leaving with his instructions.

While the manservant was backing out of the door, something else was creeping in.

'Oh, my little angel!' Ernesta cried, as the monkey I had seen on the boat came skittering across the room and climbed her body as if he were climbing a tree. He came to rest on Ernesta's shoulder. He was chattering away, as though angry he had been left behind while we were all at the Ridotto. Ernesta laughed at the monkey's remonstrations.

'That wretched monkey!' exclaimed my teacher.

'Giacomo, my monkey loves you. You can keep him company while I have my bath.'

'If he comes anywhere near me, I'll throttle him.'

'Miserable man. Come with me,' she said, taking me by the hand and leading me into her bedchamber. 'I want to talk with *you* more.'

I followed Ernesta upstairs. Once we were inside her chamber, a maidservant appeared as if from nowhere. She informed Ernesta that her bath was ready. Ernesta expressed her gratitude but then continued to converse with me as the maidservant began to unfasten her dress.

Ernesta breathed out in obvious relief as the maid loosened her corset. 'Hateful thing. Whenever will fashion be comfortable? Perhaps I should dress like you.'

'Perhaps I should leave,' I said. Ernesta was now stripped to her underclothes.

'Nonsense. You're not really a boy, after all.'

'But—'

'There's nothing here you haven't seen before.'

Ernesta was wrong. The truth of just how cloistered my upbringing had been was becoming more apparent to me by the second. I had never seen a naked female body save my own, except for statues. I had barely seen my own body until my teacher showed me what I looked like with the mirror in his room.

You might have thought that, given everything I had learned of late, I would not be so shy, but when Ernesta's maidservant left the room, bobbing her way to the door, I felt the urge to go running after her rather than be left alone with her mistress.

'Come on,' Ernesta said to me. 'You can help me get out of this thing at least.'

I untied the loose bow at her waist so that her petticoat fell to the floor and she stepped out of it at last, naked as a newborn baby, and several hundred times as wonderful.

Here were the charms that encouraged dukes to send diamonds. Ernesta's skin was more smooth and white than the pearls around her neck. Catching me marvelling, she extended her arm and let me stroke it. 'Milk. Like Cleopatra,' she explained.

That night, the bath was filled not with milk but with warm water and oil that made it opaque. The air was thick with the scent of flowers. Ernesta stepped into the bath and relaxed into its thick warmth with a sigh. She closed her eyes momentarily. When she reopened them, she fired a question at me.

'Tell me, my dear, how did you come to know such a despicable man as my Giacomo Casanova?'

My mouth must have dropped open. 'Casanova!' I squeaked. I had definitely heard of him. And nothing good. His reputation was blacker than the Devil's.

Ernesta laughed. 'Oh. He's given you an alias. I'm not surprised.'

'I have been duped,' I complained.

'Darling, you've been *seduced*,' Ernesta corrected me. 'I assume you've been having a good time of it.'

I nodded, though I was embarrassed.

'And he's helped you with your education?'

'Yes,' I admitted.

'Where did he find you?'

233

I told her the story. She listened to me with an expression on her face that grew graver the more I said. When I told her about my father's determination to keep me uneducated, she shook her head.

'He wants to take care of me,' I said, by way of an excuse.

'We all must take care of ourselves,' said Ernesta. 'Keeping a girl locked away for her own good can never work. Only a truly naïve girl would end up entrusting her virginity to Giacomo.'

Her words stung so that I was glad when I heard the bells chime two. How time had flown.

'I have to leave,' I said. I picked up my brother's cloak and wrapped it round my shoulders. 'Thank you for the wine.'

'Wait,' Ernesta called. 'I want you to have something.'

She rose from her bath like Venus in Botticelli's painting. Her maidservant rushed forward from the shadows to wrap her in a gown. Once dressed, she headed for her dressing table and a Chinese enamelled box thereon. I was dazzled by the contents, which spilled out as though they had been fighting for room inside. Here were gemstones that could have funded an armada. Ernesta rifled through them, as Maria sometimes rifled through her sewing box in search of a bone button. Eventually Ernesta found what she was looking for and held it aloft. Triumphant.

It was a pearl. Not as big as the pearl Ernesta had been wearing that evening, but still a far bigger bauble than she had any business giving to someone she barely knew. I said as much.

'Believe me, the gentleman who sent me this pearl did

not know me at all,' she laughed. 'It is entirely the wrong colour. I should like you to have it and I think he would agree. It will look very well with your hair.'

'But . . .'

'Take it,' she said. 'You never know when it will be useful. Consider it your very first asset.'

I let her give me the pearl. She placed it in my palm where it lay cool and perfect.

It was a South Sea pearl, dark as burnished coal. Where it caught the light, it glowed purple and blue. It was breathtaking.

'Thank you.'

'Now, go.' Ernesta kissed me on the cheek. 'I hope that I will see you here again.'

The following morning, I put my hand beneath the pillow and felt around until my fingers closed over the pearl. I brought it out and looked at it. My very first 'asset', as Ernesta had joked. The previous night's adventure might have felt like a dream, but here was proof everything that had happened was very real indeed. I had spent the evening with a courtesan, thanks to the most notorious womaniser in Venezia. Ernesta Donato and Giacomo Casanova. Lucifer himself might have kept better company.

40

Despite telling Marco that he would not hear from me again, it seemed that my willpower decided otherwise. Or rather my lack of willpower. Just a couple of hours later, I got out my laptop and wrote to him. Reason had not worked. Nor righteous anger. Perhaps flattery would. I just needed to know that I had been more than a diversion.

> I would like to meet you face to face. Because while we've been exchanging these emails, the face in my mind has been the one I have seen on the Internet: the 1990s playboy. I would like to see how time has treated you. I would like to see if that face is now framed by grey hair. Perhaps you're even bald! I can't help feeling you know far more about me than I know about you. I have been entirely open with you and what I have told you can be easily corroborated by a quick Google search. But you are still something of a mystery to me and I want to know more. Are you worried that time hasn't treated you kindly? I don't care. I want to know the man you are today.
>
> I know there's a possibility we could meet in the flesh and be disappointed. While our friendship is only virtual, there is plenty of room for imagination and, of course, we will be imagining each other into our own perfect fantasies. But I am confident I would not be disappointed if I met you. No matter how someone ages, there is always a part

of them that remains the same. That physical part is the eyes, don't you think? While faces may wrinkle, eyes can retain their youth and optimism for ever. You talked about the importance of my eyes in making you trust me. I look into your eyes in those pictures on the Internet and see someone I know I could be friends with. I see optimism, a mischievous sense of humour and, above all, kindness. When I first typed your name into Google, I don't know what I was expecting, but I know I wasn't expecting to find a photograph of someone who looked like a kindred spirit.

Like you I think we truly know a person through their eyes. Though God only knows who was looking through the lens when those photos were taken, I felt as if you were looking for me. I felt an immediate connection that could be something more than a working acquaintance. Didn't you? You must have done. I don't think I would be writing this email now if I didn't believe you felt the same way.

We have danced around each other for weeks. We have amused each other long-distance. Not least in the library this morning. At times, our words have crossed in space, like those of two people in a real conversation, eager to share their thoughts with the one person who might understand.

So, you ask me what I want from you and I am telling you that I want more. I want to shake the hand that presses send on your emails. I want to throw my arms around you and greet you Italian-style. I want to let my kisses linger on your cheeks. I want to hold you by the shoulders and look into the eyes I already know. I want you to smile at me, directly at me, without a screen inbetween us. I want to run my hand along the curve of your jaw. I want you to kiss me. I want everything.

While I was writing my email to Marco in the early after-noon, I'd felt invincible. I felt sure I was writing what Marco would want to hear and his response would be forthcoming and absolutely in agreement. On the one hand, it was ridiculous to feel I was falling in love when I had never met the man in person, but on the other hand, it wasn't so strange these days. Hundreds of thousands of people met for the first time via online dating sites. They flirted from a distance. Weren't they already in a relationship of sorts before they even exchanged a first phone call?

I was sure Marco didn't write in the way he had written to me to everyone who emailed him asking for access to his magnificent library. He certainly couldn't have been asking them for cybersex. We had made a proper connection. It could only be strengthened by meeting each other properly, adding sound and vision to our blossoming love.

As the afternoon ticked by, my confidence that such a bold move would have changed the game in my favour began to ebb away. I had an excuse to write to him again, having discovered that Luciana's courtesan was in fact his relative. I started that email but didn't finish it. I couldn't move the conversation back to Luciana. I had to move the game on and that meant waiting for Marco to make his play.

There was still nothing by the time the cleaners arrived at the office, hovering pointedly while I read and reread my last email and waited in vain for a response.

'We're in the bar,' Bea texted. I didn't need to ask which one. With a heavy heart, I turned off my computer and put on my coat.

At the bar, Nick and Bea were waiting with the traditional spritz. I lifted a small toast in their direction, and then let them continue a lighthearted argument about some film starring Tilda Swinton. Nick had loved it. Bea had not. Nick said it was beautifully made. Bea said he only liked it because it contained several close-up shots of Tilda's nipples. I had no opinion – I hadn't seen the film – but I was glad to let Bea and Nick banter without interruption. I didn't want to answer questions about my day.

About an hour after I arrived in the bar, the woman I secretly thought of as the legendary Chiara walked in. She was accompanied by just two men that evening. A very small entourage for her. One was carrying her dog. The other – you'd never see this in London, I thought – was carrying her handbag. A third young man who had been sitting at the bar vacated his stool so that the exotic signora could sit down.

Ridiculously, given that I had no real idea who the woman was, I felt a sudden surge of jealousy towards my imaginary Chiara. Chiara had seen Marco in reality. She had touched his face. She had felt his hands slide along her well-preserved body. Why must I continue to be kept at arm's length? Was it because of women like the one to whom Marco had lost his virginity? Could he only bring a relationship into the physical realm if he was certain the woman in question didn't want anything more than sex? Or revenge?

I felt the crazy urge to know more bubbling up inside me until, like the compressed air in the bottle of prosecco the barman had just opened, it would not be kept inside. I had to find out if this woman was Chiara. I had to ask her if she had any idea at all why Marco would be keeping me at a distance.

'I'm going to the bar,' I told my friends. Nick and Bea both raised their glasses to indicate the need for another round. I walked right up to the woman I thought was Chiara and positioned myself beside her.

'Excuse me,' I said, all nonchalant. 'But are you Chiara?'

The woman looked confused.

'Chiara Giovanni.' I plucked a possible surname from mid-air.

'I am not Chiara, no,' the woman responded. 'Is there someone perhaps who looks like me? What did you say her family name was again?'

'It doesn't matter,' I said. This was not a conversation I wanted to get into. 'I can see now you're much older than she is.'

The woman in the sable practically bristled and I felt hot with shame as I returned to my friends. Was I going crazy? If the woman I had imagined into a sex kitten had been Chiara, what could she have told me in any case? Marco said he hadn't seen her in decades. Chiara might have known the playboy he was back then, but she didn't know who he was now.

'You seem preoccupied,' said Nick. 'Something eating you?'

I shook my head.

'Come to my place for dinner?' he suggested. 'I'm going to cook *tagliatelle al cinghiale*.'

'He's going to open a jar of pasta sauce,' said Bea. 'But it's a good jar. I'd be up for it if I didn't have something even better waiting at home.'

I declined Nick's offer. 'I think perhaps I'm coming down with something. Haven't been feeling right all day. I should probably take a couple of paracetamol and go to bed.'

'You do look a bit sick,' said Bea.

I am sick, I thought. I'm lovesick. Over a man I've never met. And now he has made me humiliate myself by performing online sex in his library. How stupid can a girl get? I felt sick and angry as I thought about how vulnerable I had made myself again. And right after Steven's betrayal. I considered myself to be an intelligent sort of woman but when it came to dealing with men, I was always bottom of the class.

I got back to the flat and opened up my laptop. This time I began to write an angry email, telling Marco he could stuff his psychological games. If he didn't want to take our relationship any further than an email, then he could sod right off. It was weird, to share such confidences at a distance and not make any plans to come closer. It was plain nasty if the entire episode had been intended to get me to a place where I was willing to masturbate for his pleasure, while he remained aloof and invulnerable.

What had possessed me? I didn't know where he was. I had assumed he was emailing me from a private office, but he might have been sitting at a desk in the middle of a room full of people. They might have been looking over his shoulder while he typed the instructions I carried out that morning. They might even have been in on the joke, adding their own depraved suggestions. The house might have been full of specially invited perverts.

Why had I let myself get into this position again? The critical voice inside my head was full of answers, of course. At best I must have been trying to restore my self-esteem after the shock of losing Steven, thinking that if I could persuade someone as rich and good-looking as Marco Donato to love me, I would have proved myself worth more than the affections of a penniless academic. Or perhaps I just liked being humiliated. Perhaps I wanted Marco to make me cross the boundaries I once thought I would never cross. After all, wasn't I the one who had suggested the sex-club trip that led to my break-up with Steven? No matter what I told myself, part of me must have *wanted* to go to that club. I could not deny I had been mind-blowingly turned on by my first and last Sapphic encounter. I still thought about that threesome, too. The two men with the girl in the collar.

I was so confused. I sat at the kitchen table and pressed the heels of my hands to my eyes. What did I want? Was my true nature that of an exhibitionist? A voyeur? A masochist? Maybe I was a little of all of those things. But above all I wanted to be understood. I wanted to be loved. Marco had seemed to understand me, but now that I had put my cards firmly on the table, he was gone.

I sat in the kitchen for a long time but when I heard the bells of the Chiesa dei Carmini strike two, I forced myself up from the table and into the bedroom. I had not finished my angry email to Marco but there seemed to be little point. Such furious bleating wouldn't change his mind. Maybe I had to change *my* mind. I had to think about what I really wanted. Maybe I had to avoid these puppetmaster men and find myself someone worth loving for real.

41

When I finally got to sleep, I dreamed I was back at the palazzo, but this time the usual man in the mask wasn't there to greet me. Instead, my masked lover was Steven. His eyes may have been covered but his smile was unmistakable. He took me by the hand and I followed him into the library. We weren't to be on our own there. Curled up in a chair like the cat she longed to be was Kitty, Steven's erstwhile student and lover. She was wearing that black cat's-eye mask she had been wearing at the sex club.

'Do it for us,' said Kitty. 'Show us what you did for him.'

I sat down at the desk. My laptop was already there. It was open. The direct-message window was flashing. The instructions were already coming thick and fast. I sat still. I read them but I didn't act. Steven read over my shoulder and murmured encouragement. Kitty, growing bored of my inaction, got up from her chair.

'Let us help you,' she said.

She slipped her hand into the neckline of my white dress and made a grab for one of my breasts. She squeezed it hard. With her other hand she pulled my hair until my face was tipped back towards her. She kissed me with such ferocity, my lips bled.

Steven joined her. Four hands all over my body. No fraction of my flesh was out of bounds to them. I did not move as they stroked and kissed and pinched me. I let myself be moulded entirely as they wished. My eyes were on the

243

laptop's screen, where new instructions blinked into life every couple of seconds.

Put your fingers inside her. Pinch her nipples. Twist her clit.

I realised they were not instructions for me. They were for Steven and Kitty. It wasn't about what I should do to myself this time, it was about what they should do *to* me. I was to be entirely passive.

I lifted my arms obediently as Steven stripped off my dress. I was subservient as a small child while Kitty helped me step out of my underwear before she buried her face greedily in my soft pubic hair. I went limp as Steven suckled at my tits. I could barely feel Kitty's fingers inside my vagina.

After a while, it was as though I was no longer in my body at all. My flesh was just a conduit for other people's desires. Kitty's. Steven's. Marco's. Anybody's. Meanwhile, I floated somewhere above them, just observing their frantic efforts to please themselves and, I suppose, to somehow please me too. My body reacted like an automaton. Enough kissing, stroking and licking would make me come. It was a matter of persistence. Push the right buttons. Keep pushing. Win the prize.

I glanced down to where Steven was pleasuring himself frantically as he watched Kitty lick at my clit with ferocious determination to make me come first. On the screen, Marco's words flickered menacingly.

Lick her. Penetrate her. Make her come for me. Make her come.

Steven came first. His face was anguished and ecstatic all at once as he unleashed his load all over my body. Kitty whooped in delight when she saw it. She dived to catch his semen on her tongue. She licked at the places where Steven's cum had splashed onto my body like an animal desperate for cream. She licked a pathway up the centre of my chest and came to a halt, looking into my eyes. Staring into them.

'Sarah? Sarah? She isn't looking at me. Steven? Marco? Where has she gone?'

42

Shortly after the night at the Ridotto, Giacomo, as I now called him, wicked man, went away. He said he had business in the north. When I asked him what kind of business, he wouldn't tell me. I had learned not to press him for details. Likewise, I closed my ears to the gossip I heard about him everywhere from the kitchen to the front pews of the church.

I suppose I should have stayed at home, but I was used to my freedom now and the idea of even one night without escape from my father's house was something I could not bear. So this time, when I was supposed to be asleep, I set out along the canal in the opposite direction to Giacomo's hovel. I went to Ernesta's house.

She was happy to see me. 'I want for intelligent female company,' she said. 'Much as I like most of the men who visit me, men very rarely talk of anything but themselves.'

We sat in her salon and talked of everything. I definitely wanted her to talk about herself. I wanted to know how she had come to be so rich when she claimed she started life on the church steps, abandoned by her mother, wrapped in a piece of rich silk.

'Which suggests to me that my mother was a business-woman herself,' she cackled.

Ernesta was taken in by a wealthy family, who raised her among their servants with the hope that one day she would make a fine lady's maid. That was not to come to pass. When Ernesta was thirteen, the man of the house took a fancy to her. The price of Ernesta's silence was her first pearl.

'This one,' she said, plucking the bead from her jewellery box. 'Not much for my maidenhead, eh?'

Every jewel in the box had a similar story behind it.

'This bead was the price of my arse,' she said, handing me a ruby. Then an uncut sapphire. 'This was the cost of three days tied to a bed.'

'What about the pearl you gave me?' I asked her.

'That was from Magherini, the duke. It was the price of a first kiss.'

'That's all?'

'Darling, you don't know how well I kiss. Besides, Magherini has exotic tastes. He considered the pearl a big deposit on further adventures.'

Her eyes clouded over. I could tell she was upset at a memory.

'Come on,' she said. 'I want to show you something different.'

She pulled me to my feet and we walked down the gallery round her courtyard.

'There is my true pearl,' Ernesta told me then.

Though it was late, a small girl was playing in the courtyard. Her golden hair was brighter than any mirror in the house. She danced round the fountain, stopping from time to time to flick water into the air so it glittered like diamonds as it fell.

'All this will be hers and she will never have to take a

man to her bed unless she wants to. She can be the woman she wants to become. She can be a mother or a musician, a merchant or a muse. Hell, I don't even care if she wants to become a nun. She'd look lovely in the outfit.' Ernesta laughed.

'Wouldn't it be hard for her to make a good marriage anyway?' I asked. 'I mean . . .'

'With my reputation? Oh Luciana. You dear sweet little thing. You would be surprised at what people are prepared to overlook for a house like this. Don't you think I get marriage proposals every day of the week? Respect has nothing to do with "good" marriages. Neither does reputation. It's all about the consolidation of two fortunes. Respect? Huh. The freedom to become what you wish to become and to choose whom you want to share your bed with is worth the respect of a million doges. In any case, the Doge is a particularly close friend . . .'

We both laughed at that.

Downstairs in the courtyard, the little girl protested as a nurse appeared to take her to bed.

'Go to bed!' Ernesta called down to add her weight to the side of sense. 'It's late.'

'Mamma, Mamma! I have learned a new song.'

The girl sang a snatch of a gondolier's lament, but with lyrics I had not expected. Even Ernesta had to blush.

'Wherever does she learn those things?' Ernesta asked. She squeezed my arm.

'Come along. There is someone else I suppose you should meet, if only to know to avoid him outside my four walls.'

Ernesta paused so that her monkey could climb onto

her shoulder. I had already noticed that evening that instead of its usual jewelled collar, the monkey was wearing a string of pearls. The Duke's pearls. Ernesta held on to the monkey's tail as we walked to the salon on the *piano nobile.* The monkey held the largest pearl – the pendant – like a blackbird's egg in one tiny old-man's hand of a paw.

'You might want to wear your mask,' Ernesta told me.

I did as I was told and when a footman opened the door I waved Ernesta through ahead of me. After all, I was still a boy.

'The Duke Magherini,' said the footman with due ceremony. It was the man who had bought Ernesta the pearl that now lay in my pocket. I was fascinated to see him. In my head he was a swashbuckling adventurer. Handsome and suave. In reality, he was shorter than I expected. He was not handsome. He had a weak chin. His eyes were close-set and mean. No wonder he has to buy kisses, I thought, a little cruelly.

The Duke blanched when he saw the monkey on Ernesta's shoulder.

'Last time he was here Umberto bit him,' Ernesta whispered. 'But it was his own fault. No one holds Umberto's tail except me.'

'You've brought that bloody monkey,' the Duke complained.

'Umberto says he has forgiven you,' Ernesta replied smoothly. 'But you will have to remember to behave yourself in his company.'

'And who is he?' The Duke nodded in my direction.

'A relation,' said Ernesta. 'From Turin.'

I bowed.

'I didn't expect to have to share you,' the Duke told her.

'Come now,' said Ernesta. 'You have never really had me to yourself.'

The Duke seethed through the whole of his visit. He threw dark looks in my direction all the while. I said nothing. Ernesta led the conversation. She talked of music and art. She teased the Duke about his extravagant hat. He did not like to be teased.

Worse still, I imagined the Duke felt he had bought Ernesta's time with those pearls but the fact that Umberto was wearing them was obviously meant to tell him Ernesta expected more than baubles for her heart.

Eventually, the Duke gave up.

'It's late,' he said. 'If your relation isn't tired enough to go to bed, then I certainly am.'

Ernesta made a show of protesting at his departure but when she went to kiss the Duke, Umberto hissed and chattered.

'You are still not in his favour,' said Ernesta.

'Will I ever be properly in yours?' the Duke replied.

'He loves you,' I observed when the Duke had left us and Ernesta was undressing again.

'Perhaps he does, but he is brash and too bold and often angry.'

'Angry with you?'

'Angry with womankind.'

Ernesta took my hand and turned her face towards me so that I could see the faint shadow of a bruise now that her make-up was gone.

'He has passions far too violent for my taste. I believe he will not stop until he throttles some poor girl. That is why I will not see him alone again.'

I was aghast. I had read of such passions but hoped never to experience them myself. 'Why do you receive him at your house at all?'

'Because having him as an enemy would be even more dangerous than having him as a lover. At least when he is in my home, I can see exactly how he plans to harm me.'

I shuddered at the thought.

'I prefer my lovers to be gentle.'

She combed out her hair. I watched from a chair in the corner. After a while she put down her brush and crossed the room to take my hands.

'Dear Luciana.' She pulled me to my feet. 'I prefer lovers like you.'

I did not know what to say.

Bending over me, Ernesta brushed her rubious lips across my cheek. She had kissed me before, but this time, I felt something different. I felt intent in her embrace. A moment of silence and stillness hung between us before Ernesta finally took hold of my face and drew my lips to her own.

'You are such a beautiful child,' Ernesta whispered. 'I have wanted to kiss you since I first saw you at the Ridotto. Boy or girl, I knew I'd have you.'

'But—'

'Don't resist, my love.'

I closed my eyes tightly, shutting out the face that drew closer to my own. What would Giacomo have said?

Ernesta persisted, kissing me softly on my nose, my ears, my eyelids, my forehead and then on my lips again. Her touch was lighter and gentler than any man's. Her breath was sweet, like sugared almonds, her skin as smooth as satin as she pressed her cheek against mine. Finding my lips still tightly shut after all this gentle persuasion, Ernesta made a little noise of amusement before she set to work at prising them open with her tongue.

I did open my mouth then. To protest.

'Ernesta! What about Giacomo?'

'He would not grudge you my love. He's very generous with his own.'

Ernesta drew away from me to see my reaction. She knew she had upset me.

'Oh, come now.' She drew a finger down my cheek. 'You are not the first girl he has taken to my little house.'

'It belongs to you?'

'Yes. He could hardly take you back to his family home. You must have known that.'

I shook my head.

Ernesta led me to the bed and gently pushed me backwards onto it. She lay down beside me and lifted one of my hands. She laced her fingers through mine.

'His heart is big enough to hold many loves. Your heart will be too.'

She kissed my fingers.

'Sometimes we have to accept that a good lover stays only long enough to teach us how to be better for the next one. Kiss me,' said Ernesta. 'I am the next one.'

And soon a warm hand was creeping beneath my white shirt, caressing a nipple that hardened in spite of my misgivings. I let Ernesta's hands wander curiously over my body for a moment or two, unsure of what I should be doing in return. I guessed I should probably be doing exactly the same as she was doing to me, but the move from kissing another woman to actually caressing her eager, feminine body seemed too great a step to take.

Ernesta was patient, whispering sweet little words of pleasure and encouragement until finally I felt myself ready. But she herself was far from shy. She had struggled out of her gown at the earliest possible opportunity and happily laid her half-naked torso against mine. She pushed my clothing out of the way so our bodies rested in some places skin to skin. When I was finally undressed, my nakedness felt more than skin-deep.

'Touch me, Luciana,' Ernesta murmured, 'touch me too.' Her quickening breath softened her commanding words. I moved a shaking hand from her back in the direction of her ample breasts. She shifted eagerly to make herself more easily reached. She held herself slightly above me and to my side, jutting out her perfect breasts like fleshy battlements so the target for attention could not be more obvious.

I began to caress Ernesta's breasts, in the way she had caressed mine.

'Kiss them,' she begged me, 'suck them. They're yours to do with whatever you wish.' I poked out my tongue and her tiny pink nipples stiffened immediately. She pulled my head closer to her breast and thrust one of the quivering buds right into my mouth. 'Bite it,' she commanded softly. Part of my mind still fought against the suggestion but I soon found I had gently closed my teeth together on the stiff little bud.

'More,' she rasped. 'Bite a little bit harder.'

As I paid attention to my new lover's breasts, Ernesta's

253

hands had crept lower. Suddenly noticing the shift in focus, I tried to push them away.

'Don't,' I pleaded. 'I really don't think I want—'

'This?' It was too late.

I closed my eyes as Ernesta's fingers tangled in my pubic hair, waiting for the inevitable. Soft but insistent fingers on my clitoris made me bite my lip as the sensation sent tiny prickling arrows all over my body. Ernesta kissed me again, thrusting her tongue inside my mouth as, down below, her fingers echoed the action.

I called out.

'Ssssssh,' she whispered. 'My darling. You're so wet, so ready.' A peculiar tingle ran down my spine at these words, which echoed my teacher's so closely. 'Just lie back. I'm going to make you come all over me . . . You don't have to do a thing.'

The words, so quiet yet so commanding, stripped me of my last inhibitions. I raised my hips and pressed my body against her thigh. Ernesta smiled her approval before she ducked her head down between my thighs.

With the first flick of her tongue Ernesta found my clitoris. I bucked my hips upwards with the surprise of the perfect hit and while they were thus raised, she grabbed my buttocks and used them to lift me still further. Her tongue moved slowly at first, up and down the shiny shell-pink skin of my vulva, tantalising my clitoris. Her eyes were on mine all the time. Every sinew in my body was vibrating with sensation.

'Let go,' she demanded. 'I can feel you're almost there.'

Ernesta's face was wet from her nose to her chin and I knew that it wasn't all saliva. When she returned to her frantic tonguing this time, my hips bucked higher again, as if to drive her tongue into me. I was not thinking of my teacher any longer. My body took over. I could no longer even think of resistance as I shuddered and groaned and covered Ernesta's face with sweet cum.

When I had finished shaking, Ernesta crawled up the bed to lie beside me and kissed me carefully on the mouth. I tasted my own love juice on her lips. What had I done? I was going straight to Hell. And yet I found that I was happy.

My happiness was to be brief. The following morning, my father did not leave for his warehouse as usual, but instead called me into his office. He had a smile on his face. A horrible smile. I suppose he has not had much practice over the years. But it was a smile nonetheless as he informed me, 'Luciana, I have the most marvellous news.'

'Really, Father?' I didn't suppose for one moment he was going to tell me he had decided to get rid of Maria, but I hoped for something rather better than I was about to hear.

'I want to talk to you about marriage.'

'For you, dear Father?' For a moment, I convinced myself that all would turn out well.

'Not for me, you silly girl.' My father reached for my hand and I knew I was in trouble. 'For you. For the most beautiful girl in all Venezia.'

'But no one has seen me. How can they know I am beautiful?'

'You have been noticed in church, of course. And there can be no questioning your goodness and your purity.'

If only he knew.

'You are a true prize for any man.'

'But which man intends to make me his?'

'It is such wonderful news,' my father continued. 'You are sure to be delighted.'

'Then let me begin to enjoy my great happiness right away!'

'I have received an offer for your hand from the Duke Magherini.'

I fainted. My father assumed it was with delight.

How could I marry the Duke Magherini? I could not tell my father he was a thug and a villain. As far as he was concerned, I knew nothing of the man except my father's recommendation of him.

I made every other objection I could think of.

'I am not worthy of being a duchess!' I began.

'My darling,' said my father. 'You are worth a thousand queens.'

'But he is the first man to ask. We may get a better offer,' I said, in direct contradiction of my last point.

'A better offer than a duke? For a merchant's daughter from Turin?'

'Am I not a little young still to be married?'

'You are seventeen, my love. You are of the perfect age. Though I appreciate you may be a little unprepared compared to other girls since you lack the guidance of a mother. I will ask Maria to tell you what will be expected of you. No, hang on,' he muttered to himself. 'Maria wouldn't know. She's not yet married herself.'

Oh my father. My dear sweet father. So utterly blind to what happened under his very own roof.

'No,' he concluded. 'I will not listen to any more of your silly objections. This is the perfect match for you. The Duke will visit us tomorrow afternoon.'

'What if I don't like him?' I burst out.

My father placed his hands on my shoulders and looked into my eyes.

'You will like him. You will love him. You will be a perfect wife.'

He smiled at me. He was as happy as I had seen him since my mother died. I smiled back, though inside, worms of misery were already eating my heart.

43

Oh, I knew all about worms of misery. I'd been experiencing more than a few of my own since the day I called Marco's bluff. I had heard nothing from him. Not even a note to acknowledge he had received my last email. I felt well and truly stupid. He'd taken all that he wanted from me. He'd had his fun and probably posted the video to Rude Tube. I had been an idiot to think that he could ever want more from me. He was a man who had dated supermodels. A little virtual fun was fine, but he was never going to let himself be seen with a dowdy academic on his arm.

Neither had I heard anything more from Steven. There was no follow-up to his strange and unexpected email. Of course, I had reread it over and over. Sometimes his protestations of love chimed loudest in my heart but most of the time it was that awful, damning phrase. 'A vanilla sort of love.' To think I'd thought that was the ideal. I cursed my naivety.

I couldn't go back to the library after that morning when Marco had me pleasure myself for his entertainment. Fortunately, I had scanned some of Luciana's diary entries so I had plenty to be going on with. It was frustrating from time to time, when I found a word that hadn't scanned so well, not to be able to refer to the original, but the frustration was a small price to pay to avoid humiliation for a while. I could not face going back to the library, sitting at that desk, knowing what was inside the drawer. Assuming the vibrator was still there. Had Marco retrieved and cleaned it, ready for the next girl? I shuddered at the thought. Then there was the mirror. Was its presence why Silvio had regarded me so strangely? How many times had he seen it before?

Nick and Bea noticed that I was spending more time in the office. Neither of them knew about the cybersex, of course, but Bea knew about my flirtation with Marco and guessed that something might have gone wrong. She also knew I had heard from Steven, if not about the details of his proposal. Bea offered me her services as a confidante and I took them as far as I could bear. When I finished talking about my upset and confusion, she told me, 'There are nice men out there. Uncomplicated men. Men who want to make you happy and who don't know the first thing about playing games. Men like Nick. Nice guys can be sexy too.'

She was right about Nick in one respect. He was the archetypal nice guy. When he joined us at the bar, he fetched us drinks and paid us compliments. He jumped to his feet every time Bea or I got up to leave the table. He was self-deprecating and funny. I knew that he liked me. But he was not Steven. He was not Marco. When Nick placed his hand on the small of my back to guide me through a crowd, I felt no electricity. I could not imagine falling into his arms. What was wrong with me? Why did my idea of love have to be spiced with distance, pain and hurt? Why did I only lust after the unattainable? Steven: the arrogant academic with his heart in his trousers. Marco: the elusive billionaire. Where his heart was, nobody could know. Assuming he had a heart at all.

Then, of course, Marco broke his silence. My chest ached as I opened his email. I was ready for another humiliation. Instead, I read this:

I asked you what you wanted to happen and you answered me, at length and with an honesty I hoped for yet didn't expect. For that, the very least I owe you is my own honest answer to the same question.

I too wish that we could meet face to face. Like you, I have a very clear picture in my mind of my charming correspondent, but I am aware that a photograph doesn't tell one everything. They say the camera never lies, but in the era of Photoshop, we know for sure that's not the truth. However, I agree with you there is one thing we cannot fake, which will always give us away. It is the look in our eyes.

Though I saw you only in a photograph before I admitted you to my library, I had the strangest sense that you could see into my soul. Perhaps that we'd even known each other before. Our conversations since have only served to make me more certain that you, and only you, could really understand me. Your willingness to open yourself up for me, even though I couldn't be with you, showed a trust that thrilled my soul. You are brave and you are beautiful, Sarah. Your trust in me is a gift greater than you can imagine. I do not want to take you for granted.

So, yes, what I want more than anything is to meet you in person. Properly. What prevents me, I cannot tell you. I am afraid that even you, with your loving heart, would not be able to handle the truth of who I am. I am not the man in those photographs. For that I am more sorry than you could know. I am a coward, I suppose.

His email was ridiculously cryptic. I wrote my reply in seconds.

Don't be a coward. You could be the Devil and I would still love you.

The following morning I received an invitation to a ball.

44

News of a party at the Palazzo Donato quickly spread through the university. Several people had received invitations, including Nick and Bea. No one could quite believe it.

Of course I had hoped that my time in Venice, which coincided with Carnevale, would bring me the opportunity to don a mask of my own, but Nick had been pretty scathing about the chances.

'All the parties around Carnevale these days are run for tourists. You pay a thousand euros for the privilege of sitting next to Dusty and Sandy from Ohio, in town for their fiftieth wedding anniversary. You wanted to sit next to a count. So did they. You end up spending the evening talking about the price of gas.'

'Sounds very romantic,' I said.

But even Nick had to admit that the invitation to the party at the Donato house was rather more promising. There was no price on the bottom of it, for a start. The invitations, on stiff creamy card, had been delivered by hand. They were beautiful, decorated with a simple monkey's-head motif.

There were plenty of theories as to why the Palazzo Donato was opening its doors after so long. A favourite was that Marco had finally run out of money and agreed to open his house to some luxury-goods firm that would hold a ball that was essentially a sales pitch. But I hoped otherwise. My own invitation had come with a handwritten note.

'You shall go to the ball,' was all it said.

Marco was a man who had paid for Prince to sing at a girlfriend's birthday party. Was it possible that this ball was just for me?

I was enchanted by the possibility. But I was also a little disappointed that my first meeting with the man I had been busy falling in love with would be in a crowded room. After our cybersex in the library, I had imagined he would invite me to dinner alone. For that reason, I considered turning the invitation down. Wasn't inviting me to a party that would be thronged with other people just another way of keeping me at arm's length? I said as much to Bea, but she persuaded me that to RSVP in the negative would be cutting off my own nose to spite my face. Besides, she and Nick were raring to go.

We can't go without you,' she begged me.

'He must have had this party planned for weeks,' I said, looking for reassurance that he'd actually planned it in days. 'He's invited me as an afterthought.'

'In that case, we'll trash the place,' Bea assured me.

I didn't want that. I had come to love the Palazzo Donato and its ancient treasures as much as I had ever loved any pile of bricks and mortar. I wrestled with my conscience for a little longer. Wasn't I just doing it again? Allowing Marco to think I was at his beck and call? But if this really was going to be the only way he would see me . . . I had to go. Once we were face to face, we could sort out this stupidity. I could insist on normalising our relationship. And perhaps there was something romantic about the idea? To finally lock eyes across a crowded room? I thought of Romeo and Juliet. Star-crossed lovers. Maybe it would be just like that. Hand to hand at last.

'Who cares how long ago he thought up this party? He's trying to impress you,' said Bea. 'You must go.'

I suspected she was more interested in the ball than my heart.

'Alright,' I agreed.

Bea immediately adopted the 'headless chicken' approach to the whole event.

'What am I going to wear?'

I, too, wondered exactly what the protocol was. Did you have to dress in period clothing or could you use your mask to accessorise something more contemporary? In the end, it was Luciana who persuaded me I should go the whole hog.

Luciana's disappointment at having to go to the Ridotto in boy's clothing helped me make up my mind. How many opportunities would I have in my life to wear a full-on ballgown and not feel overdressed? Bea agreed and we slipped away from the office one afternoon to visit an agency that hired dresses by the evening. Unfortunately, they had not changed their stock since the nineteen-eighties, and while the dresses were most definitely extravagant, they spoke more of 'loadsamoney' than 'luxury'. All crushed velvet and cheap gold-coloured tulle.

That said, Bea eventually found a red velvet gown that fitted her perfectly and was not too 'Wild West casino' once she had unpicked the white lace round the neck. But with a day to go before the ball, I still had no dress and was facing spending the evening in the little black dress that had been everywhere from the Proms to London's sweatiest night-clubs. Including the sex club where Steven and I had finally unravelled. I knew it flattered me but I was just a little disappointed to have to put it on again. It wasn't exactly festive. Apart from anything else, it seemed like a bad omen. I resigned myself to making another shopping trip.

But when Bea and I got back to the office, I found a huge cardboard box on my desk. I was not expecting a delivery. The only thing I could possibly imagine it contained was some of my belongings, sent from England because I hadn't responded to Steven's email. Bea was altogether keener to know what was inside. She offered me her letter-knife to slit the parcel tape.

'It's really heavy,' said the post-boy, who was still hanging around. Any excuse. He had a thing about Bea. Most men did.

'Come on, Sarah,' Bea encouraged me. 'It won't bite.'

'I don't know about that,' said the post-boy. 'It was so heavy I thought there might be an animal in there.'

'Don't be ridiculous,' Bea took the letter-knife back. 'If you won't open it . . .'

'Careful,' I said, as she slashed at the tape.

'Oh!'

The flaps of the box fell open. Inside was another box. This box was altogether more glamorous, however. It was shiny white and embossed with just one word. Dior.

'Wow,' Bea breathed.

I stepped forward to take a look. 'Probably just used the box to send some papers,' I said, but my heart rate was definitely rising as I lifted the white box out of the larger one and set it down on my desk.

'Don't be ridiculous, Sarah. Someone has sent you a present!'

As an idea formed in my head as to the identity of the sender, I found myself wishing I could open the box alone, without Bea's running commentary and the inevitable conclusions she might draw.

Nevertheless, I lifted away the lid of the box. The contents were so tightly packed, it wasn't immediately clear what they were. It looked as though the box had been haphazardly stuffed with scraps of silk and feathers. But when I reached in and tried to pull those feathers out . . .

I didn't think I had ever seen such a beautiful dress in my life.

'Oh my goodness,' Bea sighed. The sight of the dream frock transported her as much as it did me. A fitted bodice flared into a skirt that already seemed to be dancing. Bea shepherded the post-boy out of the room so I could put the dress on. It was incredible. It fitted me closely, following and sharpening the contours of my body so that I looked like a better version of me. My perfect self.

'Whoever sent this dress knows your measurements exactly. It's from Marco, isn't it?'

I didn't need to read the card to find out for sure.

There was a mask, too. It was Bea who lifted that out of the box and stripped away the tissue paper. Having grown up in a family of four sisters, Bea had very little concept of ownership and she was enjoying this gift just as much as I was.

'Oh wow!' she breathed.

The mask was beautiful. It was not the half-face I would have chosen for myself but a full-face mask, gilded, with a serene brow and rosebud lips. It was only when Bea finally handed it over that I realised what was different about this particular piece. There were no holes at the side of the mask for the ribbons that would tie the mask in place. Neither was there a handle by which the wearer might hold it in front of her face like a fan. There was no way to keep the mask in place except for a button stitched to the back side of the lips.

'Oh my God,' said Bea. 'It's one of those. It's an actual *servetta muta.*'

The 'Mute Maidservant'. Of course I had heard of this type of mask before, but I had yet to see one in real life. I couldn't believe anyone still made them except for decoration. Surely Marco wasn't going to expect me to wear it? As long as I wore it, I would be unable to speak.

'This must be a mistake,' I said.

* * *

265

But I knew Marco would not have chosen this particular mask by accident. In which case, what was the meaning of it? Why did he want me to be silenced? A strange fear suddenly gripped me. The last time a man bought me clothes was the day Steven brought home that hateful beaded G-string. When I thought about the mask, I was reminded for some reason of the woman I had seen at L'Enfer – the one sandwiched between two men with a collar around her neck. This *servetta muta* was a similar symbol of servitude. I wasn't going to put it on. I laid it on my desk and just looked at it until, thinking of Luciana's diary entry regarding the Ridotto, I had an idea of my own.

'I want you to wear the Dior,' I told Bea.

'What? You're kidding! That dress was a gift to you. It suits you perfectly.'

'I'm not sure it suits me at all.'

'Oh, I get it. You want to send a message that you can't be bought.'

'Is it that transparent?' I asked.

Bea nodded.

'Well, good. Because that *is* the message I want to send. I can't be bought. I don't want gifts, I want to be treated as an equal, not a puppet. And that means an end to playing games.'

Bea laughed. 'Ordinarily, I would tell you not to be so stupid. A man who sends good gifts unprompted is so rare as to be almost mythical, and this is a bloody good gift. But I can see that you're playing a long game.'

'I don't want to play games,' I murmured.

'Nonsense. You're playing a long game and I am only too happy to enable you by wearing your unwanted couture. It's Dior!' she shrieked.

'And the mask?'

'And the mask. What will you wear?'

'I'll wear your red velvet, of course.'

★ ★ ★

As I donned Bea's red dress for the evening, and completed my disguise with an extravagant powdered wig, I pondered my decision. Perhaps I should have been flattered that Marco had sent me such an expensive dress. But I didn't like the way he assumed I would not have already chosen something for myself and that my choice might have had significance beyond fit and flattery. Plus, why should I be the one at a disadvantage? Easily and instantly recognisable, while I had no way of knowing who my host was until he revealed himself. If he wanted to be able to observe me more closely, then I wanted exactly the same. I wanted to be able to watch him across a room and see how he acted with his guests. I wanted to see if the old playboy was still on the prowl. How would he react when he approached the woman in the dress he had paid for and realised it was not me? Would he be offended? The worst-case scenario was that he would consider Bea a more fitting recipient for the Parisian finery.

'You look so very beautiful,' said Nick, as Bea and I entered the room in our party clothes. 'Both of you,' he added. 'I shall be the luckiest man in Venice, turning up at the palazzo with you ladies on my arm.'

Together, we three walked down to the landing-raft nearest to the university, where a gondola was already waiting for us. Marco had sent it, of course. Later we would learn that he had sent gondolas all over the city to bring his guests to the front door. Nick and the gondolier helped me and Bea into the shallow boat, which remained steady despite the unbalancing weight of lace and silk and feathers upon it. Giggling, Bea collapsed onto the cushions, sinking into her skirts. I followed suit. We squeezed alongside each other in the *felce*. Nick sat opposite. I was sure he was grateful for his mask, which made it just a little less obvious that he couldn't take his eyes off our cleavages.

'You know what?' said Bea, as we made our stately progress

267

down the Grand Canal. 'You look far better in that dress than I ever could.'

It was true I had come to like the red velvet number more than I could have imagined when I first saw Bea pluck it from its hanger. By torchlight it was almost classy.

'And you look like a goddess in the Dior,' I returned the compliment. It was such an incredible dress. Wearing it had transformed Bea from my giggly friend into a more regal version of herself. A veritable queen.

The journey by gondola was the perfect way to prepare for the evening ahead. It was so wonderful to be on the Grand Canal that night. It was the Tuesday before Lent, Martedì Grasso, and tonight the parties would be more extravagant than ever as the citizens of Venice prepared themselves for the austerity of the days to come. Not that many Venetians observed the prescribed period of abstinence these days. That said, Nick had suggested he could do with a couple of weeks off the booze. But not tonight. Tonight was going to be all about excess.

As we drifted along, we passed dozens of gondolas bearing costumed passengers. They nodded as they sailed by. It was strange, I thought, that the wearing of masks enabled people to be more friendly than usual.

From the bridges and the bars on the canalside, tourists called and waved. The flashes of their cameras glittered like stardust.

'It's like being in a film,' said Bea. 'All these people trying to photograph us.'

'And why not?' said Nick. 'We are quite the smartest gondola in town.'

We had Marco Donato to thank for that and I, for one, could not wait to express my gratitude in person.

45

Outside the Palazzo Donato, several gondolas were already moored so their passengers could disembark. As we waited for a space to dock, I looked up at the house. Usually so dark and silent, that night every window was ablaze. Flaming torches marked the corners of the landing-raft, where liveried servants were helping guests make the tricky transition from boat to, almost, dry land. I recognised none of them. They must have been hired for the evening. Where, I wondered, was Silvio? I gazed at the disembarking passengers, in their extraordinary finery. Clearly, none of these people had been reduced to the Eighties-style monstrosities in the dress-hire shop. Bea cooed over a woman in a metallic dress with the shimmer of molten mercury. Her mask was coated in the same material, giving the impression that she might dissolve into a puddle of quicksilver at any moment. Another woman wore an enormous domino, the extravagantly flounced cloak made popular in the eighteenth century. The ruffled hood made her seem so top-heavy that as she made the step from gondola to raft, I held my breath and waited for a splash.

Who were all these people? I knew the Palazzo Donato had not welcomed guests for over a decade. Were the guests walking into the house through an arcade of blazing torches old friends? What did they think about the years of social exile? They must have been curious. Just as I had been curious to see what lay behind the front door on the first morning

I came to see Luciana's letters. It was strange to be coming to the house to find it so busy and full of life. I felt oddly protective of the usually empty courtyard and the library. I hoped the library, at least, would remain out of bounds. It was my sanctuary. It was a space I wanted to share with no one but Marco. I hoped he felt the same.

At last, our gondola drew alongside the landing-raft and the liveried servants turned their attention to us. I let myself be lifted onto the raft by two strong pairs of arms. Bea, whose borrowed dress was altogether more extravagant, needed not only the pull on to the raft but a push from the gondola beneath as well. Nick joined forces with the gondolier to hoist Bea to safety, then followed quickly behind her. In his velvet trousers, he didn't need a hand at all.

'So here we are,' said Bea. 'I have to say, your boyfriend has put on quite a show.'

'He's not my boyfriend,' I reminded her.

'I have a feeling that after tonight he will be. I mean, all this *must* be for you. He hasn't had a party in what? A decade?'

'I'm sure he was having the party anyway,' I said, as I'd always said, though I still hoped I was wrong. 'Put your mask on properly. Otherwise there's no point having swapped clothes.'

The tiny courtyard that had been so tranquil the first time I visited was transformed. The fountain was in full flow, its glittering jets turned into natural disco lights by the flaming torches that lit every corner. More liveried servants circulated here, bearing trays of prosecco, turned liquid gold by the flames.

Nick took two glasses of wine and turned to offer them to Bea and me. I accepted mine gratefully, as did Bea before she realised that her *servetta muta* would absolutely prevent her from being able to enjoy it. She signalled to me with anguished eyes.

'Not yet,' I answered. 'I want to see his reaction before you take off the mask.'

She grunted her assent.

'You know what?' said Nick. 'I think those masks should be compulsory in the university. I'd get a whole lot more work done.'

Bea grunted something else.

'What's that? You'd be happy to take my students so I can prepare for the Paris conference next month?' Nick teased. 'Bea, you are so very kind.'

I scanned the crowd that had gathered in the courtyard. I had an idea of what I was looking for. I estimated from the photographs I had seen of him that Marco would be at least six foot in height. As a younger man, he'd had a swimmer's physique. That probably wouldn't have changed so much. Judging by the pictures of his father and his grandfather, the Donatos were not a family that ran to fat in middle age.

'Which one is he?' Nick asked.

'Hard to tell. Everyone's wearing masks.'

'Look for someone who seems proprietorial?' Nick suggested. 'Is there anyone who looks as though he's playing the host? Anyone with an unusual number of attractive women around him? There must be people here who could pick him out even with a mask on. No one is that anonymous. The way they walk, talk, even the shape of their ears will give them away.'

Bea grunted something along the lines of 'get on with it'. She was obviously keen to be introduced so she might swap the hateful *servetta muta* for the white mask she had brought to replace it once my little joke was over. I was very conscious of this. There wasn't a lot of time. It was a shame I would not get much opportunity to watch Marco as he moved among his friends.

We followed the crowd through to the salon on the *piano*

nobile. The doors with their monkey-headed roundels were wide open. Ernesta and her pet watched proceedings from their place on the wall.

'That's a Carriera,' said Nick when he saw the painting. 'Worth a bloody fortune.'

Bea held her mask against her face but dropped the button from between her teeth to tell me, 'Girl, you have lucked out.'

But had I?

I surveyed the room. There were so many women jostling for space in front of the mirror and, to my mind, they all had more to show off than I did. Who were they? Were any of these women the girls who had draped themselves over Marco for the cameras? Was he talking to one of them now? Was that him in the blue suit and the plague mask? Or was he the man dressed as a joker? How about the sombre-looking fellow in the black cloak and tricorn? It was impossible to tell.

In the Dior dress that squeezed her waist as small as a wasp's, Bea was turning plenty of heads, both male and female. One of them must be my epistolary lover. I longed for him to reveal himself to me. Despite the red of my dress, I felt myself fading from sight.

46

The afternoon of the Duke's visit arrived. Maria was far more excited than I was. She brushed out my hair twice as enthusiastically as usual before arranging it in a style of ludicrous complexity, which was apparently all the rage. It was especially ludicrous given that I intended to wear a veil.

When she had finished messing with my hair, she pinched my cheeks to bring some life to them.

'Ow,' I complained.

'You don't look well,' she told me. 'What is the matter with you? Aren't you excited you're meeting your future husband?'

'A potential suitor,' I corrected her. 'I have the right to turn any suitor down.'

'If you want to be turned out on your ear,' said Maria. 'A duke has come to ask for your hand and you're talking about turning him down? You will get no better offer, believe me. If I were you I would stop talking so ungratefully and do my best to make sure the Duke is impressed.'

I nodded. There was no point discussing the matter further with Maria, who could not see how any woman could be complete without a husband. In that case,

273

perhaps I should have told her to look to her own behaviour. Chasing a priest? She might as well have chased the Doge himself.

She pinched my cheeks again. This time she pinched so hard she brought tears to my eyes.

'The idea is to make me look beautiful,' I reminded her. 'Not desperate.'

'Men like to see a girl on the verge of tears,' said Maria, ridiculously.

But not so ridiculous as she imagined when it came to the Duke. Yes, I had sensed when I met him at Ernesta's house that he was a man who liked to see a woman cry in pain as much as in sadness. I held the courtesan's pearl in my hand. I grasped it so tightly that my fingernails dug into my palm. I thought about Ernesta's bruise. I would avenge my friend. Or at least, since my power was so limited, I would let the Duke know he had no secrets from me.

I planned it all very carefully. I was the picture of virginal innocence that afternoon with my face scrubbed, my hair covered and not a hint of ostentation in my plain but feminine dress, which was the very opposite of the trousers I had grown used to. But I held in my hands a string of worry beads. No one would think that too odd, I decided. After all, I was a naïve young girl about to meet a man to whom I might promise my life. I had so little experience of men, other than my relatives and the few ageing male servants my father would allow at the house. Of course I was nervous. Hence the beads. But I also held in my hand Ernesta's pearl. And what no one else knew is that I had snipped the string of my worry beads, so that the moment I wished it, they would fly apart and cover the floor of the salon. After that, I had to rely upon the Duke having at least some gentlemanly instincts.

My father looked so very pleased to have such an important guest. I was disappointed in him for that. I had not expected him to be so overawed by the Duke's title but Papà could not do enough to make the odious man comfortable. The table in the salon was laden with the sort of feast I would have expected at Christmas. The cook had outdone herself. There were enough cakes to feed all the children in the city's *ospedali*. Of course, I would not be touching any of them. Neither would Maria, though as soon as we entered the room, I could tell she did not know where to look first. At the Duke? At the cakes? At the Duke? The cakes won out. They were certainly more attractive to me than the peacocking braggart at the window. He had chosen to stand there in the hope of showing himself off to best effect.

My father introduced me to my wealthy suitor and I played the innocent girl. The Duke showed none of the nervousness he had shown in Ernesta's presence. For my part, I expressed my delight and surprise at having received such an illustrious offer for my hand. I kept my eyes to the floor, raising them only in the direction of my father to see how he was enjoying my little charade. Papà smiled at me dotingly. Oh, Papà. He couldn't wait to make me this other man's responsibility, no matter how much it cost him.

The Duke seemed to enjoy my performance too. He recounted the story he had told my father regarding having seen me in church. He claimed he had noticed me week after week, gazing modestly at the prayer book in my hands, looking up only to see our Lord's face when I took the sacrament. He could tell I was a good pious girl, unlike so many of the women in this terrible city. My father nodded in agreement. As did Maria.

'Maria is deeply pious too,' said my father. 'There is nothing she won't do for the church.'

One of the housemaids was serving the coffee and offering round some pastries. Overhearing my father's remark about Maria's piety, the poor girl almost dropped the coffee pot. Maria crucified the girl with a look as she helped herself to an enormous serving of cake. I refused.

'I'm too nervous to eat,' I claimed. Everyone was happy with that. Good. Nerves were my cover. I fiddled with the beads in my hand. Once or twice the Duke looked to see what it was I was doing as the beads went click, click, click. Perhaps he thought I was saying a rosary. He was the one who should have been praying.

My father and the Duke made chit-chat about the summer in Venezia. They both believed it was the hottest June they had ever experienced. Neither could wait for the autumn to set in. The very best time to be in the city was the springtime, of course. Before the great heat started, when the days were still cool and clear.

'What do you think?' the Duke asked me.

I told him I agreed. Venezia was best of all in the spring.

Then one of the servants came upstairs to tell my father he was wanted. A business associate had come calling with important news. The Duke looked slightly perturbed. Perhaps my handsome dowry had gone down in a ship newly scuppered by the Turks. My father excused himself.

'I'm sure it is not so important,' he said to our guest. 'But you understand that any large business such as ours requires constant attention. Maria will keep you both company. Maria.' My father turned to her. 'Please ensure the Duke has all he needs.'

'Perhaps the Duke would like some more cake?' Maria offered at once.

He demurred and so did I but Maria saw no reason to deny herself. And while she was helping herself to another *cornetto*, I saw my chance. I had been rolling the worry beads in my hand for the entire interview. Now it was time to let them go. With a flick of my wrist, I flung the beads onto the floor. The pearl went with them.

'Oh!' I exclaimed.

'You have been worrying too much,' said the Duke.

I got down on my hands and knees and began to scoop up the beads. Possibly thinking this might be his chance to sneak a kiss, the Duke joined me on the carpet and gathered as many beads as he could see. I left the pearl for him. When he picked it up, I saw his brow crease in confusion. Of course he recognised it. It was, as Ernesta had promised me, a jewel quite unusual and rare, with its glimmering surface blazing pink, orange and yellow like a sunset reflected in the lagoon.

The Duke held the pearl in his hand and stared at it. I threw back my veil. When I reached to take back the pearl, we locked eyes. I knew the Duke remembered where he had seen that pearl before. He also remembered where he had last seen me. We remained on the carpet, just staring at each other. I touched my fingers to my forehead as though I were tipping a cap. Such a masculine gesture cleared the fog of the Duke's memory absolutely. He got to his feet and looked down at me as though I had suddenly grown a horn. Or, more specifically, a tricorn.

'Oh, whatever's happened?' said Maria. Having loaded her plate with enough cake to satisfy even a girl of her appetites, she was ready to play chaperone again. And in the split-second her back had been turned, the Duke and I had ended up on the floor.

'I broke my worry beads,' I explained. 'The Duke has been so kind, picking them up for me.'

'What a lovely man he is,' said Maria, as though the Duke were not right there in front of her, glowering in my direction. His look was pure murder. 'What a wonderful husband he'll make.'

'Wonderful indeed,' I said.

My father returned. His face was flushed from having hurried back but he looked happy.

'My biggest competitor just lost a boat in the straits of Medina. It has doubled the value of my cargo. What do they say about an ill wind? What a wedding we shall have for you now, my dear daughter!'

'Thank you, Papà. I can't wait!'

'I must go,' said the Duke. 'I thank you for your hospitality, Signor Giordano, but I have business of my own to attend to.'

'I understand,' said my father. 'I hope this afternoon has convinced you of my daughter's charms.'

'She is a woman of many surprises,' said the Duke. He smiled in my direction, but the smile did not reach his eyes. It was more like the baring of teeth Umberto the monkey deployed to warn you he was minded to take a bite from your ear.

'We will see you again soon,' said my father as he escorted the Duke from the room. 'As you know, there will be no problem with the dowry. And I am certain you will not be disappointed. Luciana is a fine girl. Amiable. As intelligent as she needs to be. A musician and a seamstress. She has quite prodigious talents.'

'Indeed,' I heard the Duke respond. 'I need no convincing of that.'

With a curt bow, he left the room.

'Well, I think that went well,' said Maria. 'But you saucy minx. I know you threw those beads on the floor quite deliberately.'

I shivered at the thought that my trick had been uncovered, but it was soon clear Maria had no real idea why I'd tossed my beads to the ground.

'You wanted to test his manners, of course. And what a clever way to get a little closer to him. Did you smell his perfume? It's really quite exquisite. And his hair! Could you see if that's his natural colour?'

'I learned everything a girl needs to know,' I responded.

'Quite,' said Maria. 'You must be happy for the match to go ahead?'

'Oh yes,' I said, secure in the knowledge that it would not go ahead under any circumstances. The Duke would not want me now, knowing that I knew about his passion for Ernesta. I only wondered what excuse he would give my father. Poor Papà. When he came back into the room, he clasped both my hands in his.

'A wonderful match,' he said. 'I can tell you are going to be very happy. The Duke was very quiet as we walked to his gondola. That's a sign, I tell you. You have quite disconcerted him. I was exactly the same when I met your beloved mother. I do believe the Duke is in love.'

Of course the Duke was not in love. Not with me, at any rate. Though it was certainly possible that some passion had been aroused in him. As I got ready for bed that night, Maria asked if I wanted her to help me pray for a quick resolution to the matter of my engagement. I agreed, though I was hoping for a very different outcome.

With Maria gone to bed, I prepared for my nightly excursion. Dropping from the window held no fear for me now and I could cover the distance to Giacomo's house in a fraction of the time it had taken me before. He was back from his business and waiting for me. I told him about the Duke. He laughed, but it was a mirthless laugh.

'Clever girl,' he said. 'But I do not think you should thank God for having delivered you just yet.'

'What? You mean he might still want to marry me?'

'He might still want to marry your father's money,' my teacher said. 'Worse still, he might want revenge. He's not a man who takes humiliation lightly.'

'I didn't humiliate him. I warned him,' I said.

'Same thing.'

47

By ten o'clock the party was in full swing. The palazzo's garden, which had been such a haven of tranquility the first time I walked through it, was now as busy as any Ibizan nightclub in high season. The sound of the band was almost drowned out by chat and laughter. More liveried servants circulated with food and enough prosecco to drown a horse. After a whole bottle, Nick decided that he was drunk enough to dance. Bea joined him. Having begged me for mercy with an extravagant dumbshow, she had swapped the *servetta muta* for an ordinary mask with elastic to hold it to her face while she boogied. I hung on to Marco's mask now, though I still could not bring myself to wear it.

I was glad to see my friends enjoying themselves, but I was not yet able to relax. We had been at the party for two hours and Marco had still not revealed himself to me. Several times, I was sure that I had worked out which of the masked men was my secret lover, only to be disappointed when I got close and heard an English accent or saw that the eyes behind the mask were blue and not Marco's deep warm brown. Three times, I was asked to dance. My heart leapt upon the invitations, only to deflate when I discovered within seconds of having taken to the floor that my partner was not my secretive Italian billionaire but an accountant from Rome, a Mercedes dealer from New Jersey or, most memorably, the fishmonger from the Campo Santa Margherita.

'I never thought I would see the inside of this house,' he said. 'But when everyone's in a mask, class goes out of the window.'

I agreed. Though the fishmonger had the manners of a duke compared to the car dealer, who had tried to cop a feel through my voluminous skirts.

The dance ended. I excused myself from the fishmonger's company and went to find Nick and Bea again. Nick was loading another plate with *cichetti*, stuffing one in his mouth for every one he carried.

'Where's Bea?' I asked him.

'I thought she went to look for you,' said Nick through a mouthful of food. 'Last time I saw her she was heading over there.'

Nick waved a frilly cuff in the direction of the door that led to the library. If Bea had gone there, then I wanted to go with her.

I slipped into the library corridor just in time to see Bea – or rather the train of the Dior dress – disappear through the library door. I followed. If I'm honest, I was a little disappointed that the library door was open. It was my space. I felt proprietorial. I wanted be the one who showed Bea the room's treasures. I was surprised that she would go in there without me.

I put my hand on the door handle, ready to go in after her, but paused when I heard two voices. One was Bea's. The other was a man's voice. Without thinking, I put my ear closer to the door as I tried to get a sense of what was going on. Had Bea in fact arranged an assignation in the library? I didn't want to interrupt her if she had. Alas, the library door was too thick to allow me to hear much of the conversation inside. I turned the handle as slowly as I was able, so that the bolt slipped from its catch, then I leaned my weight against the door so that it opened just a crack, giving me the peephole that I needed.

Bea had her back to me. I was struck anew by how beautiful she looked in the dress, from every angle. The strict boning of the corset lent her perfect posture. The low cut of the neckline revealed the tips of her shoulder blades. Like me, she was wearing a wig, and its pigtail hung down the middle of her back, just waiting to be pulled.

The man I had heard speaking stood at the fireplace. He was wearing a long black cloak over black breeches and boots. On his head he wore a tricorn. On his face he wore a white mask that covered his features almost completely, with just holes for his eyes and a curve that revealed his mouth. He was tall but stooped. He was leaning on the mantelpiece but his pose was not casual. He seemed to be using the fireplace for support. He had one arm upon it while his other arm dangled loosely by his side, with an extravagant white lace cuff reaching beyond his fingertips. He had his head dropped low, as though he were looking into the flames.

As I watched, Bea arranged herself to best effect. She fluffed out the skirts of her dress. I could see that she was still wearing her mask.

'I've been looking forward to meeting you,' she said. 'It is you, isn't it?'

The man at the fireplace did not look at her.

'This is a beautiful house,' Bea continued. 'And a wonderful library. I have been wanting to get a look at this library for years. Why all the secrecy? And then a party like tonight? Fabulous party, by the way.'

Still, the man kept his masked face turned towards the flames. I could almost hear my heart pounding as I watched Bea try to engage with him. Of course I knew who she thought the stranger could be. Did he know that she wasn't me? A curious stand-off seemed to be developing. The man would not look up.

'Come on,' said Bea. 'This is getting ridiculous. You're Marco Donato. You must be.'

The man shook his head.

'Then who are you? Aren't you going to introduce yourself?'

'I work here,' said the man.

'You work here?'

I tried to get a better look through the gap. As far as I knew, the only person who worked at the house full-time was Silvio. Was it him? The voice hadn't sounded like Silvio's. It was deeper and it also sounded laboured. Rasping. As if the speaker couldn't fill his lungs.

'What do you work as?' asked Bea. I could tell from the way she asked the question that she wasn't convinced by the stranger's explanation.

'I work in the garden. I'm the gardener.'

'Really.'

I struggled to place the voice. I still couldn't. But it definitely wasn't Silvio. He wasn't that tall.

Taking off her mask with a flourish, Bea stepped towards the gardener and, before he could protest, she took up his free hand.

'Oh my God!'

Bea dropped the stranger's hand as quickly as she had taken it up.

'Oh, I'm sorry,' she said. 'I'm really sorry.'

The stranger turned his back on her, hugging his hand to himself like an injured child.

'I'm sorry. That was so rude. I didn't mean to—'

Bea gave a gasp of distress and made a run for the door. I just had time to jump out of the way before she wrenched the door open and dived through as though the Devil were on

her tail. She did not see me before she ran off down the corridor. I ran after her.

'Bea! Bea!'

She did not turn around.

48

I finally caught up with Bea at the end of the corridor. Not knowing the house, she had run herself into a dead end.

'Bea,' I said. 'What's happened?'

'Oh, Sarah, it's you! Thank goodness. I just made such a fool of myself. I went to look for you. While I was at it, I thought I'd have a snoop around. See if I could find the library. Well, I found the library but there was somebody already in there. It was a man. There was something about him that made me wonder if he was Marco Donato. I've asked practically every other man at the ball. One guy actually said he was Marco but later admitted he was a car salesman.'

'I think I met him.'

'Hands all over the place,' said Bea.

'That's the one. But the man in the library . . . ?'

'He was just standing at the fireplace. So still. Kind of defiant. I asked him who he was.'

I didn't let her know that I had heard the whole conversation.

'He wouldn't even look at me and, hey, I'm used to being looked at, even when I'm wearing a mask.'

She glanced at her cleavage. I couldn't help but laugh.

'Anyway, I pushed him for an answer and he told me that he was the gardener. I thought that sounded like bullshit so I took him by the hand.'

Bea put her hand to her mouth.

'Oh God, Sarah.'

'What is it?'

'I felt it before I looked.'

'What?'

'His hand. It was . . . it was like it was melted.'

I pressed her for more information.

'It felt like a lump of meat. And then I looked. Two of his fingers were gone and the rest were all shrivelled and stuck together.'

I shook my head.

'And I shouted out in shock. I couldn't help myself.'

She began to cry.

'Whatever must he have thought?' she said. 'Poor man, I was so rude. But I'd never seen anything so awful. Not in real life. I couldn't stop myself, it was such a horrible surprise. Oh Sarah. He's the one without his fingers. I don't have the right to cry. But I'm so embarrassed.'

I wrapped my arm around Bea's shoulders.

'I need to go and apologise.'

'I'm not sure that will make it better,' I said.

'You're right. Oh, I'm such a bitch.'

I tried to assure her that she wasn't.

'You'll be more careful about grabbing a guy's hand next time, that's all.'

'He said he was the gardener. You will tell him I'm sorry, won't you? I'm such an idiot. Obviously it wasn't Marco. I should have just left him alone.'

While Bea continued to berate herself, I began to wonder if she had been wrong after all. The library was the obvious place Marco would choose to wait for me. Was the burnt hand the extent of the man's injuries or was there something else behind the mask? Was that the real reason why Marco Donato hadn't been photographed since 1999? Was the rasping voice behind the fact we'd never even spoken on the phone?

'I'll just be a minute,' I said. 'Why don't you go and get Nick to find you a drink?'

Bea gathered up her skirts and headed for the exit to the courtyard. Meanwhile, I retraced my steps to the library.

'Marco?' I stepped into the library and closed the door behind me. 'Marco? Are you in here?'

No answer.

I walked over to the desk where I had spent so many mornings. Luciana's papers had been tidied away, of course. It would have been foolish beyond belief to leave them out when the house was full of masked revellers. But what else had been put away?

I held my breath as I opened the top left-hand drawer.

The vibrator was not there. Which meant, unless Marco had lied to me and Silvio knew all about the sex toy, that Marco must have been in the library at some point since my last visit. How recently, was the question I needed an answer to now.

I walked the perimeter of the room. As I had noticed before, there was only one door into the library. At least, only one door that I had discovered. Bea and I had not noticed her masked stranger slip out while I was consoling her, which meant that either he was hiding in the stacks, or there was a secret exit. If there was a hidden door, who would know about it except the owner of the house?

'Marco,' I tried again. 'It's Sarah. I'm on my own.'

Still nothing.

'Marco, I'm sorry I didn't wear the beautiful dress you sent me. I thought it would be fun to let Bea wear it. I didn't know—' I struggled to finish the sentence. 'I'm sorry, OK. I really am.'

The library remained silent. Ernesta's portrait gazed down on me, but this time her expression seemed pitying.

★ ★ ★

As promised on the invitation, the ball at the Palazzo Donato ended with the first strike of the bells at midnight, when the guests were corralled towards the watergate and the gondolas that would take them home. The excess and debauchery of Martedì Grasso was over. Mercoledì delle Ceneri was beginning, marking as it did the start of the forty days of Lent. Of sobriety and abstention. Of quiet reflection. I was certainly doing plenty of that. Bea's encounter in the library had left me almost as shaken as her. She felt she'd reacted badly to the poor guy's burnt hand. I felt far worse when I considered the possibility that the poor guy was Marco.

Only Nick was reluctant to go home.

'Amazing party,' he kept saying. 'A-ma-zing.'

He'd danced the night away with a girl dressed as Pierrette.

'She's from Denver. She got her ticket to the ball from a travel agency.'

'How weird,' said Bea, voicing my own thoughts. 'To keep your house closed for years, then open it up to random tourists.'

'Weird, too, not to show up to your own party,' said Nick.

'He must have been there,' I said sadly.

'He can't have been there. Otherwise, he would have made himself known to you,' said Bea.

'Perhaps he did,' said Nick. 'And you didn't recognise him.'

Or recognised him too late.

'Do you want this?'

Nick offered me the *servetta muta* that had come with the dress Marco bought me. I'd passed it to him while I climbed into the gondola. Now I let it fall into the water and float away down the canal.

49

The night after the Duke's visit, I went to see Giacomo again. We talked about my predicament and the life I might have if I could only escape my father's house once and for all.

'How would I live?' I asked. 'If I can't rely on the kindness of my father?'

'That's simple,' he said. 'You have everything you need within you.'

'What? You think I should become a washerwoman?'

'You have something far more valuable than your strong arms. You have your words.'

I had taken my diary to Giacomo's house for safe keeping. He picked it up from the place where it lay beside the bed and waved it at me.

'I will take your diary to a printer. I will have copies made and we will sell them. We will make a fortune. Your fortune,' he added.

I laughed. 'But you cannot print my diary. I am not a proper writer. Besides, can you imagine my father allowing it? He would have the printing presses stopped. He would have people killed for daring to print it.'

'Only if he knew you were the author.'

We had little enough time to be with each other

without wasting it on talk of my unsuitable suitor and how I could possibly support myself if I managed to escape his proposal. I stripped off my trousers and my grubby white shirt and skipped up the stairs to the chamber, beckoning my teacher to follow. He caught me up as we climbed the stairs and lifted me off my feet as we went into the bedroom. He tossed me into the middle of the cushions.

He ran a thoughtful finger along my body, from my shoulder, down my arm and across my waist.

'You are so beautiful,' he said. 'I will never tire of looking at you.'

'Even when I am a crone?'

'When you are a crone, my eyes won't be so good. We'll be a perfect match.'

I felt so happy. I was so sure I had avoided a bad marriage. If only I could think of a way to be free to be with my teacher for ever. If he would have me.

I fell asleep in his arms. It didn't happen often. Ordinarily, I would be so anxious about getting back to my own bedroom before sunrise I would be unable to relax into dreams, but that night was different. I was so very happy. If only I had known how fleeting that happiness was to prove.

I drifted into sleep gently. I was woken roughly.

It was the most unfortunate of coincidences. The Duke told my father he had gone to see Giacomo regarding the matter of an unpaid debt. He and his henchman had visited in the middle of the night to ensure they weren't given the slip. And whom should they find in the dreadful wastrel's bed? It was obvious from his expression that the Duke could not believe his luck. Two birds with one stone.

I hung my head. There was nothing I could say. Nothing. Nothing at all. Everything the Duke told my father was true. I had crept from my bedroom in the middle of the night. I had been found with a lover. Not just any lover, but one of the most notorious men in the city. Of course, my father understood there was no possibility this side of Heaven the Duke could take me for his wife now.

'She is worthless to the good men of Venezia,' the Duke told my father. 'When this gets out, all chance of a good marriage will be gone. If I were you, I would send your whoring daughter straight to a convent.'

'I didn't think you minded the company of whores,' I spat in the Duke's direction. I earned myself an open-handed slap across the side of my face. My father did not attempt to defend me.

The Duke left.

My father and I were alone. I tried to find some crumb of comfort for him but I knew he would never understand. Even as I tried to tell him about my education, I could see I had crushed his dream of raising his family from the merchant class to the aristocracy. He stared at me as though I were a stranger. He'd raised me so carefully. He'd gone to such lengths to keep me from bad influence and I had ended up in the bed of the city's most notorious Lothario. Giacomo Casanova. Eventually, he looked down at the papers on his desk.

'I cannot bear to look at you,' he said. 'I will arrange for you to be taken somewhere else in the morning.'

'"Somewhere else?" Where?' I asked. 'Are you sending me back to Turin?' I added hopefully.

'News of this kind will quickly reach Turin,' was my father's conclusion.

Maria escorted me to my bedroom. She didn't speak to me. To speak to me kindly now might besmirch her own spotless reputation. No doubt she would have to confess her ungenerous feelings towards me the following afternoon. But I felt sure my father would soften overnight.

Papà left for Genoa in the morning. I was right, he had softened his feelings towards me during the night. He was unable to bring himself to make a decision about my future. Possibly, given enough time, he might have reached a compromise that allowed me some measure of freedom. We had relatives in the Dolomites. Surely bad news wouldn't get that far? Unfortunately for me, my father left my fate in the hands of someone far more inclined to judge me harshly. My brother had been apprised of the situation and told he should deal with me as he saw fit.

My brother saw fit to send me to a convent.

15th July, 1753

'Vanity,' muttered the ancient nun. 'Such vanity has led you astray.'

And yet there was something approaching tenderness in the way she combed out my long brown hair. Unhappy as I was, I closed my eyes and remembered a time long, long ago when someone had combed my hair just as tenderly. I remembered my mother, singing to distract me as she yanked out the knots.

The old woman found a knot but she was not so tender or careful now. She didn't carefully hold a skein of hair above the tangle so she would not tug on the roots as she tried to loosen the mess. No, she just pulled, and tugged, until I was sure she would rip the hair straight from my head.

'Ow!' I protested. 'I'll do it.'

'Vanity,' she muttered again.

'Give me the comb,' I commanded, but my commands carried no weight in this place.

'I have to do it,' she said as I clutched at my scalp to try to lessen the pain. 'Sit still. You're making it worse.'

'You're being ridiculous. I can comb my own hair.'

While I was arguing with the horrible old hag, another nun came in. When she saw I wasn't happy with the way my hair was being dressed, she looked concerned. But not for me. She held me down on the stool by my shoulders and before I knew what was going on, the old woman had gathered the length of my tresses into a single tail and slashed it off.

I gasped. Both women laughed. They let me stand up but it was too late for me to run from the room. The old woman held my hair in her hands and stroked it. Then she held it up to the nape of her own neck.

'What do you think, Giulietta? Would Casanova make a pass at me?'

'Let me have a go,' said the other woman. She took my hair from her abominable colleague's hands and held it to her own head.

'You are a princess,' the old woman assured her.

My mouth was full of curses. 'You witches. Why comb my hair so tenderly when you knew you were going to cut it off?'

'Because your hair belongs to us now and by this time tomorrow it will belong to someone else. It will fetch a fine price, this tail will. It's nearly red in places.'

They were going to sell my hair! I put my hand to the back of my neck, naked for the first time I could remember. They had taken my hair to give it to a wig-maker. By the end of the week, some bald-headed old hag could be wearing my hair to a ball.

'My father will hear of this,' I warned them.

'I should think your father will approve,' said the younger woman. 'After all, he sent you here to learn the error of your ways. He knows it's your looks that got you into this mess. Don't get so much trouble with a plain girl.'

We were interrupted. The Mother Superior who had welcomed me on the dock had arrived with two more of the *figlie*.

'They cut my hair,' I protested.

'I know,' said the Mother Superior. 'You'll get used to it. In fact you may find there is liberation in being freed from earthly measures of beauty.'

'But they said they're going to sell it!'

'That's right. I can't say I approve of the falsification of God's natural gifts with the use of hairpieces, but we are not a rich convent, having no musicians to charm the coin out of the pockets of the wealthy like the Mendicanti or the Pietà. We have to support ourselves in other ways. Think of your hair as a gift to us in return for our hospitality.'

'But my father must have paid you?'
'You may be with us for a very long time.'

So here I am. In a convent. And this is not like the convent I heard of from Giacomo. The nuns in this convent actually seem to believe in God and religion and the Pope as someone other than a man they are ambitious to sleep with. My days pass in prayer. And it's true that I do pray, after a fashion. But I never pray to wake up with a soul as clean as the day I was born. I pray only for liberty from this place. I pray that someone will open the doors to my cell and take me far away from here.

What is my sin? That I loved too much and too freely? Had I been a man, my father would have patted me on the back. But I am a daughter. A chattel. By allowing myself to be used, I have diminished my value. I'm like a broken cup. But there is so much more to me than this stupid feeble body. If I were allowed to be free, what a contribution I could make! I believe I could be as good a philosopher or scientist as any man before me. I could create machines and discover planets. I could broker peace between the warring nations of the world. I have the wit and intelligence of any man. If only my father would believe it.

I cannot stay here. I shall leave this place even if I have to die in order to do so. But however long I am cloistered here, my mind will forever be free.

50

When I got back from the ball, of course the first thing I did was go online. The entire gondola ride home, I had been composing an email to Marco in my head, explaining why I hadn't worn the dress and how awful I felt that he'd had such an awkward encounter with Bea. It was him in the library. I was sure of that. I didn't mention my suspicions to Nick and Bea, however. Especially not to Bea. I didn't want her to feel worse than she already did. Besides, I wanted to think the ramifications through before I discussed the situation with anyone. How would I have reacted had I been in Bea's place? The burnt hand she described was very different to the hands that caressed me in my dreams. Could I honestly say I would have taken it in my stride? These were the questions that occupied me until I got to my laptop and, cursing the patchy connection, finally opened my email.

Marco had already written.

Dear Sarah,

I hope you enjoyed yourself this evening. Silvio reports that the ball was well-attended and that my guests drank enough prosecco to fill a swimming pool. Did you like the band? They have an excellent reputation for helping a party go with a swing.

What was this? I read on.

I am only sorry that I was unable to be there. I cannot tell you how much I had been looking forward to seeing you in that dress. Was the colour right? And the size? You have Silvio to blame if it didn't fit you.

And now I expect you want to know my excuse. Where was I when I should have been wowing you with my prowess on the dancefloor? I'm afraid the reason, as always, is work. A Hong Kong company in which I am heavily invested has been going through some difficulties. Last week, we had to sack half the management. I decided there was nothing for me to do but fly out and take the helm for myself until a suitable replacement can be found. So, while you were dancing, I was flying and now I'm here. This is my view.

Attached to the email was a view of Hong Kong in the early-morning sunshine, taken through a window from a high floor in an office block, or perhaps a hotel. I stared at it. I peered closely to see if I could see the reflection of the photographer in the glass. I could not. I was confused. Why hadn't he emailed me before he left? That way I wouldn't have spent the whole evening searching for him. I might have been able to have the good time he claimed he wanted me to have.

Of course, I wrote back. At the very least I had to thank him for his hospitality. However disappointed I felt that the ball had not marked our actual meeting, it was an experience that I would never forget. It was unlikely that I would ever attend such an extravagant party in my lifetime again. So I thanked him for the dress and for the opportunity to dance at a Martedì Grasso ball. I asked, in as casual a manner as I was able, when Marco was coming back to Italy. My email was met with silence. Marco did not seem to want to write to me any more.

Not so Steven. Almost three weeks after he sent his email asking me to reconsider our break-up, I heard from him again.

Dear Sarah,

Did you get my last email? I have to admit I've been checking my inbox every ten minutes for a reply. I sent you that email against my better judgment. Perhaps I should have kept my thoughts to myself. But if you didn't get it – and assuming you want to know what it said! – write back to me, please, my darling. I'm going to Paris in just over two weeks. I miss you terribly. It would be wonderful if you could meet me there.

What surprises life was throwing at me. Surprises and confusion. I continued to hold off on writing back to Steven. It felt like that could only make things worse.

There was no doubt, however, that I didn't want to hang around in Italy. Not anymore. Three days after the ball, with still no news from Marco beyond his frankly unconvincing apology for missing the party, I booked my flight back to London. When making my arrangements for my stay in Venice, I had bought a one-way fare. It seemed like the right thing to do at the time. I wasn't sure how long I would want to stay in the city. It might have been a week, it might have been a year. A lot depended on how my research went. There had been moments in the past few weeks when I thought it might even have been for ever.

I snorted at that idea now. The narrow streets that had once seemed so interesting were frustratingly dingy. The quiet canals seemed sinister. The gondoliers were too knowing and familiar. I thought I would cry if I saw another couple celebrate their engagement on the Rialto bridge. So I clicked 'buy' on a one-way ticket to Heathrow. I inputted my credit-card details and officially ended the dream.

51

Last night, I dreamed a monkey came to the window of my cell. It was a little monkey, just like Ernesta's. It chattered at the bars to gain my attention. I don't know how long it had been there before I noticed. When I finally did hear the chattering, I obviously didn't respond quickly enough because the little beast picked up a stone from the garden and threw it at my head with astonishing accuracy.

I soon leapt up then and went to the window with the intention of grabbing the wretched thing through the bars and strangling it with my bare hands. How it mocked me in my tiny cage, as it must once have been mocked itself.

As I drew closer, however, I no longer felt like throttling the gentle creature. It tipped its head to one side in a parody of human pity and observed me with such empathy in its brown eyes.

'Yes,' I said. 'I think I know how you must have felt now. But what are you doing here, my hairy friend? Why are you here in my dreams?' I stood on tiptoes to get a little closer, just as I had stood on tiptoes to see even a sliver of cloud on my long lonely nights since arriving here. When I was close enough, since it was obvious the very real stone had not properly woken me up, the monkey reached through the bars of my window and grabbed me by what remained of my hair.

'You beast! I'll have you!'

The monkey let my hair go. I stumbled back into the room, red-faced with fury. But I realised as I ranted that this was no dream. There really was a monkey at my window. It was Ernesta's monkey. Umberto.

Now I noticed that there was a silver cylinder on the collar round Umberto's neck. Ernesta had told me before about such things. How a monkey could gain access where a man couldn't and, like a bird, could thus be the perfect messenger. Umberto, seemingly knowing his purpose, sat very still while I reached up and unscrewed the cylinder's cap.

There was a tiny roll of paper inside. Eagerly, I unravelled it. My room was dark. Once the stub of candle burned down, the idea was I should have no more light until dawn, lest light in the darkness encouraged me to stay awake and think too much about my fate or, God forbid, how I might escape it.

So again, I had to stretch to my very fullest height and hold the paper at the bars to get a little help from the moon. As luck would have it, the moon was almost full and when the monkey helpfully retired to a tree opposite, I was able to read the note quite well.

Some water must have got into the cylinder, so some of the writing was smudged, but I could see at once that Ernesta had sent Umberto as Giacomo's messenger. I could make out Giacomo's fondest wishes for me. He loved me as strongly as ever. I must be in misery, as he was without me. And since we couldn't be together, if I sent word by this monkey, then he would send me . . . a phial of poison? So that this agony might be ended once and for all?

52

3rd September, 1753

The Mother Superior pulled back the blanket to gaze on Luciana's face one final time. There was no doubt Luciana had been one of her more challenging novitiates. It seemed she would never accept her fate, but lately she had been an exemplary member of the convent. She was kind and cheerful. She was helpful. She had a wit about her. The Mother Superior should not have laughed at Luciana's jokes, but even now, as she gazed upon the child's cold white face, she felt a smile play across her lips at the memory of the time she had served a live squirrel for lunch.

'Oh Luciana,' the Mother Superior breathed as she lifted the blanket to cover the dead girl's face once again. 'You are with God now and he shall be very lucky to have you.'

The other nuns, who had stepped back from the body so the Mother Superior could say a few last words, gave up a chorus of wails. Everyone had loved the dead girl, no matter how bad an influence she might have been. How cruel that she had fallen ill before her nineteenth birthday. She had been snatched from the world by the very peril her father had tried to defend her from when he sent her out in a plague mask as a child.

'She is with our Father now,' the Mother Superior reminded her charges. 'There is no need for tears. She has ascended to Heaven.' She tipped her head to one side at the memory of another misdemeanour. 'I hope.'

And so Luciana Giordano left the convent exactly as she had threatened: feet first. Four men came from the nearby island to take her back to Venice. Luciana's uncle, who had visited so recently, confirmed that Luciana must not be buried in the convent's own cemetery but taken to the chapel on San Michele to join her mother there. Luciana's father was too overcome with grief to make arrangements. Her brother was in South America. The uncle managed all.

The four men who carried the stretcher down to the funeral gondola were long-faced and solemn. They stepped slowly in synchrony, down the path to the landing-raft. Luciana's uncle was there to accompany his niece on her final journey. He was dressed all in black except for the brilliant white lace of his cuffs. As was the custom of noblemen of his rank, he wore a half-face mask.

The pallbearers gently lifted Luciana onto the funeral gondola. The nuns formed a strange guard of sorts as the gondolier pushed off from the shore. The pallbearers stood upright, working hard to keep their balance as the gondola moved away. As befitted her status in life – at least, before she disgraced herself – Luciana would be borne to San Michele with the full and proper ceremony.

The progress across the lagoon was slow. It seemed the whole of Venice loved a funeral. Fishermen gawped and let their catches get away. It was obvious from the beauty of the gondola that the deceased within must have been important.

How they would have loved to see Luciana's cold dead beauty. In death her face was even more arresting than it had been in life.

At San Michele, the priest was waiting. The pallbearers carefully lifted Luciana onto the dockside. What a sad procession made its way through the cypress trees to the Giordano vault. The door to the tomb was already open. A small table beside the door held the sacrament. It was a parody of a country home laid open for a treasured guest.

Poor dead Luciana took her place on the stone ledge above her mother's casket. The dank smell of the tiny stone room made her uncle cover his nose with one of his lace cuffs, as though he might otherwise breathe in contagion.

'Leave me here with her,' he said. 'And with my sister.' He gestured towards the casket that had been interred in the tomb some eight years earlier. 'I was not able to be by her side when she died. I want to ask her forgiveness for having allowed her daughter to go so badly astray.'

The priest nodded. He agreed it was a terrible thing to bear such guilt. He understood entirely why the uncle would want to beg his sister's forgiveness. He assured the grieving man that God's forgiveness was already guaranteed whenever he decided to ask for it.

The pallbearers left too, with instructions that they should take the funeral gondola back to Venice and ask the uncle's personal gondolier to return to fetch him at sunset.

★ ★ ★

It was September. When the pallbearers and the priest left the uncle to grieve, sunset was still some eight long hours away. No one expected the man to remain on his knees inside the tomb for that long. Not even for a niece and a sister. But when the priest passed by later that afternoon, the uncle was still there.

'Sir,' said the priest. 'You are most devout. But I must go inside for my dinner.'

'I understand,' said the uncle. 'I am happy to continue to pray alone.'

'I will leave the main gate to the island open so that you may leave when you wish.'

'Thank you. Oh, and before I forget.' The uncle reached into his purse and pulled out five gold coins. 'For your trouble. And for your gracious intercedence with God on high on our behalf?'

'I will pray for you all, sir.'

The priest would have attempted to get the entire Borgia family into Heaven for five gold coins. He would certainly pray for this poor wretch who had lost his whole family. But first, dinner . . .

53

With my ticket booked, there was still work to be done before I could start packing up my things at Ca' Scimmietta.

The last of the papers I had scanned in the Donato library before the ball and its disappointments lay on my desk at the university. This was not written in Luciana's hand, but someone else's. It had been tucked inside the diary as an afterthought. My heart fell as I translated it. It confirmed all my worst fears. It was an account of Luciana's death. She had died in the convent of 'diseases unknown'. She was taken from the convent to be buried on San Michele with her mother.

I had not made the trip to San Michele during my time in Venice. Reading about Luciana's last resting place, I decided I had to. I boarded a ferry at the quay where I had first set foot in Venice almost ten weeks earlier. Spring was truly in the air now and the lagoon was bright and calm.

I climbed off the ferry at the cemetery island along with a couple of grandmothers bearing flowers. They walked quickly and purposefully. They knew where they were going. They chatted animatedly as they walked, suggesting to me that their time for grieving helplessly had long passed.

I didn't know quite where I was supposed to start looking. I knew that space on San Michele had been at such a premium for so long, it was quite possible that Luciana was no longer on the island at all. Modern Venetians leased their plots on the island for just a short while, buying a decade or so before they were dug up and moved on. But I knew some very old graves still existed from when the island was not just a cemetery but also a working church for the people of Canareggio.

I weaved my way around the graveyard with the help of a tourist's map that pointed out the notables who'd ended their days in Venice. The description I had read said that Luciana was buried in a family tomb. I could not find it. After three hours of searching, I gave up. I sat down on a bench, defeated and depressed.

My thoughts wandered back through my time in Italy. I'd found what I came for in terms of my research, but I'd uncovered a whole new set of mysteries within myself. I decided, as I sat on that bench, that I would write back to Steven and tell him I was ready to talk. What would become of that, I didn't know, but at least my relationship with him, however dysfunctional, had been real. On the island of the dead, I decided I was through with chasing ghosts.

The ghosts, however, were not quite finished with me. To celebrate my last night in the city, Nick and Bea insisted we three go out to dinner. There were spritzes and there was wine. There was much departmental gossip and much laughter. When the evening was over, Bea started to cry.

'I'll be coming back,' I told her, though I didn't honestly know if I would. 'Or you could visit me in London.'

'Nick's going to be in London soon,' Bea told me. 'You two should definitely meet up.'

Nick smiled shyly.

'That would be nice,' I said.

Bea's security guard arrived at the restaurant to take her home for a booty call, leaving Nick and me alone. He offered to walk me home, of course. Though it wasn't icy, he offered me his arm. When we got to Ca' Scimmietta, he didn't ask to come in.

'I'm sure you've got plenty to do,' he said. 'Finishing off your packing.'

I nodded.

He helped me to get the door open one last time. I went to kiss him goodbye. Nick grasped my shoulders and suddenly placed a kiss right on my lips. I was wide-eyed with surprise but he let me go after just a second.

'You deserve love, Sarah,' he told me. 'Proper love. Not angry, not jealous, not evasive. You need someone who is supportive and kind to you. Someone who will always be there.'

I knew he was talking about himself. I hugged him tightly.

'Take care,' he told me.

I promised that I would.

I watched Nick walk away along the misty canalside and thought about his words. At any other time in my life, perhaps I would have invited him upstairs and let him kiss me again. But Nick had never been a feature of my dreams.

As I settled down under the covers on the four-poster bed for the last time, I thought about the months that had passed since my first night in Venice. Memory fragments of my stay in the city swirled through my mind, mixed up with scenes from Luciana's diaries and pictures from my nocturnal adventures with the man in the mask. Would he be with me that night?

54

This time, my dream began not in the garden but in the library. A figure, not unlike the man Bea had insulted, was standing by the fireplace in that very same pose. I stepped into the room. Glancing down at myself, I saw that I was wearing the Dior dress Marco had picked out for me. The metal-grey skirt formed a puddle of fabric around my feet. In my hand, I held the *servetta muta*.

The man at the fireplace turned to face me when he heard me come into the room. He was wearing his mask but I could see, even from a distance, that his eyes were smiling. He held out his hand to me. His perfect, strong, tanned hand. We knitted our fingers together.

'Come here.'

He sat down on one of the armchairs beside the fireplace and pulled me down onto his lap. He ran his hand over my hair and unfastened the clip that held it in place so that it fell loose over my shoulders. He pushed his fingers deep into the cascading waves and then brought my face closer to his for a kiss.

'No,' I said.

Gently, I pushed back from him.

'Not with your mask on.'

Behind the mask, my lover's eyes glittered. He smiled at me. He smoothed the curve of my lips with his thumb.

'Of course.'

With one hand, he reached up to undo the ribbon that

held his mask in place. With the other, he continued to hold the mask to his face so that it didn't fall away too soon.

'Are you ready?' he asked me.

I took a deep breath. I was. Nothing he could reveal would change my feelings for him.

Like a magician exposing the secret behind a trick, finally he uncovered his face for me. His familiar smile. Those brown eyes. His expressive eyebrows. I put my fingers to his perfect skin. He was every bit as handsome as the man I had only seen in photographs.

'Happy?' he asked.

I nodded.

'Can I kiss you now?'

I wrapped my arms around his neck and pressed my lips to his. He held me tightly as he kissed me back. There was truth in our embrace. At last we were being honest with each other. The warmth of his mouth upon mine suffused every part of my body. I had never felt so happy or so loved.

'Come on.'

We stood up. Still holding my hand, he led me away from the fireplace. We went from the library to the galleried floor, where Ernesta had once entertained Luciana, and Marco now had his own quarters. He opened a door to a room that overlooked the Grand Canal. The sunshine and the reflections bouncing off the water outside made a light show on the gilded walls. Stepping into that room was like stepping into heaven. And in the middle of heaven was a wide white bed.

I turned my back on Marco so that he could unfasten my dress. He worked quickly, occasionally dropping a kiss on my shoulder as he did so. As the bodice slowly loosened its grip on me, I breathed deeper, and relaxed. I stepped out of the dress. Beneath, I was wearing a pure white lace camisole, knickers to match and snowy stockings, like a bride. Marco smiled as he took in the sight of me. He placed his hands on either side of my waist and squeezed playfully as he kissed me again.

Laughing, we tumbled onto the bed together. The sheets were cool and crisp beneath my fingers. Sitting up, I helped Marco pull off his shirt. He sat up to tug off his boots and his trousers himself. When he lay down again, I ran my hands over his broad chest. His perfect chest. The scar I'd seen in my previous dreams was gone, leaving no trace. Meanwhile, he slipped his hand beneath my camisole and cupped and caressed my longing breasts, cooing at the softness of my skin. His palm lightly brushed my nipples, causing them to harden quickly. I begged him to take one between his teeth. When he did so, gently closing his lips around the rosebud, I felt as though I had been plugged into some magical source of electricity. My entire body trembled with excitement. I felt arousal spread to every part of me. I wanted him so much.

His shaft was already hard for me. I wrapped my hand around it and felt its heat and strength as I pulled the foreskin down. I slid down the bed so that I could take it in my mouth, making it harder still by sucking. Marco groaned with pleasure. He reached for my head and smoothed my hair while I licked the length of his penis, savouring every warm, smooth inch.

'Stop,' he told me, when I could feel he was close to the edge. 'I want to come inside you.'

I lay back down on the pillows for him, lifting my hips so he could pull off the white lace panties. He joyously threw them into the air. They fluttered to the floor like a tumbling dove.

I pulled him down towards my lips. We kissed again, full of heat and love for each other.

'Are you ready?' he asked me.

His hand was between my legs, his finger pressed into me.

He could feel that I was ready. My pussy was perfectly wet and longing to be filled by him. I parted my legs so that he could give me what I wanted. As he guided his cock inside me, I felt what can only be described as relief.

Our lovemaking was as wonderful as anything I could remember. We were like teenagers, experiencing sex for the very first time. Our sighs were punctuated by happy laughter. Our orgasms were tremendous. I came again and again and again. I felt I could have made love all night long.

Afterwards, Marco propped himself up on his elbow to look down at me.

'I love you,' he told me.

I told him that I loved him too.

He kissed me and said, 'I know.'

55

The following morning, I left Venice for London. I ordered a water-taxi to take me to the airport. It was an extravagance, but I felt I needed it. I did not have the energy to stand like a sardine in a packed vaporetto, and then drag my bags to the airport ferry stop. Nick had offered to help, of course, but I told him I didn't need help and he had accepted the brush-off with grace. Almost with relief, I thought. I didn't want to be waved off.

The water-taxi driver promised he knew the fastest route out of the city. We would avoid the busiest canals, zipping through the smaller ones instead. That was another advantage of the water-taxis. They could go where the vaporetti could not. But what I had not reckoned with was that the taxi-driver's route might take us right past the Palazzo Donato.

I tuned out of the driver's incessant chatter and gazed at the house I had come to know so well. That morning, it looked just as it had done the very first time I laid eyes on it. It was well preserved and well cared for but somehow it still had an air of neglect. The windows were all shuttered. There was no boat other than Marco Donato Senior's old water-taxi by the landing-raft. The feeling one got when one looked at the place was a distinct lack of life. A lack of love.

'Are you in there?' I asked Marco silently. 'Are you sitting in your courtyard? Are you in your library, holding the letters I was reading just last week? Are you peering out from behind your shutters? Can you see me?'

I stared at the Palazzo Donato, daring Marco to come to the window. My eyes were defiant. He had asked for my forgiveness. I wanted him to know that there was no need to ask forgiveness. He had not humiliated me. He had not left me feeling foolish or down at heart. Much.

The water-taxi driver noticed me staring at the palazzo as we passed.

'Ca' Donato,' he said, automatically switching into tour-guide mode. 'Nobody knows what goes on in there but it used to be a big party house. There are stories. There was a tragedy. Now, it is a house of mystery . . .'

I nodded impatiently.

'How much longer until we get to the airport?' I asked.

The driver took his cue and shrugged. 'Is a calm day. Twenty minutes.'

'Wonderful,' I said. 'Perhaps you can make it nineteen?'

I turned away from the Palazzo Donato at last.

56

8th September, 1753

I don't know how long I lay asleep. When I woke, I was not certain I was even still alive. I pinched my leg, but then surely, I said to myself, you would be able to feel your own leg in Heaven, too. Or did the angels go round bumping into things because they couldn't tell where their own feet were?

Certainly, I hadn't sprouted wings. But as consciousness came back to me, I was in no hurry to pronounce myself alive. There had been moments when I was convinced that the poison was a trick. How could you take a draft that would make you appear to be dead for three days then, *miracoloso*, be returned to life safely and absolutely with no lasting effects? How could you ever trust someone not to sell you an ordinary poison, intended to kill you outright? How could you tell the difference? I would have felt better had I met the poison-master but of course, that was not going to be possible.

When I agreed to the plan, Umberto the monkey returned, just as promised. This time, instead of the cylinder about his neck, he carried a small bottle. The sleeping draught. I was tempted to try the draught on the monkey first, but there were several problems with that plan. I had to send word back, of course, that the plan was going ahead. Also, how would I have explained a half-dead monkey beneath my window? The sisters would have worked out that something was afoot.

So, I tied a piece of straw to the monkey's collar as promised and sent him back to the boat with all my love both for Giacomo and for Ernesta who had lent us her dear little messenger. Then I sat down on the edge of my bed and took the draught in one, throwing the empty bottle out of the window so the nuns would not guess what had happened. A long sleep and freedom, or death? Either one was preferable to the slow death of the spirit I was suffering now.

I lay down. For a moment it seemed as though nothing was happening. The vile herbs certainly tasted poisonous, but I did not feel them working in my veins. Had we been duped? Was this poison as effective as the medicine my father had forced down my throat when I was a child? While I was pondering this my thoughts chased their tails and then . . . nothing . . .

A dreamless sleep, as promised. Quite dreamless. Still. Silent. When I woke I brought nothing with me. Indeed, the life I lived before seemed to be the dream. I was waking new and unformed, wrapped in a membrane.

Wrapped in a sheet.

'Get it off me! Get it off me!' I shouted. Giacomo obliged straight away. He was there beside me. That dear face smiling down on mine.

'Thank God,' he said. 'I thought I was going to have to leave you here overnight.'

I sat up at once. The roof of the tomb raked my hair.

'Be careful. Move slowly. You have been asleep for a very long time.'

'Hours?'

'Four days.'

'Where am I?'

'Where do you think you are?'

There was enough light to guide us to the dock where the gondola would be waiting but I was still dressed in a shroud. I argued that the priest should not be surprised to see a girl in a shroud on San Michele, but everything had been thought of. I donned a mourning dress. Boats arrived at San Michele all the time. The priest should not be surprised to see a woman in mourning he had not noticed slip onto the isle.

'Where are we going?'

'You can't go back to Venezia.'

'Then where?'

'I have arranged lodgings for you in Trentino.'

'And you with me?'

'I can't come with you,' he said. 'There are things I must do in the city.'

I understood at once. Ernesta had been right to warn me Giacomo's heart was very full.

'But you will be provided for,' he continued. 'I have taken care of that.'

'By whom?' I asked. 'Your new woman will surely put a stop to you sending me a stipend.'

'By you. You will provide for yourself,' he said.

I understood what Giacomo had put in place a few days later when a package arrived at my new lodgings. I had two rooms in what must once have been quite a grand house. As Giacomo suggested, I passed myself off as a young widow. In my new life, I was a girl with no family.

The woman who ran the house was perfectly uninterested, thank goodness. All that mattered to her was that the rent was paid on time and I didn't bring home any visitors. Had she been in the habit of opening correspondence, my new freedom might have become very uncomfortable indeed.

Inside the package was a book. Inside the book, a letter. Inside the letter, details of my very own bank account with the Monte dei Paschi di Siena. Of course, I had read the letter first, thinking it might be full of protestations of love and ways in which we might yet be together. Instead, it was brief and simple. It made my heart sigh. I turned to the book. I didn't recognise the title. Nor the author. Of course, that was the whole purpose. The author was 'anonymous'.

The Lover's Lessons, was the title. 'The sexual awakening of an innocent young girl.'

It was my story in my words.

Epilogue

Inside the Palazzo Donato, Marco Donato stood at the desk in the library where Sarah had worked for the past two months. He ran his sore, stiffened fingers along the back of the chair, imagining her sitting there. If she were there now, he would put his hands on her shoulders. She would turn to face him and look up into his eyes. She would smile and he would know that everything would be fine. She would not care what had become of him. She would love him no matter what she saw.

But Sarah wasn't there any longer. She had gone and he had let her go. What agony it had been to see her at the ball and discover he still did not have the courage to reveal his new face. Not after the moment in the library. Perhaps he should have written the truth in response to her last letter, but would she have believed it? The truth had been buried such a long time ago.

So he was alone again and Sarah had never come to see the last jewels he had kept for her. The loose pages from Luciana's diary of September 1753 had been separated from the bulk of her papers, along with a single letter. For some reason both had been tucked into a collection of correspondence by the letter's addressee: Giacomo Casanova. Marco read the letter from Luciana again.

*My lost love, how often do I think of you? I think of you
every moment of every day. And when I think of you, I find I
am happy. Without you, I do not know what I might have
become, but with you I became myself. From my window, I
look out on green hills outlined by sad cypress trees, but my
heart is with the birds. I have the freedom to walk where I
choose, to think what I choose, to be the woman I always
wanted to be. And I am the woman I wanted to be because,
my dear heart, of your love.*

Marco folded the letter closed. He might never see Sarah
again. But he felt he was just a little closer to being the man
he once hoped to be, because she had loved him.

Sarah's intoxicating story of passion and
obsession continues with

Hidden Women, Book Two:

The Girl Behind The Fan

Stella Knightley

Hurt and confused by the sudden end of her strange love
affair with Venetian millionaire Marco Donato, Sarah
Thomson is persuaded to take her bruised heart to Paris by
her ex-boyfriend Steven, who is hoping for a reconciliation.

While she and Steven rekindle their psychologically and
sexually tortured relationship, Sarah tries to forget her
yearning for Marco by throwing herself into a new project:
a study of the life of notorious nineteenth-century
courtesan, Augustine Levert, whose sensual charms parted
many a man from his fortune. But when her life begins to
parallel Augustine's story, Sarah realises she will never erase
Marco from her heart.

Faced with a choice between safety and overwhelming
passion, will both women make the right decision?

Coming out in June 2013 in paperback and ebook:
pre-order now!

HODDER

Do you wish this wasn't the end?

Join us at www.hodder.co.uk, or follow us on
Twitter @hodderbooks to be a part of our community
of people who love the very best in books and reading.

Whether you want to discover more about a book
or an author, watch trailers and interviews, have the
chance to win early limited editions, or simply browse
our expert readers' selection of the very best books,
we think you'll find what you're looking for.

And if you don't,
that's the place to tell us what's missing.

We love what we do, and we'd love you to be part of it.

www.hodder.co.uk

@hodderbooks

HodderBooks

HodderBooks